BANDIT'S TRAIL

BANDIT'S TRAIL

A WESTERN STORY

Max Brand

**BLACK
STONE**
PUBLISHING

Printed in the United States of America
ISBN 9-781-4708-6126-1
Fiction/Westerns

1 3 5 7 9 10 8 6 4 2

CIP data for this book is available
from the Library of Congress

Blackstone Publishing
31 Mistletoe Rd.
Ashland, OR 97520

www.BlackstonePublishing.com

CHAPTER ONE

Señor Don Sebastian Valdivia prided himself upon his ability to be all things in all countries. In Rome he was indeed most Roman—in Paris he was more Parisian than the French—in England he could play golf and yawn in the faces of ladies and drink Scotch and soda in tall glasses—in Switzerland he could use an Alpine stock where the hardiest ventured, and talk the language of every canton in that variegated land—in his own Argentine he could be the king that his ancient family and his measureless estates entitled him to be—and now that he was in these United States, for the moment, he boasted that he was more democratic than democracy.

Since the scene was the great Southwest where horizons grow wide and men grow big, he was turned out in the very fashion of the hour—or at least his conception of it. Upon his legs were fine leather chaps set off with silver conchas. About his waist was girded a cartridge belt that supported a holster and a pearl-handled Colt—which he could use if occasion demanded. Upon his back was a blue silk shirt; his sombrero with its high-peaked Mexican crown was banded about with golden filigree; a crimson bandanna spotted with green flowed copiously about his throat. His saddle was such a treasure as would have made the heart of any Mexican caballero swell with jealousy, and the horse that he bestrode was a glorious stallion whose thoroughbred strain was dashed with just enough mustang blood to put a shining devil in its eyes.

Riding through the crowd that flocked about the old ranch house, bidding on various items in the long list of the sale, Señor Valdivia carried his forty-five years as erectly as any youth and felt himself quite a part of the picture. He would have been most astonished had anyone told him that compared with the others, he was like the colored frontispiece in a book without other illustrations. Indeed, no one dared even to hint such a fact to such a grandee, and if the rich man noted some differences between himself and the cowpunchers and ranchers in their overalls and well-rubbed coats, he would have attributed it to the natural distinction that exists between men of blood and position and wealth compared with the nameless herd. So he went on his way sublimely indifferent to the faces around him, attributing their faint smiles and wrinkling eyes to a natural admiration of the striking figure that he made.

His secretary, Juan Carreño, rode at his side, dressed like a somewhat tarnished copy of his master and keeping skillfully half a horse's length behind Valdivia. Señor Valdivia sat his horse at the outskirts of the crowd and watched the bidding on the plows and rusted cultivators and sewing machines and mowing machines and horse rakes. What had cost $150 new, now went for $5 to $7, but Señor Valdivia did not bid. The trip to the Argentine might be considered expensive. Besides, he had not the slightest conception of what his huge cattle ranch in that southland might need in the way of implements, and, even if he had, he would not have bothered his head with the buying of them. Such matters were to be left to the discretion of his general manager and that gentleman's assistants. For his part, he had ridden to the sale only because a rumor had reached his ears that valuable horses were to be disposed of here. And horses were the hobby of Señor Valdivia.

Señor Valdivia knew them from all angles. He had hunted foxes across the grass lands of England. He had hunted again in wild Ireland on big-boned Irish horses. He had ridden Arabs of ancient blood and shuffling gait across the deserts of their native land. He had wagered his tens of thousands of francs at Longchamps and smiled at his losses; he had wagered his thousands at Epsom and smiled at his winnings. He had maintained a stud in Austria to work out some fanciful ideas of his own connected with the breeding of the equine race.

On this particular trip to the States his one purpose, if he really could ever be said to have a greater purpose than amusement, was to pick up horses that might be used by his ranch riders in the distant southland. He had already collected two hundred. He wanted still more, and the ship that was to convey them south was already chartered and lay in the harbor of New Orleans awaiting his pleasure. Such was the scale on which the señor worked his will—kingly in all things—like a king in this, also. Time pressed upon him now. But he could not resist the temptation of this last sale before he departed.

But there was a dreary interval before the horses were produced. First came the furniture of the house, from enlarged photographs of the ancestors of that extinct family to the rocking chair with the tattered lace headrest in which Grandmother Garrison had sat while she knitted stockings and dreamed upon the world. These things were bought by a junk dealer who also acquired most of the agricultural implements.

"Suppose that we return to the town and come back this afternoon when the horses will be offered?" suggested the secretary, whose spirit was failing him.

But the master was iron. Fatigue was to him a thing unknown, and at the end of the fifth hour the points of his waxed mustache bristled out as sharply as when he started forth in the cool of the morning. For he was one of those rare fellows who always seem impervious to blowing dust and burning suns. There was always a hint of color in his sallow cheeks. There was always that champagne sparkle of liveliness in his eyes.

"I must tell you for the hundredth time, Carreño," he said, "that culture is in the mind, not in the body, and that the mind never drinks more freely or more deeply than when the customs of foreign lands are under observation."

Carreño, said some who had malice in their hearts, had been chosen by his master as secretary because he presented a contrast that was so flattering to the king of the Pampas. He was a dumpy youth who still lacked something of his thirtieth year, but there seemed more weariness of age in his dull, flat eyes than in the sparkling glance of Valdivia. He was one who did not find it possible to contradict Valdivia even in his own heart of hearts. He was like some churchmen. He revered high position and established custom so much that to deny the righteousness and the all-pervading wisdom of the Valdivia was like denying the same qualities in the Creator.

Now he winced a little and blinked the running perspiration out of his eyes, but he nodded in agreement. "Yet as you yourself said yesterday, sir, a land of such barbarians …"

That was his only weapon against the tyrants. He kept in his mind an unexpurgated text of all the past sayings of the Valdivia, and in time of need he could draw forth with either hand a stout quotation and level it at the head of the master like a gun. The master now shrugged his shoulders.

"Yesterday was yesterday," he said. "Today is today. Your body has always been fat, Carreño. Take care of your brain, my lad. Take care of your brain."

Just what was meant by this last warning Carreño did not understand.

"Very well, señor," he said, and fell back to his accustomed place to ponder that last remark. Yet it remained a mystery. Once or twice dawn seemed to be flickering upon the verge of his struggling intellect, but the light went out and remained in darkness. But, for that matter, the Valdivia usually left him in such a condition. Therefore the burden was the less heavy.

Noon came. A lunch was brought out of two sandwiches, a pickle, an apple, all wrapped in strips of brown butcher's paper. The crowd sat down in circles wherever it could find shade, and poor Carreño found himself compelled to squat in the dust and sink his teeth in this miserable fare. The dancing heat waves before him flowed into another picture of little round tables, of striped, broad awnings, of saunterers under parasols, and somewhere the delicious music of ice chiming against thin sides of glasses.

"Alas, Paris," Carreño sighed.

Sometimes, into his brain darted the wild suspicion that his master was not quite balanced. Otherwise he could never have left such a place for such a torment as this, with the thick, stale sandwiches, and the hungry flies buzzing and darting, and the hot wind lifting the dust in clouds. But when the thought fluttered into his brain it was chased furiously out again. For this was hardly less than heresy; this was indeed almost atheism.

Poor Carreño. He looked to his master and saw him sitting, cross-legged, in the dust—he—the Valdivia! And by his side, a tall, limber-backed cowpuncher answering the vivacious conversation of Don Sebastian with grunts and shrugs of the right shoulder—the left having probably been broken in a fall from horseback. But there sat Don Sebastian talking as blithely as though this were a charming boulevard café. The secretary shook his head and told himself, for the millionth time, that it was better to observe and note down than to try to comment upon such matters.

In this, perhaps, he was right, for no one could have understood the Valdivia—not even Don Sebastian himself. Neither would the rich man have desired to do so, for what he understood he detested, and he was continually looking for new corners simply in order that he might get around them.

The lunch was quickly finished and washed soggily down with lukewarm water, flavored with a few drops of vinegar. Then the sale recommenced still more drowsily, still more hotly.

The heat of the morning had been a mere prelude and warming of the oven. Now the baking of human flesh began.

However, Don Sebastian would miss nothing. He pruned his little mustaches stiffly out on either side and advanced into every corner his inquisitive glances. He had not the slightest idea that he would ever use this knowledge. But he loved information for its own sake and for its very uselessness he loved it all the more. He was as full of statistics as an almanac, as full of anecdotes as a joke book, and if his statistics were out of date and his jokes stale, he cared not a whit. They amused him in the getting.

There was an end to torture at the last, and finally the horse sale began. The crowd packed closely around a large corral into which, from time to time, the horses were brought, one man leading the more docile saddle ponies, and two men controlling the colts and the vicious part of the stock.

Even Carreño now threw off his dullness and began to prick up his ears, for though Carreño was rather more of a pig than a man, yet even pigs are interested in horses—or should be. As for Señor Valdivia, he was like a man at a play, smiling and nodding as the exhibits were brought on, one by one.

CHAPTER TWO

They brought on the poorer stock first, for the auctioneer who stood on a box just outside of the fence knew his business and how to work up his crowd to a fever pitch of excitement with the smallest possible means. And the stock of the Garrison Ranch gave him an opportunity such as rarely was in his hands. For there was not an animal on the place without a dash of the thoroughbred, and in many cases the blood was high indeed. The horses that the cowpunchers rode to their common daily tasks were never more than half mustang and even some of these were pictures of beauty. They were snapped up eagerly by the attending ranchers and even a cowpuncher, here and there, put in a bid, particularly those who had worked for years on the Garrison place and knew the animals and loved them under the saddle. And many a wise-headed horse that was none the best in looks was furiously bid for by two or three contending cowpunchers until some sharp-headed rancher, perhaps, guessed at the hidden qualities of the animal and stepped in to buy.

The auctioneer supplied the stimulus with well-chosen words. His voice was unimpaired by his efforts of the morning, and if some of the edge had been taken from it by much talking, he had restored its volume by a discreet drink of moonshine whiskey, colorless, strong as lye. He had been in his youth a singer of some ambition and had even appeared for a time on the vaudeville stage until too much beer and too little study had wrecked his opportunities. But he could still carry the air for an improvised quartet and occasionally "fake" a tenor to the delight of an audience of cowpunchers. Or, what he lacked in voice, he could make up with enthusiasm and his manner. It was known that he had been upon the stage, and the reputation made his bearers deaf to his faults. But if the gold was gone from his tones, there was still volume enough to roar and ring over the corral above the occasional neigh of a frightened or lonely horse. His tongue was never still. It rattled like the chattering dice in a gambler's box, only breaking into a wailing note when he announced a new bid.

His little eyes flashed continually from one side to the other, surveying every face, and not a change of expression that might mean an approaching bid escaped him. Instantly his attention was focused upon the prospect, and all his talent went to draw forth the larger sum. In his own way, he was an artist. He wore a derby hat, grease marked at the brim from much handling with unclean fingers. It was pushed far back on his head, and the downright rays of the sun had painted the end of his blunt, fat nose a brilliant red. He wore a wing collar, but he had long ago discarded the necktie and undone the collar in front for the sake of more air, so that now the ends of his collar curled up around his face. From many violent gestures, too, his coat sleeves had worked into thick wrinkles above his elbows and displayed a length of purple-striped shirt.

He carried a sort of truncheon, which was an old, broken cane with a great knob, and with this he beat time to the bids upon the top rail of the fence. He had a word for every turn of events, for every creature that was brought before him. A spindle-legged two-year-old was brought in, snorting, flirting at the dust with a restless forehoof, staring at the audience out of red eyes.

"There's a horse that is a horse," Jim Bradley, the auctioneer, said. "Look at them legs. What d'you say, gents? Look at them legs! There's bone for you … there's substance … startin' a horse like that under a hundred dollars is a crime. There's a horse that'll fill out to a whale. Did you say twenty-five? Twenty-five it is. Who gives fifty? Who gives me fifty? Sound as a fiddle … straight as a string! Who gives me forty? Gentlemen, this here is an outrage. Ain't there nobody left in ol' Texas that knows a horse? Give me five dollars, then! Who'll make it thirty? Thank you, Mister Kelly. There is somebody in Texas that knows a horse. Goin' to Mister Kelly for thirty! Gents, this is only startin'. This ain't no common cow horse. This is the makin' of a racer! Who says thirty-five? Thank you, Mister Smythe. But Kelly ain't goin' to let you have him. He knows a horse, I tell you. Now, Mister Kelly … forty! Now forty-five! We're gettin' up to where we should've started from."

He began to jab his truncheon first toward one and then toward another, wrenching the bids from them, until the perspiration poured down his face in streams. One would have thought that apoplexy must claim him, but still he went on through the long, dusty, hot moments.

"Here's a mare with the look of a mother in her eyes. Look at her, boys. There's a mare that'll give you horses to ride on. Good an' roomy … disposition like a saint of heaven … look out, Joe!"—as the saint out of heaven nearly whipped the head from the shoulders of a too curious bystander with her flashing heels. "Lovely nature, but some spirit. Nobody wants a horse that can't take care of itself on the range."

The colts were worked through, the matured horses and mares were brought on and disposed of, and half a dozen times Señor Valdivia said to Carreño one word: "Buy!" That meant that the animal was to be purchased regardless of the price. And it was done. Carreño had an irritating habit. His bids went in fives only.

For instance: "An upstandin', hundred percent horse … a credit to Texas … this horse is a gentleman, friends. This horse is out of Thunder Blossom by Bay Ridge. They ain't no common or garden blood in this horse, gents. This here horse could stand stud on any man's ranch. He's got the blood lines. He's a racer. Do I hear five hundred? One hundred? I don't, hear you, Mister Garret. No, I ain't goin' to hear you laughed at for biddin' a hundred dollars for a horse that ain't got his like west of the Mississippi."

"One hundred and five," said Carreño, who had received his marching orders from his master.

"And fifty!" Garret called.

"And five," said Carreño.

"Which says two hundred?" bellowed Jim Bradley.

"Two hundred!" Garret cried.

"And five."

"Three hundred!" Garret yelled angrily.

"And five."

"Five hundred dollars!" shouted the rancher.

"And five," said Carreño, showing his white teeth while the fat of his face wrinkled back in a smile.

And Garret turned with an oath and strode from the crowd.

So it was always with Carreño. To have wasted a dollar of his master's money by making a bid higher than was absolutely necessary would have been, in his eyes, the blackest of crimes as well as a manifest folly.

In the meantime, the herd in the reserve corral grew smaller and smaller, and still the audience had not thinned.

"Why does everyone stay?" Señor Valdivia asked of a neighbor, for he himself was ready to depart with his purchases.

"They's some fun comin'," said the cowpuncher. "The Crisco Kid is apt to lose his horse, and, if he loses him, they'll be a gunfight, sure."

"Ah?" Valdivia said politely. For he loved a bullfight as well as the next man, whereas even a fool could tell that a man fight was far more exciting. So he pricked up his ears and made conversation. "It is enough to fight over," he said. "A fine horse is a rare possession."

"But this here horse ain't no good to nobody but The Kid," said the cowpuncher.

"How can that be?"

"He's a plumb outlaw, till Crisco tamed him. He found this here horse down under a fence where he'd rolled and got cast … couldn't get up. Crisco got him out, and, after that, he got plumb gentled to The Kid. But all he's got for other folks is hoofs and teeth … and plenty of them. That's the horse that killed Jack Renau."

"I have always held," said the Argentinean, "that proper handling, and the right men, will manage any animal, no matter how stubborn."

The cowpuncher turned and stared blankly at him. Then he made a careful gesture, as though explaining a difficult point to a child. "I said that this here horse was the one that killed Jack Renau," he explained.

"Ah?" said the other.

"Now Crisco has been ridin' the horse for a year, but he's got a gent in town that hates his liver. He knows that nobody but Crisco can sit still for more'n a minute on this Twilight horse, and he knows that nobody but Crisco will bid for him. And Twilight wouldn't be no good to him. But he's out here … there he is yonder … to buy that horse away from Crisco if he can. Just because he hates Crisco's heart."

"Yes, yes," Señor Valdivia said, as though this matter were something that he could understand far more easily than the Texan could comprehend it. "I see how it might well be so. Which is the man who wants to buy the horse … Twilight, did you call it?"

"That's because of his color. Doggoned if the name don't fit him. You'll see that when he comes into the corral. There's Bud Carew yonder. He's the gent that'll mingle with Crisco when they start biddin'."

"Which has the more money?" Valdivia asked, growing more

and more interested. He looked over Bud Carew. There was nothing about Bud to suggest any particular malevolence. He was a broad-built youth with rather handsome face, his sombrero pushed on the back of his head, a cigarette turning between his lips.

"I dunno about the money," said the informant. "I guess they are about a set-up. They been borrowin' all month to raise all the coin they can. They say that Carew had near pawned his gizzard to get coin. And I know The Kid has done the same. They'll be pushing that money up pretty high before the game is over ... unless one of 'em loses his nerve. But no matter which one of 'em wins, they'll be a fight afterward. That's doggoned sure and certain. That's why Twilight's goin' to be the last horse knocked by ol' Jim Bradley. Jim don't want no livestock hit with slugs before he's sold it." He chuckled at this practical thought.

"But the sheriff?" Valdivia suggested tentatively.

"Him? He's mighty busy. The Clark boys come down and busted things up over to Rangel Crossin'. He's got some help and started chasin' them. He won't be on hand to stop no shootin' that might start."

"Ah," said Valdivia, half closing his eyes and drawing in his breath slowly. "There are some few delightful customs left. But civilization is a plague that works very fast, my friend. I am glad to see that it has not yet wiped out everything. Which, then, is this gentleman with the odd name? Crisco, did you call him?"

The cowpuncher chuckled again. "I dunno nothin' about him. Nobody don't know nothin' about him. Except that he come ridin' in from the north, an' he talks book-made langwidge like a doggone' schoolteacher. He looks mighty good-natured, and he is. But his idea of chicken an' ice cream is a fight where everything but the beer bottles is used. He'll come to a fight like a range cow comin' in for water. He'd walk ten miles and swim a river for the sake of swattin' some gent that had been bustin' things up. Take a bad man ... with two guns and a lot of reputation ... them kind are raisins and nuts to Crisco. Doggone me if his mouth don't water when he sees 'em comin'. All he does is to take a flyin' hop onto his horse and go to meet 'em. And when the dust dies down, there's The Kid joggin' back, smokin' a cigarette ... and yonder is the two-gun man lookin' at the sky and wonderin' what's hit him."

"He is a man, then, of some talent," Señor Valdivia said with another of those delighted indrawn breaths.

At that moment The Crisco Kid appeared, and the cowpuncher explained: "There's Crisco now."

Señor Valdivia beheld a handsome youth in his early twenties who had just taken off his hat to mop his head with his handkerchief. He thus exposed a thatch of yellow hair clipped short to discourage its tendency to curl. And he had in common with Señor Valdivia himself a pale skin in spite of his life in the open sun. Valdivia looked him over with instant approval.

How strange that he, though a most superstitious man, had no suspicion of all that would come to pass through this handsome young Anglo-Saxon.

CHAPTER THREE

The last horses of the sale had now been disposed of with a single exception, and when this final animal was brought forward, there was a stir of interest keener than even the beginning of the sale had caused. Purchasers left the corrals where they had been receiving, or looking over again, their newly acquired stock. Men who had been loitering under the shed to escape the blast of the sun—cowpunchers and idlers—now hurried up to view the closing bidding. There was a hasty jostling around the corral, and Señor Valdivia managed to get himself a place next to the rail with his informant by his side.

And here came Twilight. No one man held his head; no two men held him. There were no fewer than four ropes attached to his halter that was made doubly stout, but the four men at the ends of the ropes clutched tightly and looked with awful eyes upon their captive as though it were a tiger, ready to spring upon them.

As for Twilight, he regarded these fellows with the most magnificent disdain. With proudly raised head, he looked calmly over the faces of the crowd and then above and beyond them as though a floating wisp of white cloud in the great distance had attracted his attention. He canted his head a little to one side like an intelligent dog or a thoughtful child, and seemed to be studying the contents of that far-off bit of moisture. A whisper and a hum of admiration went through the beholders.

What could be said of Twilight? There needed some old Arab bard to describe him, one whose horses carried him fifty miles across the desert and came majestically home in the evening with ears pricking and tails proudly arched; one whose mares nosed open the flap of his tent and entered to beg for bread or to smell the newly brewed coffee in the egg-shell cups from which their muzzles must be put gently aside, like a baby's too inquisitive hands; there needed a poet whose hands knew the corded strength of perfect thighs and haunches and the glorious slope of shoulders, one who had dwelt long upon the dreamy lights that lived in the eyes of the brood mare when she touched her foal nose to nose and let the youngster tyrannize.

Such a one, so knowing and so loving horses might have described Twilight, but no other. But when he stood in the center of the corral with catlike lightness on his four hoofs, it seemed as though he could leap into the thin air and stride away through it with flashing legs. It seemed as though all the others, thoroughbreds and the rest, had been mere dull preludes and preambles leading up to this perfect thing. As for his name, his color indeed explained it. He was a black dappled chestnut—not the dark of night, but a deep and burnished chestnut mottled over like a leopard with dark splotches. His mane and his tail were silken black; there was not a white hair on him. And the fingers of Señor Valdivia yearned to run over the glistening shoulders where the muscles were marked softly beneath the skin.

Someone said: "Talk soft, Jim. Shoutin' might start him playin' the tiger. An' my brother Al is holdin' one of them ropes."

There was a laugh at this, a laugh made gentle out of respect for the hidden devil in the stallion. Even Jim Bradley admitted the importance of the advice he had just received by the modified voice in which he now spoke.

"Gents," he said, "there is horses and horses. There is some that'll cut out a calf from a herd before its ma could bawl twice. There is some that could smell water on a desert fifty miles away. There is some that'll carry you soft as a buggy all day long. There is some that'll come when you hollers for 'em. There is some horses that a baby could ride. There is some that is made for womenfolk to sit on. And, gents, there is some horses that're made for men!"

Alas for the power of habit, especially in orators! The mild voice with which the auctioneer had begun rose and rose during this brief address until it had swelled to considerable proportions and the last sentence was delivered in his usual bawling note. And as his tones began to rise, the stallion withdrew his glance from the distant cloud and pricked his ears. He did not glance at the auctioneer, but a slight shudder went through his body, and, when the voice ascended suddenly into a roar, Twilight plunged straight up into the air while poor Jim Bradley paused in midgesture with his truncheon extended, agape to see four stout-bodied men twitched so lightly from their feet and suspended at the ends of their ropes.

Twilight, landing, reached for one of his captors with his teeth and, securing a shoulder hold, ripped the coat from the fellow's back with a force that tossed the owner head over heels in a far corner of the corral. Then his heels shot like twin speeding rifle bullets at the head of another of his jailkeepers. The fellow avoided death by dropping flat, and then rolling through the thick velvet dust toward the fence and safety. The other two waited for no more, but turned on their heels and fled for their lives.

Only sharp wits and matchless agility saved one, for as he raced for the fence, Twilight was a tiger at his heels.

"Shoot the devil!" yelled the frightened man, as though he felt the yawn of those bone-crushing great teeth just behind him. "Shoot the …!" Here he reached the fence. There was no time to climb it. Instead, he made a dive as into water, and by good luck managed to pass cleanly between the second and third bars, landing on his head on the ground outside.

There was no laughter to greet this mishap. The crowd stood by in awe, for Twilight, like a disappointed cat that has been playing with a mouse until the little creature has escaped, now went raging around the corral, squealing with fury, beating at the air with his forehoofs—hammer blows that would have cracked a man's skull like the shell of an empty nut—shaking his head, gnashing his teeth, and whipping his heels into the air behind him.

He lurched at some of those who stood too close to the fence. They retreated in terror, with yells. He whirled about, and, speeding across the enclosure, seemed as though he would dash himself to pieces against the stout bars sustained as they were by posts ten inches square of new wood. But, at the last instant, he rose like a bird, floated across the uppermost bar with half a foot to spare, and landed outside. Not to flee. That was not in the devilish mind of Twilight. His ears were back, his eyes were red, and he wheeled to do further execution.

Those who could flee fled. Those who were blocked away by the thickness of the crowd before them yelled for help.

But Señor Valdivia, with his eyes half closed and the singular faint smile upon his lips, drew out his revolver and held it ready.

He had no chance to fire, for a madman—or a hero—leaped into the path of the charging horse. A great voice shouted above the noise: "Twilight, you doggone' fool!"

And behold, yonder stood Twilight with his head down, inside the arms of The Crisco Kid, who patted the sleek neck and muttered words with the soft voice of a lover.

"Get that devil back inside the fence, Crisco!" yelled someone, panting.

The Crisco Kid obeyed. He led back Twilight, docile as a lamb, into the enclosure, and there he stood at the head of the man-killer with not even a rope in his hand but with his fingers resting lightly upon the arched and trembling neck of the great stallion. That little touch was enough to dissolve all the ferocity of the wild horse.

The drama was at an end. Or, perhaps, it could be said that it had entered upon a new phase.

Once more the crowd assembled, their faces still pale. And Jim Bradley, weak at the knees and breathing hard, climbed back upon his box.

"Gents," he said heavily, "gents, I was sayin' … I was sayin' …" He fumbled for the lost thought, found it, recovered his courage and his color. "I was sayin' that there's some horses for children, some for women, and there's some horses for men."

His voice was ringing harshly again, and the stallion, wincing a little with flattened ears, swung his head around toward The Kid, touched his nose against the man's shoulder as though for reassurance, and again was calm.

"Somebody has raised hell with that horse when it was a colt," said the cowpuncher who had previously given so much information to Valdivia.

"Not at all, my friend," said the Argentinean. "Let me tell you that there are horses like that … and women … born with the devil in them." And then he added, fixing his glance upon the careless figure of The Crisco Kid who stood at ease, stroking the horse and paying no attention to the battery of eyes that were fixed upon him: "It seems to me that our friend, Bud Carew, will have some difficulties before him when he undertakes to dispose of … The Kid."

"Sure," said the cowpuncher in ready agreement. "But Carew is one of them nacheral killers. He's got rid of three men already. And when a gent has done that much, he's pretty sure to figure out that there ain't nobody in the world that he can't handle. He's got about one chance in three, the way I figure, of beating The Kid to the draw. After that … they both shoot too doggone' straight to suit me."

Señor Valdivia nodded and sighed again in that peculiar way of his—smiling, and with a softly indrawn breath as though he were sitting in a box at a most delightful play.

"There's some horses meant for men, and men only," the

auctioneer was declaring, "and I say that that horse in there is one of the last kind. I say that horse is meant for a man."

"Ain't you a man, Jim?" asked an inquiring voice. "D'you want him?"

Jim Bradley grinned broadly. "I'm retired," Bradley said, after the laughter had died down. "I'm a retired … man. Like a lot of the rest of you. But I say ag'in, there's a horse. They ain't a flaw in him, inside or out. I say that a gent that knows a horse knows that Twilight is one in a million. Maybe some of you has seen finer horses, but … has one of you ever seen a slicker jumper than Twilight?"

There was more laughter. Jim Bradley held up his scepter and then beat it against his palm for silence.

"What do I hear for Twilight? What do I hear for a horse worth … what anybody can afford to pay for him?"

There was a pause.

"I'll start it at a hundred," The Crisco Kid said quietly.

CHAPTER FOUR

There was one of those quick murmurs of excitement, dying almost as soon as it is born, because there is more to come than has as yet been revealed. Half a dozen men were seen crowding around Bud Carew, persuading, while Bud, very red of face and with his jaw thrust out, shook his head grimly in denial.

"Let The Kid have the horse!" shouted someone. "God knows he's the only one that can get any use out of the brute! What would you use him for, Carew? Dog feed?"

Carew brushed back his persuaders and leaned across the corral fence. "They's some men that I might use for my dogs," he said grimly. "Jim, I'm in for a hundred and fifty on that there colt."

Men drew a long breath. It was decided, then, and the battle was to continue to the bitter end. Who had the more money to buy the horse? And after it was bought, how would the fight turn out? There could be no shadow of a doubt now. They saw Bud Carew vault to the top rail of the fence and sit there—carefully pulling his cartridge belt around so that the gun swung easily on his hip, ready for the draw. They saw The Crisco Kid turn to face his competitor, and they saw his hand steal down to the butt of his gun, loosen it, and slip away again to rest once more, with control, upon the graceful neck of the dappled chestnut.

And men who watched, no matter how hardy their nerves might be, began to tremble and frequently they had to moisten their lips, and if their glances were forced away for an instant, they jerked back suddenly to the central figures of the tragedy that was to come. It was as though one could watch a thunderbolt forming in the sky—watch it descending perceptibly through the air, but remain ignorant of what head it was doomed to strike, knowing that it was foredoomed to shy.

"It's a hundred and fifty, gentlemen," said Jim Bradley. "It's a hundred and fifty. Do I hear two hundred?"

"Two hundred," said The Kid.

"And ..." the auctioneer said, turning toward Bud Carew and thrusting out his cane at him. "And what?"

"Fifty."

"You, Crisco?"

"Three hundred!"

"That's bidding like gentlemen! But can he have him? He cannot! You, Bud?"

"Three-fifty!"

It was rather high bidding for cowpunchers who might work for a tenth of that sum per month. Another interest was now added to that of the coming death scene.

"Three fifty from Mister Carew. Now, Crisco, what'll you bid for your horse, the horse that nobody but you can ride ... the horse that loves you like a brother. What d'you say, Crisco?"

"Five hundred," Crisco said, his hand going slowly back and forth, soothing the great stallion."

"Five hundred!" repeated Jim Bradley rather huskily. "Five hundred up to you, Carew. Look there on a horse that's a horse. Suppose you wouldn't want to ride him? You ain't got to ride to get the worth of a thousand out of his hide. He's worth a thousand, just to look at him a couple of times a day. Am I wrong? I'm not wrong!"

Carew was biting his thin lip nervously. "Five-fifty," he said gloomily.

"Six hundred."

"It ain't enough. No horse like Twilight can get knocked down for six hundred," said Jim Bradley. "Boys, for the honor of Texas, where they know horses ... what you say, Carew?"

"Seven hundred!" shouted Carew, furious at the long contest.

The Crisco Kid winced, and automatically his hand twisted into the mane of the stallion, as though he would hold the beautiful animal by force.

"Seven hundred to you, Crisco?"

The Kid looked wildly about him.

"I'll go you twenty-five, Crisco," said a friendly voice.

"Seven twenty-five," The Kid gasped out, and stared at Carew.

"Seven-thirty," Carew snarled through his teeth.

There was a long pause—a long, heartbreaking pause. Once more The Crisco Kid looked toward the corral fence, but the strain seemed too terrible for the voice of any friend to break in. Even now Carew glared around the circle, challenging anyone to dare help his rival. And slowly The Crisco Kid looked back to the man on the fence and began to straighten and stiffen. His right hand slipped down and hung with spread fingers above the butt of his gun. He would take no further start, though Carew, muttering savagely beneath his breath, was frankly gripping the handle of his Colt.

"Seven-thirty, gentlemen," Jim Bradley panted. "The horse is worth a thousand ... for heaven's sake, boys, don't do nothin' that you'll regret later on. Seven-thirty is bid for Twilight. He's worth a thousand of any man's money that loves horseflesh. Kid, and you, Bud, bullets don't mean nothin' ... but death. Seven-thirty, boys. Do I hear seven-fifty? Do I hear seven-fifty? Goin' to Bud Carew for seven-thirty. Do I hear forty? Do I hear forty? Goin' to Bud Carew for seven-thirty. Goin' to Bud Carew ... goin' ... goin' ..."

"Eight hundred," said a quiet voice.

It caught at all those tensed heads and jerked them suddenly around where they beheld the smiling face of Señor Valdivia. And there was a groan of relief—and perhaps of disappointment.

Jim Bradley relaxed his clenched hands and turned, half reeling, toward the Argentinean. "It's Mister Valdivia," he mumbled through his thick lips, which were suddenly grown numb. "I guess … goin' to Mister Valdivia … sold, thank God!"

Bud Carew swung his legs slowly across the top bar of the fence. Then he climbed down, slowly still. He had to help himself with his gripping hands, and when he reached the ground, his knees sagged under him. Then, jerking the brim of his sombrero low across his eyes, he went stumbling toward his horse, which was tethered at an adjacent fence.

But the others did not move. They were watching The Crisco Kid, whose fingers were still wound in the mane of the stallion, though he had faced around upon the new man who had taken Twilight from him. And in his wild, uneasy eyes a score of resolves could be seen to be born in flashes, dying slowly and replaced by new ones. Perhaps, in the space of five seconds, his mind wavered back and forth between a fierce determination to draw his gun on the purchaser—or to leap upon the back of the dark chestnut and vault him over the fence and so away to outlawry, perhaps, but to freedom with the horse he loved.

Jim Bradley extended both his hands, letting his truncheon fall. "Don't be a fool, Crisco!" he pleaded

Sometimes a single word will win an argument and sometimes the lightest unexpected touch will take the strength of a strong man. At the voice of the auctioneer, the big cowpuncher suddenly dropped his head and his body seemed to shrink and his muscles grow loose beneath his clothes. He was beaten, and a sigh of relief, perhaps of pity, also, came from the watchers.

They saw The Crisco Kid gather himself together and approach the fence. Behind him, Twilight followed like a dog at the master's heels. They saw the cowpuncher rest a hand against the fence and peer through at the Argentinean as though at some far-distant figure.

"You're Valdivia?" he asked.

"I am, sir," Don Sebastian said.

"Señor," the cowpuncher said slowly, and speaking perfect Spanish of the true Castilian brand, "you have beaten me. Where shall I take your horse?"

Some half dozen times in his life the man from the Argentine had been touched. He was touched now, and, stepping close to the fence, he studied the drawn, haggard face of The Kid. One might have thought that the labors of a hard day had been condensed into the last two minutes, so greatly was he changed and aged.

"*Amigo mío*," Don Sebastian said, "we have not yet shaken hands."

"My name," said The Crisco Kid, "is Charles Dupont."

"Señor, I am honored."

They shook hands gravely between the bars of the fence.

"I am covered with sorrow," continued Valdivia, "because I have had to take this horse away from a man who was worthy of it."

"There is only one Twilight," The Kid said calmly. "I don't blame you. Where shall I take him for you?"

"I am collecting my horses at a little house just outside of the town. I think it is known as the old Montfort House."

"I know the place."

"If it will not too greatly trouble you …"

"Not at all."

"Señor Dupont, you place me under a thousand obligations by your courtesy."

They bowed to each another, and The Crisco Kid, stepping back, leaped lightly upon the back of the stallion. One hand held the ropes of the halter. It seemed bridle and reins enough for his purpose. With a low cry he brought Twilight into dancing life. Like a tiger the great horse rushed at the nearest rails, reared, and floated across it. Then he flaunted away across the open fields, the rider guiding him with perfect ease with touches of the ropes now and again. And the crowd, having remained to see this odd situation come to an end, stared for a time after the departing rider, saw him dip out of sight below a hillock, and then broke up hastily.

Carreño approached his master with a worried face and found the Valdivia fallen into a brown study, half smiling.

"But, señor ..."

"Ah, Juan, what is it now?"

"He is gone with your horse and eight hundred dollars of your money. Is it possible that you expect to see him ever again?"

Valdivia smiled coldly upon his secretary. "You are in many ways a good fellow and indispensable to me, Carreño. But you will never learn that men cannot be judged by their clothes alone. Let me tell you, Juan, that a million pesos could not persuade my friend, Charles Dupont, to steal the horse for the very simple reason that I have entrusted it so freely to his keeping. Consider him again, Carreño, and you will see that in spite of his appearance, this Crisco Kid as they call him, is a gentleman."

So they mounted and rode, after Carreño had left word for the purchases of the day to be forwarded after them.

"There is only one thing," he added when they had gone some distance.

"And that?" asked Valdivia, who seemed in the most inextinguishable high spirits.

"Of what use to you will this eight-hundred-dollar unmanageable animal be?"

"Tush, Carreño," said the master, "I have paid eight hundred pesos not for a horse, but for a man."

CHAPTER FIVE

A rush of hoofs across the night, a spattering of gravel against the front wall of the shack as the horse was swerved away in its charge, and then a little weighted bit of an envelope darted through the door like a bird, hung for an instant in the air, supported against a fall by the impetus of its flight, and settled like a fluttering bird toward the floor.

Before it reached that resting place, Bud Carew had skulked swiftly into the open doorway, catching out his revolver as he went. But he could see nothing for the instant, so blinded were his eyes by the black night and the radiance of the lamp by which he had just been reading. But, when he squatted, he could see a flying rider whip over the top of the nearest swell of ground, sketchily outlined against the white blur of the stars for an instant, and then dip out of view.

He stood up again, relaxing, but still with a scowl upon his wide mouth. Then he approached the fallen envelope with caution. For Bud Carew had been in a state penitentiary, and any man who has served five years behind the bars has learned long and valuable lessons in catlike discretion. The discretion of Bud had become so great that he had even risen to the position of a trusty.

Now he touched the bit of paper with the toe of his boot. He kicked it a little distance, discovered that there was at least no hidden explosive in it, and then picked it up. When he opened it, he discovered that it had simply been weighted down with a large pebble, and when he had removed that, he took out a slip of paper. Upon it was written neatly with a typewriter:

Carew,

    The Crisco Kid is at the Montfort House.

    He's alone there.

—A Friend

This communication, after it had been perused with care, Bud Carew crumpled in his large hand and dropped into the stove. Then he stood a while in thought, smoking a cigarette until his brain had cleared and he had adjusted himself to the new thought. So, standing there and smoking, an evil smile grew upon his lips, and his eyes, wrinkling from the corners, grew small and bright. Finally he went to the bunk at one side of the room and jerked the blanket from a sleeping figure there. The clatter of horse hoofs and the fall of the envelope had not sufficed to disturb the slumber of the man. Now Carew caught him by the shoulder with small ceremony and dragged him to a sitting posture. It revealed a fellow with a sun-browned face, now swollen and reddened with sleep, for he had been lying on his stomach with his head pillowed in his arms.

He now brushed the dangling hair out of his eyes and twisted about until his feet fell limply to the floor. "Are they after me?" he croaked.

Carew made no response. And the other pushed his hand under the blankets and brought out a small flask that he uncorked and poured half of the contents down his throat. They were so fiery that they made him blink and roll his red eyes. Then he fumbled at a vest pocket with a numbed hand for his makings.

"You've slept twelve hours," Carew informed him.

"The first sleep in two days," muttered the other.

"Wake up, Jerry."

"I'm awake. What's poppin'? You heard word about me? About them, I mean?"

"They're watchin' the border for you."

A grin of unholy glee transformed the fat face of Jerry. "You knowed that they'd do that, Bud," he said, staring fondly at his companion. "I'd've been runnin' straight into their arms, if it hadn't been for you, old pal."

"Lay off that chatter," said Bud Carew without emotion. "You can do me a turn tonight, boy."

"Say where, Bud. I'm yours to the limit. You've cached me away right under their noses … damn 'em. Tell me … did the old one die?"

"He died last night. I heard about it today, at Garrison's."

"You did?"

"It was the slug that went through his belly that turned the trick. You ought to've knowed that it would do it. Gents don't live after they been drilled there."

"I forgot about that. Well … he's done up, then." He shrugged his shoulders. Just a trace of a frown walked across his forehead. Then he puffed at his smoke.

"What's the party for tonight?"

"The Crisco Kid."

"You didn't get him today?"

"I didn't have no good chance," Bud Carew said, his face changing color a little as he recalled the strange and terrible duel without weapons that he had fought with The Kid that afternoon. "I didn't have no good chance, but tonight I got the chance that I want."

"That's good. You been layin' for him for a long time, ain't you?"

"Sure. Here's the beauty part. You're goin' to give me a hand, Jerry."

Jerry hesitated—only a fraction of a breath. Then he nodded, and, automatically reaching for his cartridge belt that lay beside him, he began to buckle it on. "Might as well be two as one," he said. "If the old guy has croaked, I might as well tackle another. Might as well be a hundred as one, eh?"

"Looks that way, old son."

"What's the scheme?"

"He's at the old Montfort House ... alone."

Jerry stood up and stretched himself. "Son," he said, "that's a cinch. Let's blow."

They were in the saddle within five minutes and rolling across the fields at a steady canter. In a brief half hour they were in sight of the Montfort House. It lay in a hollow near the flat, silver face of a tank whose stagnant waters took the faint reflections of the stars. One half of the Montfort House had fallen through age and neglect. One half remained standing, and from a window shone the uncertain glow of a fire.

"Easy," Jerry said, and chuckled, "this here is made to order for us. I don't need you, Bud."

"You don't know him."

"I've heard about him. He's hard, I guess."

"Harder'n you think. Long as he can draw a breath, he'll be able to shoot ... and shoot damned straight. You hear me talk?"

"I hear you, kid. Let's start."

"What's your idea?"

"Drop the horses here, and then go down to the house together. We'll find him and finish him easy. He ain't lookin' for nothin'."

"He's always lookin' for something. A gent that has had as many gunfights as him is always lookin' for trouble. You lay to that. We'll sneak up on that window and take our chance. But go easy, old son."

They went down the slope as noiselessly as a pair of snakes, and, creeping through the ruin of rotten timber and of sprouting shrubs before the standing part of the house, they came to the window that was dimly flushed by the firelight within.

There Bud Carew peered in, and all he saw was a wreck of a room with the plaster broken from the ceiling and dripping down in tenuous strips. The fire burned lazily on the open hearth. In a corner was a blanket roll, and a rifle stood against the wall nearby. A faint aroma of coffee and of cigarette smoke was in the air. That was all. The only sign of life was from the corral behind the house, where a pair of fighting or playing horses began to squeal like two mischievous children.

"Maybe he's back with the horses?" whispered Bud to Jerry.

And at that instant, from not far behind them, a strong baritone voice called: "You want me, fellows?"

"It's him!" gasped out Bud, and dropped for the ground, whirling as he fell.

And as he whirled and fell, with Jerry following that excellent example, he saw against the sky the tall form of a man, looking gigantic above the ground gloom.

Before he struck the ground, Bud's gun spoke, and at his side Jerry's barked in a higher note. Very deliberately, or so it seemed to the feverish eyes and nerves of Bud, the tall man drew his own weapon. Four bullets had whirred around him before he leveled it and fired, but in response there was a scream of agony from Jerry, and beside Bud his companion began to twist and kick. One driving heel caught Bud on the hip and half turned him over, bruising the bone and the flesh above it.

Desperate, feeling that a curse was on his effort on this night, he rose to his hand and his arm's length to plant a finishing shot. But the gun in the hand of the tall man spoke again, and Bud saw a flash of red lightning, felt a heavy blow upon the head, and dropped into smoothly pillowing darkness.

He wakened with the shiver and play of the red-yellow firelight upon his face. And beside him he looked up into the face of The

Crisco Kid, who was calmly finishing a cup of coffee and smoking a tailor-made cigarette. The fumes of the Turkish tobacco were sweet and heavy through the room. That, in the beginning, had been one of the causes for the hatred and the scorn of Bud. He could not understand a full-fledged cowpuncher smoking these effeminately luxurious cigarettes. He raised a hand toward his head. It was swathed with a thick bandage.

"I thought that you'd never come to," The Crisco Kid said in his quiet way.

"What happened?" murmured Bud.

"I don't know nothing except the last part of it," The Crisco Kid said, and he smiled down at Bud.

But there was something terrible in that smile to Bud Carew. In that smile was everything he had always hated and feared in The Crisco Kid—the cool aloofness from other men, the self-content, the leisurely criticism of those about him, and a thousand other things of which Bud Carew could make only dim guesses. He only knew that he hated them all.

"Jerry?" he gasped out as the whole truth came back upon him.

"Unfortunately," The Crisco Kid said, "Jerry died almost at once."

CHAPTER SIX

There is something old about even the most modern parts of New Orleans; the very hotels have a quiet dreaming atmosphere. As the Kentuckian said: "The whiskey is thicker and the hours are longer down heah." And on this quiet morning, with the stir and the hum of the traffic in the distance like a lullaby, even the subdued voice of Carreño crackled like an exploding gun in the deep silence of the hotel room.

The burring of the hotel phone bell was a rude alarm that brought him sharply out of his seat.

"Mister Dupont is calling on Mister Valdivia," said the voice of the clerk.

"One moment, please. Mister Dupont," he repeated to the master, "is calling upon Mister Valdivia."

The Argentinean stirred in a deep upholstered chair and yawned above his newspaper. "Tell Mister Dupont that Mister Valdivia will be able to see him within ten minutes."

"Mister Valdivia," translated Carreño, "will be unable to see Mister Dupont for ten minutes." He hung up and turned to his master with the usual wonder in his eyes.

"Say it, amigo," Valdivia said, smiling.

"I cannot help but wonder," Carreño said, "unless you have found something exceedingly interesting in the newspaper."

"*Bah!*" exclaimed Valdivia. "Newspapers are the invention of the devil. They are intended to make the human race weak-minded."

"Exactly," Carreño murmured feebly, fumbling to follow the thought of the master.

"Which is something you cannot understand. Let it go. But I tell you, Carreño, that newspapers exist and grow more popular only because they skillfully nourish an illusion that they convey to the reader all of importance that happened in the world the day before."

"Exactly," Carreño said, still more baffled.

"Whereas," said the master, "they convey nothing, saving the price of wheat and barley … the latest notes issued to foreign embassies … sporting returns … and a few of these foolish surface evidences of life. But all that lies beneath is unnoticed."

Señor Valdivia rose and paced the room. He was dressed in immaculate whites, with wing collar and a blue bowtie, faintly dotted with a dust of orange. As he walked, he studied how the sharp creases of the trousers broke in folds above the knees.

As he walked, he continued the conversation. "As a matter of fact, nothing that is truly of importance gets into a newspaper, unless it is by accident. For what is truly of importance in this odd little world of ours is what takes place in the hearts and souls of individuals. What made the cloud upon the brow of my taxi driver of last night is of greater importance than the note that was sent by England to France and that fills the headlines this morning. What the prime minister of England had for breakfast, for all we know, may have dictated the contents of that note. Let us understand, then, when and what he had for breakfast. All of these things are of the greatest significance. But the note itself is so many words. What lies beneath them?"

"Exactly," Carreño agreed, the perspiration standing on his fat brow as he strove to follow the master. He added: "But concerning Dupont."

"What concerning him?"

"Why must he be made to wait?"

"For full and sufficient reasons. Dupont is a shrewd fellow. Unless I watch the fall of every card, he will begin to suspect that he is necessary to me."

"Exactly," Carreño said, rolling his eyes wildly.

"And, if I am to use him, he must suspect nothing. He must feel only that I desire to take him out of the greatness of my heart to the Argentine."

"To the Argentine!" Carreño gasped.

"I said ... to the Argentine."

"E-Exactly," stammered Carreño. "And yet ... but of course these American cowpunchers are of use on our ranches."

"Tush," Valdivia said. "Do you think that I could only use such a man as Dupont as a cowpuncher? Such a heart of honor and such a soul of fire? Tush, Carreño, you have passed into your second childhood." And he leaned upon the back of a chair, laughing merrily.

It may be observed that the fat secretary was retained in his important office for the very reason of his fatness of body and of brain. A more intelligent person would have been an entity to be considered, but Carreño, to the master, was simply a creature who took the place of a blank wall. Carreño served to reflect the thoughts of Valdivia and show them back to him in highlights.

He was paid a salary, which was greater than the salary that would have been paid to an intelligent man. The reason was that whereas the diligence of an intelligent man could have been bought and that alone, in the case of Carreño, Valdivia was buying mind and body and soul. The check that came to Carreño each month was so great that, figuratively speaking, he bowed the knees of his heart and wondered over the greatness and the goodness of his master. He would rather have cut out his tongue than repeat a single syllable of the utterances of Valdivia, partly because he did not understand most of them and partly because it flattered and tickled the very cockles of his heart when he understood and knew that the master was opening his conscience before him.

"Such a man," went on Valdivia, "in another day would have been a great captain. Thousands would have followed him to war. Kings would have consulted him. And for the purity of his heart, a priest might have confessed to him as other people confess to a priest. Such a man, had his thoughts been given another bent, might have been a saint … duly canonized. Consider only what he did in the case of the dog, Carew."

"It was very strange," Carreño sighed.

"What would you have done?"

"Killed him, certainly, at the least."

"But to let him go freely, Carreño. Think of that. To let him go free, with no hindrance. To put the entire blame for the attack upon the dead man, whose life was already forfeit to the law. What will you make of that?"

"I have pondered over it. It is most unusual."

"You are right. For once in ten thousand times, you are very right. Because, my friend, do you think that Carew will repay his benefactor with even so much as the most naked gratitude?"

"One could expect so much and very much more."

"And be deceived Carew will hate him. Because to be forgiven by him that one has attempted to wrong is the most deadly and the most damning of injuries. One may forgive hatred, but scorn never."

"It is very true, señor."

"If Carew hated this fellow before, he now loathes him. Poison has entered his blood. To be revenged upon his benefactor, even for that benefaction, he would follow Dupont around the world."

"Concerning that," Carreño said, "is it not odd that this man who all the others knew only as The Crisco Kid should have told you his true name?"

"Tush," murmured Valdivia. "This is nothing. You must understand that he knew, instantly, that he was speaking to a gentleman, and therefore he could not use anything but his true name."

"Ah?" said Carreño, glad to thresh out something that had often troubled him of late. "But what could have induced such a man, with some culture, with some education, to go to the Far West of his country and live as a simple cowpuncher?"

"To answer that properly," the master said, "one would have to be an Anglo-Saxon, with the brain and the soul of an Anglo-Saxon, which we may daily thank the Creator we do not possess. But suppose I put it in this fashion ... having displeased his parents in some small affair ... perhaps of the heart ... this man feels that he is disinherited. You have no idea, Carreño, how finely strung are the sensibilities of these English ... of these Americans. A hint is to them like a blow. A gesture is an insult. A word is a catastrophe. It is buried in their hearts. It is never referred to. It is never forgotten. So, because of a nothing, this foolish boy has probably left his home and has come, by the grace of God, into my hands." He rubbed those thin, graceful hands together, exulting over the mere thought

"Are you sure that you have him?"

"I shall be sure before I have ended my conversation with him this day."

"Then, if it is of such importance, why do you make this proud man wait?"

"Because he must feel that every moment of my time is employed with matters greater than he. Otherwise, he would cease to value me."

"Ah?" Carreño said, again at sea. He added: "But I cannot see for what you could use him?"

"I shall tell you this only. I shall use him in a matter that is of greater importance to me than the welfare of all my physical possessions. Do you understand?"

"Exactly," breathed Carreño.

But his eyes were like the eyes of a fish. Striving to comprehend, he could see nothing, saving the endless leagues of the ranch of his master, flushed with the yellow-green of new verdure, flocked with many cattle beyond the counting. How could anything upon earth be of greater importance than that *ranchero?* Nothing, saving, perhaps, the fabulous fortune of yonder captains of American finance of whom one could read but could not conceive—figures great as the wealth of a whole nation, well-nigh.

"I shall use him," continued the master, "as the knight in the old days used his sword. It saved his body. It also saved his soul. Consider this for a time. You will not understand, but it will do you good to consider it."

"Exactly," Carreño said, and sighed.

"As for another thing, you must understand that I have proved the temper of the steel before I have used it. I had the great thought first when I saw him standing in the corral at the side of the stallion. For a man who can control a horse will also be able to control a man and many men. I saw then that he was a true weapon for my use, but still I wished to make sure."

"You mean, señor, that you had seen him manage the horse, Twilight?"

"To use your own word ... exactly! But I had guessed at more than this. I had guessed at powers locked up within the heart and the soul of this man. He who can love a horse can love a man. Will you understand, Carreño, that it was through love that he had conquered the stallion?"

"I hear you say it," the secretary said. "And yet ... the bridle, the bit, the spurs ... these are what we use to control wild horses, are they not, señor?"

"That, of course, is very true. But what reins, bridle, bit, or spurs did Dupont use upon Twilight? None of them. The control existed within his mind and his heart only. Be sure of that. The stallion loves him as a mare loves its foal, and the man loves the stallion as a woman loves her child. Than this, there is no greater love, and than love there is no greater power."

"Exactly," Carreño said, and gasped again for breath.

"It could be seen, also, that of that entire multitude of chosen men … all men of battle … all men born to the use of the gun, two stood out preeminent. Is it not so?"

"Ah, yes," whispered Carreño, glad to be upon ground where he could speak with surety and authority.

"One was this Dupont … this Crisco Kid, as men call him in this barbarian land. One was Carew. For when Carew ran his eye along the crowd, remember what happened. Men who would have offered a thousand dollars to the Crisco Kid to buy the stallion, shook their heads and were abashed. The enmity of Carew meant more to them than the friendship of The Kid. At that moment I made up my mind that I must test the two. And test them I did."

"Señor?"

"Why, Carreño, do you think that it was chance that brought The Kid and Carew so quickly together? Not at all. It was I! For I, Carreño, needed a gallant spirit and a generous one for my work, but above all I needed a formidable fighting man. Do you comprehend me?"

"Vaguely, señor," the poor Carreño admitted, shaking his head. "Only vaguely I fear."

"Have I not said it in plain words?"

"To be sure. How could the señor speak in words that were other than very clear. And yet … how can the señor fear anything under the sun?"

"Your imagination is haltered. Think again. Is there truly nothing that I can fear?"

Carreño raised his head and stared at the ceiling. He thought of the power of his master, and it was as a monk might think of the power of God. For what was beyond the reach of the hand of the owner of those great stretches of Pampas, those numberless herds of cattle—each so great, so fat, so filled with energy to live, each but a pawn in the hands of this millionaire.

"I have tried to think," he faltered. "But I can imagine nothing."

"*Bah*," said the master. "Open your mind. There is still one man. You have been hushed to sleep at night many a time in your childhood by the mention of his name."

The eyes of Carreño grew suddenly great, but still he stared at his master half without comprehension, as though a human being should have dared to match his forces against the mighty hand of the enemy of man—Satan himself.

"Speak it, Carreño. I think that surely it is now in your brain, because I can guess by the rolling of your eyes."

"Señor, it was only a foolish thought that came to me."

"Tell me the foolish thought then, my good Carreño, for sometimes the veriest fools have *guessed* at great matters."

"Señor, it would be to invite your laughter."

"Perhaps. And yet, have I never laughed at my good Carreño before this day?"

"After so much has gone before, and after you have said such great things of this enemy of yours …"

"Well?"

"The thought came into my brain that it might be …"

"Well?"

"I cannot say it. The thing is too terrible."

"Why so?"

"Because even to conceive that such a man is your enemy is to wish you terrible fortune."

"Nevertheless, Carreño, tell me the thought that came into your brain."

"It was this … that the only enemy that so great a man as Señor

Valdivia could fear must be no other than … I dare not name the thing that I have thought. Forgive me, señor."

"Tush, man. There is no harm in naming a name."

"Then … in one terrible word … El Tigre."

Valdivia started a little as though, no matter how he had been prepared, the name shocked him a trifle. Then he said: "It is he."

"In the name of heaven, señor, how did he come to be your enemy?"

"Ah, Carreño," said the rich man, "he has been my mortal foe for twenty years and more."

"And yet you live!" Carreño cried.

"I live," Valdivia said bitterly, "though my life has been little other than a curse. However, as I started to tell you, I knew that to match this El Tigre, I must have a man among men. At the Garrison sale I saw a bright opportunity to find a chosen warrior among many fighting men. There were two preeminent. They were Carew and Dupont. Do you think that I could rest content? I saw that if they fought in the presence of so many men, the victor must be sure to be taken by the others who stood by. Therefore, I waited until afterward and sent to Carew a short and unsigned missive that was sure to bring about a meeting between them. And, when that meeting took place, I set about making the victor my man."

CHAPTER SEVEN

Carreño was a good man, as men go, but what he would have called the basest villainy in another seemed to him, in Valdivia, sheer adroitness, and he smiled upon his master as though to say: "Still I learn lessons from you, señor, in the ways of the world." He said aloud: "But do you dream, señor, that this man Dupont might stand for an instant before El Tigre?"

"Carreño," the master said "an honest man is always a terrible foe … unless he is a fool. And Dupont is honest. Besides this, he will be made doubly formidable because he will know, my friend, that this task, if he undertakes it, is a well-nigh lost cause … a forlorn hope. Such desperate adventures are dear to the hearts of these Northerners. Show them a great danger and for its own sake the danger becomes a delightful thing. Show them a North or a South Pole surrounded by hundreds of leagues of terrible ice, of blizzards, of deadliest famine, and they cannot rest until they have pressed forward to find it. Hundreds die. They are forgotten. One man breaks through to victory. All the agony of a century of effort is overlooked because of the one triumph. What use is all the labor and the peril? Of what advantage is the North Pole or the South? None whatever! But the labor is its own reward simply because it is great. Danger is the fragrance in the flowers they seek … these wild men. You will see in Charles Dupont that the great task will appeal to him because of its greatness. The more formidable he learns El Tigre to be, the more he will yearn to be at him. I admit that the chances are great against him, but, considering him as he is, I say that he has one chance in three or four to win. Do you understand?"

Carreño studied his master's face like an astronomer into whose ken a vast new nebula is swimming. He could not understand or name the things he felt. He only knew that he was filled with awe and reverence for such power of brain. Then a tap came at the door—it must be he, The Crisco Kid, Dupont, for his ten minutes had now elapsed. So Carreño slipped into the adjoining room.

He would have given a great deal to have remained to hear the conversation that followed, but the walls of that old hotel were thick, and the doors were massive, of solid oak, so that he had no hope of overhearing. How great was his surprise when he found that the voices of the other two followed him rather clearly into the adjoining bedchamber to which he had retired. He could see the reason at once. Solid though the door was, it was poorly hung, so that there was a considerable gap at the bottom. To that crack the ear of the worthy Carreño was instantly pressed. He had missed the first part of the talk, but he could hear now. Sometimes he missed low-voiced fragments of the conversation, but on the whole he learned the general tenor of the talk. And he remained until his knees ached, against the hard flooring, and his head was swimming with what he heard. Still he listened.

They talked of the horses, first of all. Dupont reported that the shipping of the animals to New Orleans had been smoothly accomplished and that the horses had, to the last one, been safely put aboard the ship.

"Your work, then, is ended?" asked the rich man.

"I hope," said the deep and gentle voice of the cowpuncher, "that it has only begun. Señor Valdivia, if you have a need of an experienced cowhand on your estancia, let me go south on the boat and take care of Twilight on the way."

"Dupont," Valdivia said with a sudden change of tone, "do you think that I would let you leave me? No, no, my young friend. If I bought your horse at the sale, it was only to prevent the fight that I saw impending between you and the young man, Carew. If I bought the horse and then brought it to New Orleans with the rest of the animals, it was only because I wished to bring you the first step toward the Argentine. But if I could not induce you to go with me, I always have intended to return Twilight to you. He is your horse, señor. By your courage and your gentleness you have made him yours, and no money could take him away. Indeed, Señor Dupont, if you intend to make this journey only because you wish to remain near to your horse, tell me the truth now, take Twilight, receive your pay for the work you have done for me, and then ride when and where you will."

To this astonishing speech Carreño listened with starting eyes, for certainly it seemed that his master was giving up every advantage that he might have taken in order to bring this warrior to the Southland. Indeed, if he so desired, he could deftly hang Twilight before the gunfighter as a reward that would be received only after the great effort had been made to destroy El Tigre. But all of these opportunities were now cast away. Carreño could not believe his ears.

Then he heard the astonished and delighted voice of Dupont exclaiming: "Señor, whatever may have been in my mind before, I swear to you that after your magnificent generosity, you may consider that you have bought both Twilight and myself. We are both at your service, if you can use us!"

Carreño started. Here was a most unexpected turn—a man to whom freedom and a great gift were offered who refused to accept of either and entered into voluntary slavery. This could not be understood no matter how he attempted to look at it. And was it not doubly strange that he offered himself to Valdivia in almost the very words that the master himself had used? For Valdivia had stated that he was buying a man, and not a horse.

"Use you?" the Argentinean echoed gloomily. "Alas, my friend, consider me as one who, when he returns to his home land, returns to the most deadly peril. Consider me as one who journeys back to a daily dread of destruction. Then ask me if there is a use that I can make of one with your fearless heart and your sure and swift hands. No, you will not ask, Señor Dupont. You will see that the service of such a man as you becomes a surety of life to me."

It was a speech and the tone of an equal addressing an equal. And again Carreño wondered a little bitterly. For no matter how confidentially the master addressed him, there was always a little difference—a talking down. The very kindness of Valdivia tasted to Carreño like charity. But here was an equal, or at least one whom he found it expedient, in the matchless duplicity of his heart, to treat for the moment like an equal.

Then Carreño heard The Crisco Kid protesting boundless astonishment. Was there no law in the Argentine to protect her most eminent citizens?

"Consider," Valdivia said, "that this man is a devil. Men cannot handle him. He is a devil, and he has picked me out from the rest of humanity to practice his torments upon me."

"In the name of heaven, señor," cried the young American, "why don't you gather half a dozen good men together and ride after him?"

"Consider, my young friend, that half a dozen would not be enough to master him. He is surrounded often by a score of devoted adherents. Besides, he has friends, here and there among the poor, scattered over the country. The fools! Because when he robs a rich man of a thousand pesos, he gives ten to a few starved wretches, and they call him a benefactor and forget his crimes. Do you see?"

"I've heard of the same thing in the West," answered Dupont. "The long riders do the same thing. When they blow a bank, they give away a few hundreds here and there and this keeps them in friends up and down the range. If they are pursued by a posse, these friends give them shelter, tell them where and how the posse is reported to be riding, and furnish them with fresh horses if they are hard pressed."

"Exactly so! And it is true in the Argentine. The poor gauchos swear by El Tigre."

"A pretty name," Dupont said thoughtfully.

"Diablo would be a better one for him, however. Tiger is far too mild. But he is as secret and bloodthirsty a murderer as the tiger, Señor Dupont. He has covered the face of the country with his eyes and ears, as these stupid adherents of his are. He can afford to ride alone. When he needs men, he need hardly more than whistle, and they start up out of the ground, so to speak. Do you understand?"

"A shifty rat," muttered Dupont.

"If vengeance could have reached him, be sure that I should have taken him long ago. But money is not strong enough to defeat him."

"How has he come to hate you above others?"

"Because twenty years ago he wronged me, and those who we have wronged, we are apt to hate. Is that not true? You, for instance, had been wronged by this man, Carew. Therefore he hated you. You forgave him and freed him. Therefore, believe me, he hates you now more than ever before and would follow you around the world to destroy you."

"Do you think so?"

"I know it. But El Tigre, having robbed me of the woman I was to marry ..."

"What!" Dupont cried, and Carreño heard the soft, heavy

sound of his feet as he leaped from his chair.

"It is even so."

"Ten thousand devils!" Dupont groaned. "Is it possible?"

"It is true."

"He stole the girl you loved?"

"He did."

"He carried her away … by force?"

"True again. Do not ask me to speak of this thing, Señor Dupont. It sets my heart on fire."

Then Carreño heard a long, soft stride go up and down the room, swiftly, and the floor quivered with the weight of the walking man. He began himself to tremble, and he shrank a little from the door. He forgot that it was a man walking up and down. It seemed the slouching tread of a terrible lion.

"And this all twenty years ago?" Dupont breathed.

"Twenty years of sorrow. I have lived my life away from my homeland. To return to my country is to return to sad memories."

"Tell me, then, if nothing can ever be done to destroy this fiend?"

"There is only one way, and that is a desperate one that only a madman, desperately regardless of his life, would follow."

"However, let me hear it?"

"Suppose," said the voice of Valdivia, "that some hate-crazed man … cunning, nevertheless … were to pretend to be outlawed, were even to commit a crime to give truth to the appearance. Suppose that he were then to make himself so well-known among the criminals who haunt the foothills of the mountains that El Tigre would be forced to take notice of him. Then you may be sure that El Tigre would strive to button him to himself and make him one of the dependents. Suppose, then, that this wild-hearted madman and hero should play the part of a member of the band until he found an opportunity to face El Tigre when the two were alone together, and shoot him down like a dog … then leap onto a horse and flee ... flee with all the speed of a fast animal ..."

He paused, and Carreño could hear the hard breathing of his master.

"In such a way, in such a desperate way, the thing might be done. But you will hunt through Argentina in vain to find a man willing to stand up before that destroying beast."

"Señor," the husky voice of Dupont said, "one thing at least is true ... all things are possible."

"But here," Valdivia said, "is another matter. The woman he stole away from me bore to the beast, El Tigre, a girl baby and died in giving it birth. The child has grown up wild as an animal, but beautiful as a blessed angel. What will come of her in the hands of El Tigre and his mates?"

"Dear God!" cried Charles Dupont. "No power under heaven could keep me from Argentina. Señor Valdivia, we are agreed I travel south with you?"

"I am a thousand times delighted."

"I shall see you again. *Adiós*." The door closed heavily.

"Carreño!" shouted the master. He tore open the door. "Did you hear?" he gasped out.

Carreño had never seen the Valdivia in such a convulsion of joyous excitement. His whole body shivered with it. His eyes glittered. His face was pale with happiness.

"I heard ... señor. It is very wonderful. He intends to go to El Tigre and to ..."

"Ah?" Valdivia said, his expression changing suddenly. "It is as I thought! You have dared to eavesdrop?"

Seeing that he was so neatly caught, two thoughts flashed into the brain of the poor secretary. The one was wonder at the shrewdness of Valdivia in pretending such headlong impulse in order to find out if his man had been prying at his secret conference, the other emotion of Carreño was utter despair if he should lose his place.

He searched feebly for an excuse. Then he clasped his hands

together and gaped upon his master. His knees were unstrung and began to sag.

"Señor, señor … in heaven's name," he whined.

"Stand up!" Valdivia snarled. "I have always known that you were a dog. I see that I have always been utterly right. But … there are dogs that have their uses, and you happen to be one. Stand up … but so long as you live, never forget …"

The pale raised hand was to Carreño like a flashing thunderbolt. He shuddered beneath it.

"I shall never forget. I shall remember beyond the grave, señor!"

"Tush," Valdivia said, suddenly smiling again. "But did you hear him?"

"*Sí, sí*, señor. He talked like a man eager for this terrible service."

"It was the mention of the woman that did it. The fool has gone to dream of a blessed saint who is forced by her brute of a father to lead the life of a wild Indian."

"E-exactly," stuttered the cowed Carreño.

"And he will never rest by day or by night until he has found her," Valdivia said, and he broke into laughter so hearty that he had to hold his sides.

"But she is beautiful, señor!"

"What of that?"

"Why, if all should go as you wish … if he should accomplish the miracle and be able to join El Tigre … if he should see Francesca …"

"Well?"

"But, adoring her, how could he find it in his heart to lay a hand upon her father?"

"You do not know these men, Carreño. It is impossible for you to conceive the iron of which they are made. He is now a madman … a crusader. To destroy El Tigre and bring the girl away is now his only thought."

"Bring her away? Impossible!"

"Nothing is impossible. To climb to a star is a small thing to such a man as this Charles Dupont. And when he brings her back … as I swear I believe that he will … why, Carreño, I have reached an age where I must marry soon or else give up hope of having an heir."

"Señor!"

"It is true. Having bearded the devil in his den and taken the girl away to be his bride … I cross his game and marry her myself." He laughed again. "Is it not perfect, Carreño? But it is still a dream … it is still a dream … I must not think of it too much."

CHAPTER EIGHT

From any viewpoint it was a dull trip. The *Charlotte P. McGuire*, which was the name of the old tramp freighter that the man of the Argentine had chartered, had slogged her way south across the oily waters of the Gulf and bent down around the blunt elbow that South America pushes east into the Atlantic, and south and south along the Brazilian coast, and south and west toward the Argentine with no more excitement than the long, monotonous swells that the southern trades kick regularly toward the equator. It was in every way a musty, drowsy trip with the strong smell of the stabled horses between decks and the moist, warm wind wafting lazily across the prow.

The crew grew tired of gambling or lost all its money, then played cards for nothing until the spots were rubbed thin on the packs, then listened to one another telling tales until they were thrice repeated, then cursed the diet on which they lived, the air they breathed, the ship they sailed in, the sky beneath which they sailed, and one another's faces.

Only three men endured the passage with any equanimity. These were first Carreño, who found any scene exciting that embraced his master; secondly there was the master himself, whose whistle could be heard sounding shrill from the bridge as he watched the ship roll on her course, or whose light shone in his cabin where he read his books until late into the night; thirdly there was the tall form of Charles Dupont standing usually in the prow, sometimes looking back where the smoke of the *Charlotte P. McGuire* rolled out of the stack and drifted in immense curves up to the clouds, sometimes staring far ahead to a cloud or a star on the horizon, sometimes leaning over the rail to watch the blunt bow squash through the dull blue sea. Through all that dreary passage he was like a man rushing home on a ferry at the end of a day's work or at its beginning, his eye on fire with the things that he would do. Perhaps he was closeted in the cabin of Señor Valdivia, where he learned to regard the fat face of Carreño as no more than a design against the wall and in whose presence one might talk as one pleased, unroll the very scroll of the heart and see no more than the blinking of dull, uncomprehending eyes as the secretary stared from a corner of the cabin. Perhaps, with his head full of the tales that the owner of the great estancia told, he went to his own cabin to read, or try to read, but always fiery visions of the things to be crossed his mind, and he was forced to put the book aside. Perhaps, and this more often than any other thing, he drew one of the Argentineans, who mostly made up the crew, into conversation about their land.

There is no one like your man of the Argentine when it comes to talking of his own country. Perhaps because that country is fairly new, at least in the bulk of its population, the inhabitants are more militantly eager in their defense and their praise of it. But, lying on the southern rim of the world, with a greater actual acreage of truly cultivable soil than any other country, with only the surface of the natural resources scratched, with wealth increasing dizzily, swarming with native millionaires whose fortunes even they themselves cannot compute, the Argentinean declares himself to be at the center of things and by no means upon the outskirts. They talked to Charles Dupont of the huge tropic forests and immense rivers of their northern domain, where the great Plata rolls out like a vast muddy sea to meet the ocean, of the measureless horizons of the Pampas, and the frozen steppes of Patagonia. They talked of their cattle that swarm thickly over the rich plains, of their roads that pass on day after day, with never a turn or a bend, through the heart of the dead-level cattle country, of estancias as large as kingdoms, of millionaires greater than kings, dollar for dollar.

But, now and again, he turned their eager chatter to El Tigre. It was not hard to do, for just as they boasted of the extent of their plains and the height of their Andean Mountains to the west, and of the size of their rivers, so they boasted, also, of the deeds of El Tigre. Through the space of almost a full generation he had lived in outlawry, and therefore he had become an almost legendary figure among them. They talked of him with all their fire, and their fire was that of a religious man striving to make a convert. They were trying to convert Charles Dupont, and just as they boasted of their country's wealth and glorious future, so they boasted, also, of owning the very most terrible of all the bandits in the world.

Of how the career of El Tigre began he could learn little. Every one of his narrators had a theory and a gaudy tale full of circum-stantial details to give it substance. But each tale differed from the others. And so did the accounts of his exploits. They would begin, for instance, somewhat as follows.

"My father's brother, señor, was a waterman who worked on a ship that plied up and down the Panama River, and he himself knew a man very well who lived in Corrientes. Therefore this story is very true. My father's brother was a very honest man, señor, and therefore does it not hold that his friends would also be honest men? What I tell to you is the story just as this man told it to my father's brother, who told it to my father when I was a boy, and I remembered it, every word. For who could forget when El Tigre was named?"

This story was told to The Crisco Kid by a tall, thin youth who was in the last stages of consumption, his sallow skin wrinkled and dry as parchment, his eyes alternately filmed with dullness and again fire bright. He had a faint, husky voice that was to Dupont unspeakably touching, and he talked with a sort of desperate enthusiasm, as though he would forget in the narration the dreadful death that was every day creeping closer and closer upon him. But at least he was sure to live until he reached the country of his birth and the land of his love. And this fact gave him some happiness. And, as his story was no more extravagant than a hundred others that were told to Dupont by the Argentineans during that voyage, while the *Charlotte P. McGuire* slouched steadily southward at ten knots an hour—except when the wind freshened and cut her back to seven—it may as well be told in toto and in the words of poor José himself.

He told that story three times. And each time he omitted not a syllable of the opening assurance concerning the honesty of his uncle and his uncle's friend. In fact, he could not vary his story. He had told it so long that the words of it were like part of his flesh.

"You must know that there was in Corrientes a very great man. He was a Spaniard. His name was Alvarado Sandoval. In the old, old days his family owned much land and was very rich. After we were freed from Spain, that family continued rich. Alvarado Sandoval was the last of his family … he had no child, nor would he ever have one. And as though he might be repaid for that great loss, he succeeded in everything else that he could desire. There were not twenty men in the Argentine who were richer than he. I dare to swear it. If he wanted more money, it came to him by magic. If he wanted more land, he found a way to take it almost for nothing. He always succeeded in his undertakings.

"He grew as big with money as a pig is big with fat. Do you understand me, Señor Dupont? He was not a rich man as Valdivia is rich, for Valdivia is like a king … kind and gentle to those who are poor. But this Sandoval had a devil in him. If one begged for more time when money was due, he said … 'I am in a hurry. I have no time myself. How can I give you time?'

"His reason was that since he could not leave his name and his money to a son who could go on making it grow, he swore that he would make his own name so great that people would never forget him. He swore that, when he died, he would leave all his money for the building of the tallest building in the world. Such was this Sandoval. You will say that he was a fool. Perhaps he was. But for money-making he had a great talent.

"This is why I tell you so much of Sandoval.

"On a day … it was in June, when the calves are weaned and the alfalfa is sowed and the sheep are dipped for scab … the great El Tigre was riding near Corrientes, and, being hungry at the end of the day, he stopped at a house and asked for food. The fellow in the house was a fool who did not know him. He was a bully, likewise, this stupid man in the house. He told El Tigre that if he had not earned by honest work enough money to buy his food, he could starve. He told El Tigre that the crows might pick him, for all of him.

"So El Tigre tied that man by the thumbs against the wall. Then he took food and ate it. Afterward he rode away. Do you understand? So long as that man could stand he was well enough, but when his legs grew tired and he fell down, then all his weight would come on his thumbs … ah!" Here José always paused to rub his own thumbs affectionately, as though he were very glad indeed that they were still with him.

"When this fellow was found it was night, and they heard him screaming in the distance. So they cut him down from the wall and all he could say was this … 'A devil has been here.'

"Afterward when he could talk, he described the man who had tied him there and everyone knew that it must be El Tigre.

"Now that house and that estancia were owned by this Alvarado Sandoval. When he learned what had happened, he was very angry, and he said he would have El Tigre caught and boiled in oil, slowly. He offered a great deal of money … I think it was fifty thousand pesos … to those who might bring him El Tigre. Do you see?

"However, many others had offered great sums of money for that outlaw, and he had never been caught, so all of Corrientes thought very little of that promise of fifty thousand pesos. But El Tigre, while he did not mind the money that was offered … for that was any man's right against an outlaw … was very angry because of the boiling in oil that was promised him if he were caught.

"One morning in that same month of June, he flew down on Corrientes with forty of his men like forty great, lean, ugly condors. They were all forty of them fighting devils with scarred faces and rifles in their hands. They went first to the house of Sandoval and took the señor from his house and marched him down before them in his nightgown … for they had come very early, do you see?

"They made him go to his own bank. They made him unlock the vaults. Then they marched him out again with sacks of gold and sacks of paper money across the pommels of their saddles. They walked him down the largest street of Corrientes. Had I but been there to see and to laugh.

"Some went before him and some went behind him, and as they rode, they shouted that Señor Sandoval had come to do penance because he had thought an evil thought concerning El Tigre. Great crowds came out to see and to laugh at the rich man in his bare feet and his nightgown. But as they went, they gave Sandoval sack after sack of his own money. They made him throw it into the crowds on either side in handfuls.

"He went shouting for help and for the police. But what could the police do? When they tried to come near, the people kept them back, laughing and shouting that this was a holy thing … this was a penance. Then they scrambled for the money on the ground.

"Ah, but that was a bitter day for Sandoval, sowing his paper money in the air and his gold coins in the dirt. Perhaps it was sorrow and perhaps it was only rage, but as he walked, he began to weep. Still they goaded him with an ox goad from behind and made him dance and yell and then throw more money out of the sacks. When all that money was gone ..."

"What? Did they keep none for themselves?" Dupont interrupted.

"Not a single peso. It was holy work, do you see? Would such a man as El Tigre profit by the penance of another? No, no!"

And José would break into the heartiest laughter in his husky voice.

Then he would continue: "When all the money was gone, El Tigre and his forty men rode on out of Corrientes. And they left Sandoval, unharmed, behind them. He offered a hundred thousand pesos to those who would catch the rascal. But who would ride in such a hunt? Who would ride after El Tigre and his forty devils? No, no! Their pockets were already full of the money of Sandoval, and they did not care to work any more that day. Besides, their ribs were so sore from laughter that they surely could not have sat in saddles on such a hunt.

"After that, Señor Sandoval fell into a decline. He swore that he had thrown away the income of two years and that his heart was broken. And, perhaps, it was. For six months after that he lay on his deathbed, but El Tigre was still free and riding through the country where he would. He was not yet boiled in oil."

CHAPTER NINE

Such were the stories that Charles Dupont heard concerning El Tigre as the *Charlotte P. McGuire* wallowed south and south through the rolling Atlantic. And though he did not believe a tithe of what he heard, he knew well enough that where there is so much smoke there is sure to be some fire. And whatever else could be said of the great bandit, certain it was that he had impressed the minds of his fellow countrymen and had impressed them, on the whole, favorably. These, of course, were the poor men, and the rich would have quite another tale to tell. To them doubtlessly the outlaw was but the scum of the earth—a worthless vagabond, a murderer, and a thief on a large scale. To the others, he remained a jovial dealer out of charity from the funds that he took from those whose wallets were filled. This, too, was of significance—that not a single member among all the unruly men who, from time to time, followed El Tigre had ever been tempted by the huge rewards offered here and there and everywhere for the apprehension of the bandit.

Such a man was a tower of strength, and certainly a project similar to that which had been roughly sketched for him by the rich Valdivia seemed the crowning folly. And yet that first idea lingered in the mind of Charles Dupont like a great dream, filled with fire and wonder. Not that the owner of the great estancia ever referred to the idea again. He might even have been thought to have forgotten the outlaw, for he never mentioned El Tigre saving when Dupont brought up the subject, and then it was with a manifest regret that he spoke the name of the outlaw.

"Yet," he would say to Dupont, "I swear to you, señor, that I could not enter my land again with a feeling of safety if I did not have such a man as you by my side."

"Do not your friends know that this fiend is your enemy?" Dupont asked him once.

"Why should I tell them?" asked the millionaire with a graceful wave of his hand. "It would only mean that their minds would be clouded with anxiety so long as I were among them. There would be no point served."

In this fashion, he left Dupont convinced that in the world there was only one perfect gentleman with a soul of gentleness and grace—and that was Señor Don Sebastian Valdivia. For his own part, he could not even think of the Argentinean without a swelling heart. When he contemplated that serene goodness of heart that had, in the first place, sought to prevent the combat between himself and Bud Carew by buying the horse, when he thought, in the second place, of the exquisite delicacy of soul with which Valdivia had induced him to come to the Argentine—yet offering Twilight freely to him if he did not wish to make the long journey into a foreign land—the very soul of Dupont was moved, and he vowed to himself that this was a man for whom he would willingly die.

And when he marked, too, the gaiety of the Argentinean, unaltered from day to day, he swore again that there are more sorts of courage than that which is based upon conscious power of mind or adroitness with weapons.

They had sighted the shore, a low-lying rim of blue to the west, above the gray-blue sea. Steadily they skirted south and south through the flawless weather, making for a small port out of which they could ship the horses by rail straight for the home estancia.

On Thursday night the sun went down over the land in a red splendor. On Friday morning they turned out of their bunks early. For the *Charlotte P. McGuire* was doing her best to stand up her nose in the trough of every wave, and she was creaking and straining through every one of her ancient beams, and a thousand loosened bolts and nuts were rattling and chattering in her as she staggered into the teeth of the gale.

They came out on deck to find that she was keeping headway, and that was all. It was more than a mere cupful of wind. It was a true gale, blowing from dead ahead. The sky was sheeted with gray. The tops of the leaping waves were sliced away by the fury of the storm, and level-driving clouds of mist whipped across the waters and rattled against the ship. They stung the face of Dupont like many needle points.

Then he saw Don Sebastian come out of his cabin and walk gingerly down the deck, whose pitching surface made him eddy about like a waltzer. Yet he reached Dupont with a smile and clung to the rail near to him.

"Is everything going well?" asked the cowpuncher.

"Between you and me," said the Argentinean, "I think that we are going down."

He spoke so calmly that Dupont would have thought the remark a jest. He stared at his companion, bewildered.

"We are holding our own, at least," he said hopefully.

"Oh, more than holding our own. But we are far from shore. So much the better, is it not? If the wind should veer around and cut in toward the land ... that might be much more serious, I should think. Then we might be in danger of being driven on the shore, though I can't make out the shore just now ..."

"We have been blown somewhat off our course. We are heading straight in for the coast now."

"Straight in!" Dupont cried, and he frowned at the rancher.

For, in what he had read of ships and shipways, it was usually well to have plenty of sea room in a heavy blow.

"Yes," Valdivia repeated, smiling still. "We are rushing for the beach as fast as we can make it, which is not very fast against this storm, as you see. But … I have my doubt."

"About what?"

"About getting where we want to get. In one word, my dear fellow, the only time in my life that I have been economical now proves that economy is a sin."

"I cannot understand you, señor," said Dupont, gravely guessing at very serious matters.

"No doubt you cannot. But when I chartered the *Charlotte* it was chiefly because she was so ridiculously cheap. I now understand the reason. The rotten old tub should never have put to sea, believe me. She has been straining and heaving enough during the past few hours to open her seams, and she is now leaking like a sieve."

"Leaking!" Dupont exclaimed, and turned pale.

Valdivia looked curiously at him. "Are you nervous?" he asked.

"In the name of heaven," Dupont said, "are not you?"

"Why," said the Argentinean, "what will be, will be. Nothing that we can do will effect what is predestined to come to us for evil or for good."

And with this cold consolation he went up on the deck, as gaily as ever, while Dupont, staring after him, felt that he had seen the man for the first time. If he needed any confirmation of the serious nature of the predicament in which they then were, he received it the next moment when he saw the captain go by him, running, his face gray and stern. He was a fat old Hollander who wobbled before him as he ran. There was no doubt that he was an able seaman and would do what he could for the ship as well as for himself, but it was also plain that he was worried to the bottom of his heart.

The pumps had been laboring furiously for the last hour or so, Dupont learned, and that accounted for a curious, staccato throbbing that he had noticed from time to time. It had even waked him from his sleep that morning.

Then he went below. He found pandemonium among the horses. Wedged closely together as they were, there was still room enough for them to stagger and slip as the ship heeled from side to side or else pitched up and down, head and tail, like a little toy boat on a lake, struck by a low-sweeping gust. Twilight stood with his ears flattened to his neck and his eyes listening. That was his way. Where other horses were hysterical with terror, the gallant stallion was merely angered by the presence of danger. He wanted to find this mysterious enemy that rocked the deck beneath him. Instead, he was roped there helplessly.

And when Dupont thought of that brave spirit floundering helplessly in the wind-wracked water, his heart turned cold and he stayed only to rub the nose of Twilight until the sharp ears pricked forward. Then he returned to the deck.

The wind was unquestionably abating. One could open one's mouth now without having an air pocket blown stiffly out in one's cheek. And the *Charlotte*, with her engines working their best, was eating into the teeth of the storm steadily. The mist cleared, also, to some degree, and presently he could see the low-sketched line of the shore before them.

José passed him, laboring and gasping under the weight of a great coil of cable. "The good God will save us!" he yelled to Dupont. "Pray to Him, señor!"

The whole crew, then, knew the condition of the vessel, and that did not augur well for discipline. But here he had counted without including the spirit of the captain. That hearty soul might be daunted by the catastrophe that now looked him in the face, but he was in no wise unnerved. He seemed to be everywhere at once, and Dupont had an impression that through the single efforts of the captain the *Charlotte* was being held together in the crisis.

For another hour they struggled on, with the wind still mercifully falling, but the *Charlotte* was now manifestly settling. She had gone down so far that the heave of the waves no longer jerked the propeller out of the water with a roar from time to time. She had gone down so far, in fact, that she presented a smaller surface to the wind, by far, and for this reason as much as any other, perhaps, the old ship made better headway toward the land.

Yet how slowly that shore was drawing toward them. Then, as suddenly as it had begun, the wind dropped away to nothing, and a wild yelling broke out through the vessel from the happy sailors with half the burden taken from their hearts.

Dupont found Valdivia on the bridge, standing with his arms folded inside his cloak.

"There are ten degrees more color in your face, my friend," said Valdivia, "than when I last saw you."

"Because, I suppose, there is now no doubt that we'll get to the shore. And that smooth beach should make an easy landing place. I saw it through my glasses a little while ago."

"Exactly," said the master of the *Charlotte*'s cargo. "But unfortunately we have discovered that there is not a single lifeboat on the old tub that will swim five minutes after it has been loaded."

Dupont turned gray again. Then he shrugged his shoulders. "For those who cannot swim, that is a tragedy. Thank God that I do very well in the water." He added hastily: "And you, señor?"

Valdivia had begun to whistle. He broke to add quietly: "I have never swum a stroke in my life."

There was a little silence between them.

"The waves are falling rapidly," Valdivia said as calm as ever. "And if …"

The *Charlotte*, settling with a dropping wave, came to an abrupt halt and flung them both forward against the railing of the bridge. When they picked themselves up, there was a wild tumult of yelling voices through the ship. But only one word came from the lips of Dupont: "Twilight!"

He turned to go, but paused to catch Valdivia by the shoulder. "The horses might make shore," he said. "We must cut them loose and herd them overboard if we can. Then, señor, remain close to me. I swim strongly. We will make the land together or ..."

In such a time men do not pause to give thanks. Valdivia, without a word, hurried down to the deck after his companion.

There they found that riot was the word of the hour. The *Charlotte P. McGuire* had not yet heeled over, but she hung shuddering in her tracks, twisted due northwest, with the waves crashing against her port side in a series of thunderous shocks. One of the lifeboats struck the water at the same moment and was instantly half filled with men—whereat the rotten craft sank suddenly beneath them and they were left to clamber up the side of the boat as best they might, clutching the ropes that were thrown down to them by their companions from above.

"There is still the port boat," Valdivia said. "I think we may as well try that ..."

CHAPTER TEN

They ran to the port side of the ship, but found that the captain, in spite of all his fat, was already before them, bawling out his orders, intermixed with stentorian oaths. According to his directions the lifeboat was lowered from the davits while men from the deck strove to push the craft away from the side of the ship as it swung in the air.

They succeeded. It touched the water, but had no sooner done so than a great wave picked it up like a gigantic hand and flung it against the solid plates of the side of the *Charlotte P. McGuire*. They could see, then, that the report of Valdivia about the condition of the boats was even less than the truth. For a shock that a sound boat should have withstood with the greatest ease stove in the whole starboard side of the craft and it instantly filled and sank, followed by the wild yells of despair of the crew.

"There remains swimming ... but the horses first!" Dupont yelled through the uproar and in the ear of Valdivia.

"Let the horses go ... our own lives, my friend ..."

Perhaps never before had Valdivia received such a glance of wonder and of scorn as he now received. But at least he did not repeat the suggestion, following mutely on at the side of his friend.

Dupont paused again to grip the fat captain by the arm. "Your cargo?" he shouted.

The captain turned grim eyes upon the questioner. He was a man of few words, however, and more intent upon action. The fate of the *Charlotte P. McGuire* was now sealed. She could not be budged from her bed, and the thunder blows of the waves that crashed against her port side gave strong assurance that, before long, she would break up. The lifeboats being gone, it was now a case of every man for himself in what best manner he would work for his safety. Those two items were, therefore, very largely taken from the conscience of the captain. He could now afford to think of his cargo.

"What of the horses?" he asked. "They are lost, eh?"

"They'll swim as well as men swim," Dupont said. "But we'll need help to cut them loose and to drive them up the runway to the deck, and then force them over the side."

But the captain was already forging in the lead, thundering commands. That voice that made the crew tremble in ordinary times was now powerless, however, or nearly so. Only two fellows detached themselves from a wild attempt to make a raft on which they could float to the shore. The two made a corps of five with which they were to handle nearly two hundred horses. First they erected two strong, high barricades on the sides of the entrance of the runway. Then they beat open the sliding gate that closed the rail. All was now prepared for the drive of the horses.

It was descending into an infernal region to enter the crowded hold of the vessel now. Every horse was snorting, stamping, raging, squealing. All eyes were red with fury and with terror, while the deck shuddered and quaked with their stamping and with the terrible hammer strokes of the waves upon the port side. The violence of those had now greatly abated, but they still swelled high enough to complete the work of ruin that their stronger forerunners had begun. Through half a dozen opening seams along the side of the vessel the salt-water spurted, plainly visible in the dull lantern light of the 'tween decks, while the horses, nearby, snorted and neighed in a frenzy of struggling terror.

They were ready to stampede. There was no doubt of that, and if they could be stampeded toward the runway …

With that thought half formed in the brain of Dupont, while he made for Twilight, the whole mass of the *Charlotte P. McGuire* shifted its position and rolled upon its side with a heavy groaning. At the same time there was a loud scraping and bumping noise from the deck above, followed by a wild shout of fury and grief.

"The raft!" shouted the Dutch captain to Valdivia.

There could be no doubt of that. The half-made raft had been tilted from its position and slid overboard before anyone could get a position on it.

In the meantime, the heel of the vessel gave the horses a sharply sloping position on the deck and brought fresh squeals of terror from them. Dupont started the work of liberation. He started at the very foot of the gangway, where the animals were almost sure to rush up the slope toward the irregular rectangle of light that showed above. There he cut loose half a dozen of the frightened creatures as fast as his knife would work. And they started forward in a cluster, while he waved and yelled behind them, and he heard them groan with the violence of their struggle and their fear.

Up the gangway they fled with flattened ears, flying manes, and straight-stretched tails behind them, jostling one another, terrible in their strength and their speed. They shot up from the gangway to the narrow strip of the deck at the side of the ship. There, in vain, they strove to check their flight where they saw the edge of the vessel and the gray, restless sea beyond. But it was too late to hold back. The wet deck was as slippery as oil beneath their planted hoofs, and the whole thick cluster of horseflesh shot off into the thin air beyond.

A steady stream of the other fugitives followed. They had seen the game begin. They had even seen the forerunners falter and hold back at the head of the gangway and perhaps each intended to do likewise, but, once they were under way, the rush of other animals behind them drove them frantic, and the crash of the waves behind them, from which they were escaping, the yelling of the men above and below, whipped them forward up the gangway and over the side just as the first cluster had gone. In a trice every horse in the hold was raging with eagerness to join that thin swift procession.

Three-fourths of them were already gone when there was a fearful crashing on the port side. A whole section had been beaten in, as the half-rotten side of a big tin can crashes in when it is kicked. It was the blunt foot of the sea that had done that work, and the sea itself followed, rushing over the nearest horses and shooting far up along the floor.

"Save yourselves!" screamed the two sailors who had kept their nerve up to this point. "Save yourselves!" And they bolted up the gangway.

"Señor Dupont!" Valdivia shouted, and caught the arm of the cowpuncher. "It is too late for the rest of the horses … ourselves … unless we are to be drowned here like filthy rats … come!"

His hand was struck away. And Dupont leaped on to his work.

There was not time to have saved them all with only one man setting them free, and undoubtedly the prediction of Valdivia would have proven true for Dupont if they had abandoned him. But abandon them they would not. His example shamed them into imitation, and, muttering through their teeth, glancing aside with frightened eyes as the waves leaped through the gap in the side of the *Charlotte*, staggering through the lunging water, they worked on until the last horse was freed. And that last horse was Twilight.

At the heels of the frightened animals, when the last horse had been set free, ran the captain and Valdivia. Behind them came Dupont, his hand clutching the halter of the black chestnut. He heard the stallion panting with terror; he felt the body of the big horse shuddering with his fear and eagerness, and yet Twilight kept to his place behind the master and attempted no burst for swift freedom.

They had hardly gained the gangway before the whole remaining side of the *Charlotte* gave way and the empty stalls where the horses had been tethered were instantly awash with the swishing seas. The wave followed on with a strong head and smote Twilight and Dupont as they struggled forward, but it only served to wash them higher. As it settled back again, and as the *Charlotte P. McGuire* rolled more heavily upon its side, they came out upon the side of the deck.

Everywhere before them the rolling seas were marked with the heads of horses and with men clinging to bits of wreckage. The fat captain, clutching half a broken door, now plunged over the side. But Valdivia waited, his arms folded, rather like a spectator of the scene than one wrapped in the peril of it.

Dupont shouted to him to find something that would serve him as a life preserver, but he had to take up a piece of broken railing and put it in the hands of the Argentinean. Then Valdivia stepped to the side, paused to wave farewell, and sprang out into the thin air.

Dupont saw him sink beneath the water. He was down for a long moment before the white painted strip of rail appeared again with the *estanciero* clinging to it. He could see Valdivia kicking out blindly with his legs and paddling with one hand. In that confused effort he would never make the shore.

Then the cowpuncher turned his attention to the stallion and strove to drag him forward to the edge of the ship. It was a useless effort. What point there was in leaving this firm footing for the treacherous and terrifying waters beneath, Twilight could not see. Neither could he understand why he should leave the master.

Cold perspiration of horror formed on the forehead of Dupont, but there was no strength in his arms to handle twelve hundred pounds of bone and muscle, now resisting with braced hoofs. He could only hope against hope that the stallion would follow him if he himself leaped down.

He paused to take that magnificent head in his arms and stroke the wet, glistening neck. Then he stepped to the side and dived. It was a long, shallow dive that carried him to some distance from the *Charlotte P. McGuire*, and, as he reached the surface, he turned on his back and looked up.

Twilight stood at the very edge of the ship, cowering back on account of the slant of the deck and for fear of the rolling seas, but with pricked ear, searching the waters. So Dupont waved an arm and shouted. At that, the great chestnut straightened. His neigh came like a trumpet call over the waters, and he sprang out into the air.

He landed not three yards away. The foam and spray leaped high above his body. In another instant he was swimming like a dog at the side of his master—his sharp ears pricked joyously. There was another object in the mind of Dupont, however, and that was Valdivia, who he had seen struggling so clumsily through the water. Then, as a wave tossed him gently upward, he saw the estanciero clinging to his bit of wood in the nearest hollow. Dupont was instantly at his side, and over the desperate and set face of the Argentinean he saw a smile of welcome flicker like a light over a dark room.

"You have not forgot, *amigo mío*," Valdivia said.

"I have not forgot. Let the wood go. Put a hand on my shoulder ... so. Now it will be better."

Swimming strongly, he brought Valdivia in behind Twilight. There he showed him how to hold the tip of the stallion's tail with one hand and kick with his legs and paddle with his free hand. He showed him how to lie low in the water, so that there might be as little weight as possible to tow. Then with a practiced, swift stroke, he gained the head of Twilight again and led the way toward the shore.

Weighted with this burden from behind, the stallion, though he swam more strongly than ever, made only slow progress. And had he continued in his self-selected course, he could never have gained the shore. But the master led him quartering across the waves where their sway would not catch them full in the face and throw them back and where the sharpness of the crests bothered them less.

In this fashion they worked on slowly, slowly to the beach. Other unhampered swimmers were already on the white sands. He could see them wringing the water out of their clothes, dancing for joy of their deliverance and embracing one another. But they had no thought, it seemed, for those who were still struggling in the sea.

From time to time, he turned his head and studied Twilight as the gallant stallion struggled in the rear. For a time there was no change, then he could see the nostrils straining wider and the eyes glare with exhaustion. At that, he reached for the floating rope, found it, and, swimming on ahead, he caught the end of the rope in his teeth and began to work with all his might. Perhaps it would have seemed a foolish thing for a man to attempt to help a horse through the water, but where the salt sea water already buoys the body, there needs only a little added power to make a huge difference.

So Dupont strained on with all his might. He dared not look behind him at the exhausted head of the stallion. He knew that his own strength was running out of his body like water through a sieve. Mists of blackness tinged with red began to float across his eyes, and still the shore seemed farther and farther away when, from a wave top, he looked ahead.

The end came with heavenly suddenness. Something with a snake body cut the water ahead of him and a distant shout ran in his ears. It was a rope thrown from the shore, and, clutching it with one hand and holding the halter of Twilight with the other, they were drawn toward safety.

So terrible were those efforts that he had made as he swam that, when he found the soft beach at last beneath his feet, he reeled up the gentle slope like a drunkard, with one arm hanging over the drooped neck of the chestnut stallion. But at last they came into the dry, white sand, and the hot sun burned upon them, and the keen breeze clipped against their faces, and above all the joy of deliverance restored them.

Out of the great distance—or so it seemed to his roaring ears—he heard a cry, and he saw the fat form of Carreño, painfully outlined in all its flabby truth by his clinging, wet clothes, wobbling toward Valdivia, shouting, staggering with exhaustion and with joy and throwing up his hands to heaven.

"The dog is glad that I am saved," Valdivia said to Dupont, "but he allowed a stranger to save me. Señor, I shall never forget. And look ... there is the last of the *Charlotte*."

The hold of the freighter had been gradually filling as her sides were staved in. Now she pushed her nose high as though she were striving to leap from the ocean that was destroying her, and she sank suddenly by the heel. In five minutes there was nothing left but the narrow strip of the prow, covered thick with spray with the beat of every wave.

CHAPTER ELEVEN

It was mid-December when they reached the camp; the locusts were already there and gone after laying their eggs, and now the *saltonas* were creeping everywhere. Being mid-December, the Argentine summer was beginning, and a hot beginning it was, but to The Crisco Kid, accustomed to the furnace days of August in the Arizona desert, all degrees of heat were endurable. He could withstand the fiery blasts of the winds and the focused brilliance of the sun and the strangeness of the country. But the creeping locusts, or *saltonas*, he could not stand. They filled him with an unspeakable loathing. And Jeff Slinger, the majordomo of the camp, as the Argentinean calls a ranch, assured him that he could spend years and years without losing that horror of the crawling multitudes.

A friendship had risen at once between Jeff and The Crisco Kid. It originated on the second day after the arrival of Valdivia with his horses and his men, when Dupont sat out the furious antics of a three-year-old Cleveland bay stallion that had never been backed before by a man. It was a hot battle during which the peons stood about the corral and muttered: "*Muy gaucho.*" And when the big bay was subdued, Jeff Slinger deigned to open a conversation with the following eloquent praise: "You've rode a bit, stranger?"

Slinger was a man who had seen a great deal of what the world has to offer and who had suffered as much as he had enjoyed. His body was wrecked. His left arm was badly stiffened as a result of a mine explosion in Colorado; he was crippled with rheumatism from long exposure to icy water in a shipwreck on Lake Michigan; a great scar furrowed the right side of his face, gathering the flesh to it and distorting his thin mouth to a mirthless grin at all times. A lion's paw in South Africa had made that scar. Both legs had been broken several times while he was breaking horses in Texas in his youth, and on the ground his gait was a hitching, shuffling, sidewise thing, painful to behold. But in the saddle the little, broken man was still graceful and there was still in his eye an undimmed fire. Here, in a strange land, he had finally worked himself up to the second position of importance on a domain of five hundred square miles. His word was the second in command in dictating the laws that controlled three hundred men and sixty-five thousand cattle and twenty thousand sheep. In a year or so opportunity would come that would make him, perhaps, manager of another camp and give him his $10,000 or $15,000 yearly salary. Yet he remained that which he was born, a slangy Western cowpuncher with no more personal dignity than a child.

From Slinger, The Crisco Kid learned many things about *criollo* and *gaucho* and the ways of the land, but, first of all, he learned about the coming of the locusts.

On a mid-October day, the gulls about the estancia became excited, rustling their wings, flying in confused directions, and gaping their beaks as though in anticipation that their crops would soon be fatly filled, and then Jeff Slinger had seen a thin drift of transparent gauge and sparkling points of light high above him—the first drifts of the locusts, with whirring wings and bright-armored bodies in the sunshine. Myriads and myriads in each transparent, high-flying cloud of the insects, yet these enormous armies were but the forerunners, the flying outer scouts of the masses that came behind. For when the main body hove in view it came in cubic miles of purple haze, a living fog.

By night, the willows were covered with dun-colored locusts so thickly that the green of the trees were streaked and overshadowed. Here they roosted at night above the reach of the dew. When they descended for the business of laying, the great instinct took command of them. Fear left them in the mighty urge of maternity. They huddled on all the firm ground they could find—roads or dry, beaten, naked patches among the fields, monsters of the insect world with a five-inch spread of wings and a three-inch body. With two talons at the end of the tail they dug holes bit by bit until their bodies were buried to the thorax, then they filled the hole with a hundred or more eggs, covering these with glutinous foam.

In two weeks from the time of their coming, the laying locusts were gone. No harm had been done. The green things remained everywhere. Only, thousands of miles of road surface were honey-combed with new life waiting to come forth. There lay the plague asleep, as it were, and patient under whatever hand would destroy it. But how could they be destroyed? The earth was too hard to take a plow, and even had plowing been possible, there were not enough hands available to perform the work.

At the end of December over the roads and the beaten patches of firm ground everywhere, swarming multitudes of green things appeared, and with white specks among them—little locusts a quarter of an inch long still attached, here and there, to the egg skin. Through the weeks that followed, the tiny creatures fed until their shell cases were bursting, then changed the old skin for a looser dress, fed that fat in turn, and so through half a dozen skin changes until at last came the alteration from the creeping *saltona* to the flying locust. Red, yellow, black, and green, the roads were soon packed with them issuing from the shell, or streaming across from one pasture to the next, voracious feeders all, strong-jawed, but tender of body so that they climbed above the dew at night and wriggled up posts and stout grasses on the hottest days to escape from the scorching touch of the earth.

They were moving as water flows, when Dupont first saw the horrible armies. Sometimes the tide stretched suddenly far into the fields, blotting out the green as it went. Sometimes it put out a curling arm toward the big vegetable gardens near the main house, and then by scores the peons were called to stop the rush.

But it was not a rush. It was a slow, jumbled progress, tumbling against one another, crawling over the backs of the fallen, clumsy, awkward upon their feet at the first mosquito stages of active hopping, unable to climb up a smooth surface, unable even to clamber to the tops of riding boots. It was the uncountable billions with which they executed their slightest maneuvers that made their coming seem swift. Sometimes The Crisco Kid dreamed of the world depopulated by this grim pest. For though the march might be a little delayed here and there, it could not be stopped.

As for saving the fields, that could not be really attempted. The battle front was too far-flung, the hosts were too dense. The real struggle was only to postpone the destruction of the gardens. When the thin, disgusting flood of life moved toward the vegetable fields, smooth-faced barriers were erected before the army front. There was no question of a diversion to either side from before such an obstacle. The stupid creatures merely knew, by the gnawing in their empty bellies, that somewhere straight ahead there was or might be green food. Therefore the dense battalions packed closer and closer before the small wall, then swarmed upon each other's backs until the wriggling life was sheeted thick in innumerable billions. When that time came, the massacre was prepared.

Quantities of the dry stalks of the linseed, useless for any purpose saving bedding and this, were brought out and placed before the wind, at angles that would converge upon the barriers. Then the straw was ignited and rolled by pitchforks and the wind toward the barriers. In front of these the flames were pooled and the blasts of fire, aided by the wicked power of the sun, made the whole stretch across the front of the walls a furnace. It was not hard to kill these things individually.

A touch of the fire and they withered, then they turned white and red. But again their power was seen in sheer masses of prodigious numbers. For when the top layers were destroyed and the flames grew less, the hidden myriads beneath, protected by the roasted bodies of their uppermost comrades, wriggled forth to the top—and devoured the dead. Yet persistent burning could destroy even these, and at last the earth reeked with the slain—an odor that The Crisco Kid could never forget.

They grew larger. They became, on a general average, an inch in length by the time Dupont had been on the ranch for ten days. Then pits of two hundred cubic feet apiece were dug—dozens of such pits—and with ten-foot iron scoops, drawn each by two horsemen, the creeping things were swept helplessly into the graves where they were beaten down solid by a boy armed with a bit of brush. Then earth was heaped over the top and the whole trodden firm. Who could compute how many billions went to the filling of any one of the scores of graves? And yet when the labors were ended, nothing seemed to have been done. A day or two, and the earth had given forth fresh billions to replace the fallen.

Indeed, as Jeff Slinger said to The Crisco Kid: "We do this here work to save the garden and to keep from bein' fined by the state for not tryin' to down the locusts. But it ain't no good. All we kill makes just a few less that are goin' to starve to death before they turn into *voladoras*."

Fresh pits were dug. The larger hoppers were driven into them with naphtha machines, spouting fire. Still all was nothing.

They grew still bigger. They reached the last stage before *voladoras*. They became inch-and-a-half *saltonas*, covering the face of the country with horror. To walk was to crunch them to death by the score at every stride. The horses were stained with their juices above the fetlocks. Dupont, venturing out without smooth-topped boots was instantly covered to the hair of his head with the swarming horror. Vaster pits were dug. Runways fenced with corrugated iron were constructed, and into these the stupid, huge-headed *saltonas* were shunted by the cubic yard. But when the pit was filled and the grave filled hastily in at the top, nothing had been done except to pick a handful of sand from the beach.

They crawled over the edges of the watering troughs, perhaps to seek the green mosses that grew on the inside, and presently the watering trough was filled solidly to the brim with the mass of drowned locusts. Gulls, eagles, and hawks that appeared at no other times, and a myriad of smaller birds, flocked by thousands through the air, flying sluggishly and low. To them, the world had received the touch of Midas and the very surface of the earth was covered with feebly crawling food. But though they filled their crops with the voracity of which only birds are capable, though they ate and ate again of that disgusting fare, they were merely as fishing birds that take from the surface waters a scattering few of the dense bank of herring. The big threshing machine that was preparing the linseed for the market began to turn out an oily stream of seeds and pulpy bodies beaten in together.

And there were smaller enemies living upon the flanks of this host. There were other insects. The warlike praying mantis came and ate them alive by the thousands. Parasites destroyed more than all other agencies of man and nature put together. But still nothing availed. They still pressed on. Their bellies were emptied. They must be filled, and whenever there was a green thing, they must go.

They clambered up the poles of the clotheslines and ate the clothes to rags. They mowed down stout, well-matured fields of alfalfa level with the surface of the soil. A thousand tons of alfalfa disappeared from the face of a five-hundred-acre field. But what was a thousand tons of fodder to these creatures? Each could digest only a trifling bit of every trifling plant. But mouthfuls by the thousands of billions will eat up the earth, in time. *Saltonas* that began to change their skin, and were helpless in that process, were furiously attacked and devoured by their brothers. They swarmed up through the trees. They ate the leaves; they ate the bark; they ate the wood itself, down to the solid and dry old heart of the trunk.

Then, by sudden myriads, the locusts of the last stage began to appear, hung for a few days drying their new wings, and then flew off to pick up the crumbs of the feast. There was little left for them—twigs, dead *saltonas*—a few billions of these only, and, of course, the vegetable garden. They could not be kept from this by any defense that the peons could devise.

Still, voracious feeders though they were, the sweet William and the foxglove, watermelons and pumpkins, cucumbers, onions, and best of all the beautiful *paraiso* trees were never damaged by the locust swarms. A field of maize well-cultivated, twelve feet high, a wall of green a thousand feet across, was so devastated that Dupont could look through it from side to side, with only enough stalks standing to give an impression of solitary skeletons.

In February, when the camp was bare and brown, the locusts drifted away to the north, glimmering fogs of life against the sun. And, at the same time, El Tigre showed his face.

CHAPTER TWELVE

The position of Charles Dupont at the camp had been something of an anomaly. He might be considered in a way one of the hired men on the ranch, for he received regular pay, and he insisted upon being out in the open and working with the others. If a horse were to be broken, he volunteered for the labor, among the other young fellows on the estancia who were the regular *domadores*—that is to say, tamers. What a contrast between them and the cowpunchers and waddies among whom The Crisco Kid had learned the arts of the saddle.

Their skin was smoked with the stain of Indian or Negro blood, or both; the whites of their black eyes were yellowed that significant trifle that tells of mixed blood, and their faces were full of tigerish ferocity. Not that their manners lived up to their appearance in this respect, for they seemed to be cheerful and merry enough, but Dupont felt no desire to treat them familiarly. They had high cheek bones, smallish eyes that were very bright and were apt to settle ominously upon a stranger and stay fixed to him for a long time, wide mouths, and across the upper lip a long streak of black mustache, not worn long but allowed to grow in a very broad semi-circle whose ends were well beneath the corners of the lips. These fellows wore linen drawers secured at the waist with broad leather belts called *tiradores,* ornamented with silver medals and coins. With short jackets and caps they were equipped for a life of great activity and ardor. And indeed they needed such equipment, for it seemed to The Crisco Kid that in their breaking they spent more time upon the ground than in the saddle.

The Argentine saddle he was inclined to blame for this. It is a fearful and wonderful contraption that, to be understood, must be described in detail—or layer by layer. There were first of all some soft clothes next to the skin of the horse, or these clothes might be replaced with supple, well-worn skin of almost the same texture and softness as cloth. Next, upon either side of the back, came a bolster or *basto* made of reeds covered and stiffened with leather. The bolsters are of course connected over the back, and beneath the belly they are fastened by a cinch. Next come several skins topped by a larger, soft, and woolly sheepskin, and, since this would make too hot and dirty a seat, the actual pad upon which the rider sits is a smooth skin. These upper layers of skins above the bolsters are secured with a second cinch.

The stirrups, to The Crisco Kid, seemed strangest of all. For they were simply wooden disks with holes punched through for the toe of the rider's boot. But no doubt they answered excellently well. Such a saddle as this could not be thrown on as a waddie throws his in the West of the States. It has to be built up like a house, and a faulty construction may make the whole mass twist awry. Yet, much as Dupont preferred his own saddle, when he offered it to the *domadores* they were frightened and plainly ill at ease in it. The smooth, slippery leather of the seat was not to their liking. They were at a loss with the narrowness of this saddle, compared with the wide *bastos* of their own mound of skins, and they quickly dismounted and went back to their native ways. Nevertheless, though they had been raised with this saddle and though they understood many of the tricks of keeping in place on the back of a horse, the great width of their saddles kept them from acquiring that exquisite sense of balance that, after all, is the main essential in horsemanship. Across what would have been the pommel in a waddie's saddle, the *lazo* or the antique *boleadoras* was tied, and this gave a wadding against which the knees could press up and so help to secure the rider in his place.

Among such riders the exhibitions of The Crisco Kid were like light in the midst of darkness. He rode thirty unbroken horses and secured a single fall during that time, which was a record nearer to perfection than the gauchos dreamed of.

He worked, too, in the futile war against the locusts. And he rode through the pastures and watched new ways of handling cattle. As to the Argentine fashion of doing these things, Jeff Slinger was remarkably eloquent.

If they rode across the flat of the country with always that narrow circle of horizon drawn in closely around them, no hill, hardly any tall trees to break it, the majordomo of the estancia on sighting a group of the Durhams that composed the entire stock of cattle on the ranch would break forth: "D'you know why them shorthorns are so doggone' popular down here, Crisco?"

"Why, Jeff?" The Crisco Kid would ask with a grin, hoping for a new variation on a theme that he had heard developed before.

"Because a real, upstandin', self-respectin' Hereford would be ashamed to live as doggone' easy as these here cows live in the Argentine. They ain't no rustlin' for them to do. All they got to do is to waller out and chew their stummicks full. What would a Hereford do in this man's country? They'd get bored and die. That's all, Crisco."

He said on another occasion: "This here is a land of milk cows, old son."

So The Crisco Kid, learning as he went, with the avidity of a true Westerner, fell in with the ways and the knowledge of the Argentine. He liked it well enough, partly for its newness of land

and grasses and men and manners, but mostly on account of that limitless sweep of the plains. During the day it was always the close-drawn circle of the horizon, but at dawn and sunset and in the night the horizon stepped back—infinite miles, so it seemed. Mountain dwellers may come to love the heights and the depths, and sea rovers have a passion for the sea, but the love of the plains is a fever that, when once it has entered the blood of a man, makes it impossible for him to draw free breath in any other surroundings. So, all the day, The Crisco Kid waited for that sense of immensity that came with the drawing down of the evening.

Working roughly as he did through the sunshine hours, at night he found himself accepted in the inner circle of the family of the estanciero. That is to say, he had a spacious room in a wing of the great estancia that, built of adobe bricks, wandered aimlessly around huge patios and big gardens, a house of mystery, of old memories, of many surprises. And the meals of Dupont he took at the same table with the manager, Pedro LeBon, a keen-faced, silent man whose name reflected his mixed French and Spanish blood. At the same table were Jeff Slinger, Carreño, and Valdivia himself. The last had lost half of his good cheer since his arrival at the ranch.

At first The Crisco Kid thought that this abstraction might be most seasonably attributed to the devastations among the crops of the great camp where the locusts were making havoc, but the locusts passed away, and still his eye remained dark. He rarely left the big house, unless it was to look to the breaking of some of the horses, or to examine the fine point of a new colt. On the whole, he was confined day and night to his own suite of rooms, reading, or playing on a great grand piano, for he was an excellent musician. But it seemed to Dupont the loneliest life of which he had ever heard.

Once he asked Carreño: "Señor Valdivia sick, Carreño?"

"No, no," Carreño said, starting and staring at the other as though he had been asked if the world were about to come to an end.

"He seems very down-hearted," suggested Dupont.

"He is, perhaps, not happy," Carreño admitted cautiously.

"What's wrong, then? Bad news of some sort?"

Carreño shrugged the question away and hurried off. But he watched Dupont with a thoughtful eye for some days, and finally, when they chanced to meet in a corridor, he said suddenly to him: "You asked me a question the other day, señor …"

"I remember."

"Let it be a secret never to be repeated … it is El Tigre, *amigo mío*."

And this remark was carried away in the mind of Dupont for further reflection. He had fully made up his mind. Eventually he was determined that he would go upon the trail of El Tigre and do his best to accomplish a double mission—destroy the monster and bring his lovely daughter to poor Valdivia. But in the meantime he must learn something of the manners and the customs of this strange land. Otherwise, he would begin his search as a man whose eyes have been blindfolded.

Therefore he would not confide his purpose to Valdivia. Before he had a chance, the lightning struck.

They were riding across a huge field whose fence could not be sighted before, behind, or on either side. That single field was enough in itself to have composed an entire ranch in a country where estates went in units of a reasonable size. Of the domain of Valdivia it was a mere corner. In the group went Jeff Slinger and the two young fellows who were among the six score peons who worked for daily pay on the estate. It was one of the latter who first sighted the solitary form of a horseman cutting up from the horizon and riding across their way.

As the stranger drew nearer, they could make out a blood-bay horse, a magnificent animal as the expert eye of Dupont could be sure, even in the distance, by its manner of going. It swung over the ground with the stride of a thoroughbred. This horse presently came near enough for a closer examination, and they could see that the man who mounted it was a slight-built youth of not more than fifteen years, perhaps, riding with much grace and ease.

This youngster turned his head and surveyed them with great indifference. To their shouted greetings he returned not a sign and presently disappeared beyond a group of willows. He was no sooner out of sight than Jeff Slinger and Dupont found themselves looking angrily at one another.

"If I was back in Arizona," Jeff said, "that'd call for a little disciplinin' ... a young skunk showin' no more manners than to pass by some growed-up folks and say no more'n that. Might as well tell us we was beneath his noticin'."

"Suppose," said The Crisco Kid, with a faint smile that sundry unfortunate people had seen before, "that we introduce a lesson in manners even down here?"

His companion regarded him with new interest. "*Humph!*" he said, and turned to the gauchos.

"Lads," he said, "can you catch that young brat?"

They showed their white teeth to him. "A *peso* to the fellow who catches him," said the majordomo.

And the whole quartet started off at a round pace. They turned the flank of the willows, and there was the stranger floating away across the plains. Perhaps the wind blew the noise of showering hoofbeats to his ears. At any rate, without turning in the saddle, he suddenly slunk forward to a jockeying position and started his animal away at great speed. The race was on.

CHAPTER THIRTEEN

It was apparent that the gauchos were not in it for an instant. Though they whipped and cursed and yelled, they could not maintain the gait that was necessary to keep with the speeding bay before them. Even Jeff Slinger's long-legged half-breed was strung out straight in another moment, but still the color of the bay grew dim and dimmer as it drew away.

"The young devil has the wind under him," Slinger snorted. "Let's see what your horse can do, Crisco."

And saying this, with envious eyes the majordomo watched the other slacken his pull on the reins. It was all that whip and spur could have done. Twilight bounded away as though out of a walk. One leap and his tail whisked in the face of Slinger's mount. Another, and he was pulling away swiftly. For there was much running in Twilight that day. The little work that he had seen around the estancia had been only enough to keep him in good trim. He was used to the new diet and the saline water, by this time, and he was as ready for a duel of speed as a bird is ready to fly from a cage.

A blast of wind rose into the face of Dupont from that mad running. It curved the wide brim of his hat straight up above his eyes. In another moment he saw that he was gaining fast. But the fugitive found the same thing and at the same moment. He saw a ray of light flick up in the hand of the boy and fall again. The blood bay straightened to its work like a hero. In a trice, the black chestnut was held even. The Crisco Kid could not believe his eyes.

For he had ridden that fleet-footed stallion against the pick of picked horses; he had matched speed even with racers, and over any distance Twilight had never failed him. Yet here was Twilight held even. He straightened the great horse a little to his work. No whip or spur was needed. To punish such a runner as Twilight was merely to insult him. And still the blood bay floated ahead of them. The whip rose and fell in the hand of the youngster in the lead. That alone gave The Crisco Kid some confidence, for he told himself that a horse that can hold another even without punishment must eventually win. But on the other hand, his hundred and ninety pounds must be fully sixty more than that of the slender form before him.

For a long minute of anxiety that breathless duel continued. For half a mile the ground flew back beneath the swinging hoofs of Twilight. Then his flattened ears suddenly pricked forward and the rider knew that the race was won. Slowly, for a stern chase on sea or land is ever a long one, they began to overhaul the smaller pair that ran in front. Another moment, and the gain became perceptible. The blood bay, running gallantly as it could, must have marked the big horse gaining with every stride, and no doubt that took the heart from it, for let no one think that a horse does not race with his heart as well as his legs.

Dupont looked back. The rest of the pursuit swept far away behind him, growing smaller every instant, but every man still desperately flogging his horse with the exception of Jeff Slinger, who sat still, letting his fine animal work as it would, which was fast enough to keep well away from the two gauchos.

Something hummed sharply in The Kid's ear, like a dozen hornets in close flight darting down a gale of wind, and as he turned his head to the front, the crack of the revolver rang before him. It shocked the red blood into his face. Then he did two things that might have been a sufficient warning to any who knew him. He sat up in the saddle a little straighter and he loosened his Colt in its holster.

To one who loves a gun, there is nothing so grimly suggestive as the smooth touch of the butt of a revolver to the hand, a butt that the fingers have polished with much use. It was not yet time to draw, however. A seat on a galloping horse is a most unsure position from which to open fire, and even on smooth ground, firing with careful deliberation, it would have been a long shot. So he leaned forward again, watching and waiting, while Twilight narrowed the distance with gigantic strides. Presently the fugitive twisted about again with a sort of tigerish suppleness as a sleeping cat turns when its tail is touched. The revolver flashed up.

If he can down me at this distance, he deserves to win, Dupont thought to himself, and rode straight on into the danger. The gun exploded, but plainly the first bullet had flown close by luck only, for this second one passed out of hearing distance.

In a hundred yards the hard-pressed youngster fired again, and then as though in an angry fury, blazed away three times more, as though enraged by the failure. And, indeed, the horses were now close enough to have made execution very possible. To The Crisco Kid, for instance, it would have been a simple thing to have emptied the saddle on the blood bay. But something in the youth and the grace of the rider restrained him. After all, violence is the privilege of childhood. Had it been a grown man, Dupont would have killed him out of hand and given the matter no further thought as simply part of a day's work.

To be merciful, however, he must get at close quarters with the fugitive at once, before the latter was able to reload the revolver, which he was now attempting with desperate eagerness to do, holding the reins in his teeth. The first cartridge slipped from the anxious fingers. Then, as the second was drawn from the belt, Dupont shouted to Twilight and the good horse found in himself an extra burst of speed. They swept down upon the blood bay mare like an eagle stooping at a heron scurrying across the sky.

The other saw that there was no time, for the shadow of the pursuer swept across him. He turned in the saddle. Dupont caught a glimpse of a convulsed face, and the heavy gun was hurled straight at his head. He ducked it barely in time. The next stride brought him next to the pursued, and, swooping from his saddle, he caught the youngster into his strong arms.

Two strange things came to The Crisco Kid then. The first was the faintest breath of a delicate perfume. The second was the softness of the body in his arms. His iron fingers sank into that flesh until the captive cried out in pain, fumbling the while to jerk out the knife that every Argentinean wears. But Dupont, with a faint cry of horror and alarm was bringing Twilight to a halt. He slipped from the saddle and allowed the prisoner to stand free before him, making no effort, apparently, to escape the deadly blow of the knife whose handle the slender fingers were gripping.

"Señorita!" breathed Dupont. "In the name of heaven ... señorita!"

The blood flared up across her face and the big eyes avoided his, glancing quickly down.

"Señor," murmured a low musical voice. "I am sorry ... I thought that it was an enemy to be dreaded. I did not know that it was a gentleman who rode behind me."

He bowed to her, still too dazed to speak again. And as he stared, the truth of her and the beauty of her steeped deeply into his mind as a man walks far and farther into a room surrounded by wonders.

Then, with a rush, Jeff Slinger and the two gauchos were around them.

"What'll we do to the kid?" Slinger asked, dropping a hooked knee around the pommel of his saddle and beginning to roll a cigarette.

The change in the girl was admirable. That touch of softness that had passed over her when her identity was discovered was lost again in a trice. She lifted her head, and, dropping upon her hip a hand whose exquisite delicacy should have been in itself a sufficient betrayal of her sex, she stared boldly about her at the faces of the others.

The two gauchos, grinning at the prize, now suddenly drew together and began to whisper. What they had in their minds puzzled Dupont, but he had no time to make inquiry.

"The kid is too young to get more than a lecture," he said quietly to the majordomo.

The latter blinked at him. "How come, Crisco?" he said curiously. "This little rat turns around and blazes away at you with a gun. You come up and grab him and then … you want to turn him loose?" He shrugged his shoulders.

"He's had enough of a scare," said Dupont.

"Scare? The devil," murmured the majordomo of the estancia. "The little devil ain't scared at all. Look at him, and then tell me that he's scared. There's poison in this brat, partner, I know it."

"Look here," Dupont argued with great earnestness, "when the boy saw us coming after him, and when he hadn't harmed us in any way, he naturally was afraid and tried to fight us off. That's only natural, isn't it?"

"Natural?" Jeff Slinger repeated. "That kind of nacheralness gets a rope halter in Arizona. Gets a rope for a man, and for a kid like him, it gets a quirtin' across a bared back. That's what this kid gets from me. I'll teach him enough manners to make his back sore for a month. Doggone me if you ain't a surprise to me, Crisco, takin' this so easy. But you're a happy-go-lucky sort." With this, he drew his long-lashed quirt through his fingers and made the whip sing through the air. "Peel off your shirt, kid," he said in swift Spanish, turning to the girl. "You get a taste of this that'll teach you not to target practice at strangers you meet on the road."

The girl, at this, grew a little pale. There was a single flash of her eyes at The Crisco Kid, then she stared steadily and silently back at the other.

"Wait a minute," Dupont said. "In my part of the country, we always hated to see a horse flogged. And that goes for a man, too ... to say nothing of a youngster like this. Let him go. Slinger, you've frightened him enough for one day. Besides, I was the target, and, if the target forgives him, I imagine that's enough."

"Enough like the devil!" Slinger burst out, coloring with impatience. "Stand aside, Crisco. If the little fool ain't goin' to strip himself, I'll do it for him." And he urged his horse straight at the girl.

The Crisco Kid stepped swiftly in between. "Hold up," he cautioned gravely.

Slinger reined in his horse with a jerk and glowered down at his compatriot. "I'm a patient sort of gent," he said to Dupont in a trembling voice of passion that quite denied his assertion. "Doggone me if I ain't a quiet gent, but you push me pretty far, Crisco. You make a doggone' fool out of me this way. The gauchos seen me start to do this here job, and they'll think I'm a poor pup if I don't finish it. I'm the boss on the place next to LeBon, old-timer. Remember that."

"I'm remembering it. I'm simply giving you some good advice, Slinger." It was quietly spoken, but the challenge was very apparent, for Crisco had not stirred from his position protecting the girl. And Slinger grew a dark and ugly red and, as always happened when he became greatly excited, the scar tissue along the side of his face began to pucker, so that his mouth was drawn into a terrific smile.

"Crisco," he said, "d'you know what this means?"

"That you'll use your head, I hope," the latter said smoothly.

"It means," snarled out Slinger suddenly, "that I'm goin' to have my way about it."

Now, in the old days, Slinger had been a man of some reputation, and that reputation had not grown less since his advent into the southern land. He had ammunition in plenty and targets enough to keep his hand and his eye in good trim. Being braved before the gauchos had infuriated him to the point where he would have drawn a gun on Crisco without another thought, but one thing held him back. For after all, Slinger was a discreet fellow. It was through discretion that he had risen to his present post of preference out of the ranks of common cowpunchers.

And now, at the very instant when the hot blood was raging through his brain, he recalled certain tales that had been brought home by the men who had accompanied Valdivia to the States. The gossiping Carreño, above all, had told how two gunmen, men of reputation wider than the boundaries of the state, had closed in on The Crisco Kid and driven him to bay, and how one man had died and another had fallen and been allowed to go free through the contemptuous confidence and generosity of the conqueror. Remembering these things, Slinger thought again and changed his tactics.

"I got to have my way, here, young fellow," he said sternly to The Crisco Kid. "If you ain't goin' to get out of my way, I give the word to my two boys, yonder, and we'll have to lift you out of the way."

"Really?" The Crisco Kid said, smiling without amusement in his eyes. "You'll *lift* me out of the way?"

"Don't be a jackass, Crisco!" the majordomo yelled hastily, and the perspiration began to start out on his forehead. "You ain't goin' to stand up ag'in' three men for the sake of a little rip of a fool kid that ..."

"Three men?" The Crisco Kid said, apparently running his eye over the majordomo and yet at the same time apparently never taking it from him in a tigerish watchfulness. "Three men? It doesn't look to me as though there were more than a man and a half, partner." It was a sharply stinging insult, and The Crisco Kid added rather hastily: "You being the man and the other two the half, you know."

Jeff Slinger rubbed a hand across his brow. Half an instant before he felt that he had been driven against the wall and that he would have to fight for the sake of his honor. But the final speech left him a way out.

"Crisco," he said, "I'd ought to force you ..."

"You're too fine a fellow to do that, Jeff, or to take advantage of numbers."

Slinger sighed. It was plain that Crisco was opening a way for the majordomo to retreat from his former haughtiness. And though Slinger promised himself that he would never forget this humiliation, yet he was very glad of the opportunity to withdraw.

"I'd only like to know," he said, "why you stick up for the worthless little brat the way you do."

"He's young," answered Crisco. "That's the main thing. Besides, he has a straight pair of eyes. I like courage … in a kid like that."

"Looks like impudence to me," the majordomo said. "Still … I ain't a man to fight you about nothin'."

The two gauchos both gestured.

"Señor …" they said to Slinger, and he rode toward them hastily as though glad to turn away.

CHAPTER FOURTEEN

"Ah, señor," said the soft murmur of the girl behind Dupont, "you have been a thousand times brave and kind to me. A thousand, thousand times. I pray to God to reward you, and to forgive me for what I attempted to do to you. You have forgiven me for that. Your actions and your kind, brave words show it, señor."

He faced her slowly, a little confused, a little red in face, but certainly far from unhappy. "You speak English well," he said.

"Only a small bit, sir."

She answered with a broken accent—an accent, it seemed to The Crisco Kid, that gave a fragrance and a beauty to her speech. His own blush grew far deeper. He had not dreamed that this waif of the plains would be able to follow the colloquial dialect of the rough cowpuncher.

She added: "But there is a greater trouble and a danger coming to me." Her eyes widened as she looked past him to the three who were consulting. "Help me to my horse, señor. Let me ride away ... in the name of the dear God of mercy ..."

Here she was interrupted by a startled exclamation from Jeff Slinger. "Seventeen devils!" Slinger exclaimed. "D'you mean that? The young wildcat ... herself?"

The courage of the girl melted away. She was clinging to The Crisco Kid.

"They know everything ..." she whispered.

"Steady, steady," he commanded. "No harm will come to you. I'll promise you that. No, no, señorita. These are men, and therefore they are your friends to aid you, as I am your friend."

"You do not know ..." moaned the girl.

The Crisco Kid turned and confronted the majordomo, who had ridden back to them.

"I see now, Crisco," he said to the latter, grinning very broadly as he spoke. "I guess that there ain't any doubt that you got a lot better reasons than I've had. You been right, old-timer, all the time. Doggone me if I ain't sorry for actin' like a fool. I ought to've used my eyes ... I ought to've seen ... but throwin' a gun on you the way she done ... that was what set me in wrong."

He swung down from his horse and approached the girl. There was no gentleness or courtesy in his face or in his voice, however. Indeed, it made the blood burn in the checks of Dupont to think that any American could look upon a woman in such a fashion. It was as another man might have looked upon a snake. And the long, smooth-striking muscle of his upper arm swelled and grew hard.

"You ..." said Slinger to her in Spanish, "take off your hat and lemme see your face."

A frightened hand caught at Crisco's arm and clung there.

"You hear me?" snapped out Slinger.

"Señor ..." breathed a whisper of terror at the ear of Dupont, a whisper wild with appeal.

"Slinger," he said through his teeth, fairly shaking with his astonishment and his fury, "are you talking to a dog or to a lady?"

The other merely shrugged his shoulders. "Don't be a fool, Crisco," he said. "You don't know, but I'll tell you something about her. The boys, yonder, recognized her at last. This here good-lookin' kid ... what do you think she is?"

"A woman," The Crisco Kid said in the stern and yet gentle voice of one to whom that name has one meaning, and one meaning only.

"Sure she's a woman"—the majordomo grinned—"but I'll tell you something more that'll make you look at her like a snake … the way I do. Crisco, she's the daughter of old El Tigre himself."

It staggered Charles Dupont as he had never been staggered in his life before, not even in that grim moment some weeks before when he had seen Twilight taken from him. He turned to the girl, and he saw her looking up into his face with a sort of desperate appeal, as though she still hoped against hope that he would be a protector to her, though reason told her that such a hope was folly. It made his young heart grow great.

"What if she is?" he asked. "Suppose that this El Tigre, as you call him, has some checks against his name. But what of the girl, Slinger? Does that ruin her? Has she no chance left in life because her father happens to be someone most people don't like?"

"Why," burst out Slinger, "the little …"

"Hold up, partner," Dupont snapped out. "The girl understands English, you know."

"I might've knowed that the little fox would. Well, partner, lemme tell you this … that takin' her is one big bright day in your life. You know why?"

"Be brave," Crisco said gently to the girl. "You still have a friend."

"God bless you, señor. But he will talk you away from me, I know."

"Lemme tell you why, old-timer," Slinger said.

"I'm listening."

"And lookin' at her. She's too pretty for you to hear me while you look at her." He took Dupont by a muscular shoulder and turned him around until they were face to face. "Now listen."

"I'm listening, Slinger."

"When Valdivia hears about this, he'll be the happiest man in the Argentine. Do you know why?"

What Valdivia had told him rushed back across the brain of the young cowpuncher, but he said nothing. It did not seem possible that Valdivia had demeaned himself so far as to confide the secrets of his heart to every man working on his staff.

"Tell me," he said curtly.

"Because this here is bait that El Tigre will have to rise for, and, when he comes, we'll trap the old devil. You understand?"

"You'll take her back to the ranch for that purpose?" Dupont said slowly. "To trap her father?"

"Does that sound sort of sneaky to you? Lemme tell you, partner, that, if you knowed about El Tigre what the rest of us know, you'd see that nothin' good could be on the earth that has any of his blood in it. That's a fact. She looks all right. I tell you, she's all wrong. Why, you seen her turn and empty a gun at you. She'd've killed you and laughed about it afterward. She's a snake, old son. Speakin' by an' large, I'd go as easy with a woman as anybody. But the daughter of El Tigre ... she don't figger in that class. She goes back to the ranch with us. I guess you'll call that fair enough?"

There was a ring of almost hysterical terror in the voice of the girl. "No, no! Señor ... señor!"

"I want to do what's right for you," Dupont said slowly to the girl. "But what can I do better than to take you where you will be safely cared for?"

"Ah, señor, brave and honorable señor ... you hear him say it. He hates me. I am not a woman to him."

"To Slinger? Perhaps not. But he is only the majordomo. From Señor Valdivia," he added with a little warmth creeping into his tone as he remembered how the estanciero had spoken of the girl, "you will receive the courtesy that a gentleman should extend to a lady. I give you my word of honor for that."

"And my father?" she said to him.

"Ah," Charles Dupont said, his brows clouding a little, "that is quite another matter. I believe that your father has never taken any great care of the wishes of others. Why should I now take any great care for him and what he desires? It is only for you that I think, señorita. And I swear that I cannot see how I can serve you better than to take you to the house of Señor Valdivia.

"Ah!" cried the girl, and she added savagely: "You fool! You blind fool! You blind, blind fool!"

Dupont bowed to her, his jaw hard set. And then he stepped back as though he thereby resigned her to the control of Jeff Slinger. She herself seemed to realize that abuse was not the thing. He saw her beat her hands together in self-reproach. Then her lips parted, but, although her eyes spoke to him, she said not a word, as though she realized that she had ruined her cause.

After that, with no more argument, she mounted her horse and rode on ahead between the two gauchos. As for Dupont he fell behind and the majordomo dropped in at his side. Whatever might have been the secret emotions of Slinger, he chose to put on an air of great good nature.

"We come pretty near to a run-in, back there," he said genially to Dupont. "But I'm glad that we had the sense to pull up our horses at the last minute. Besides, Crisco, I tell you straight. She ain't worth fighting for. Look at her now. Them gauchos are watchin' her like mice watchin' a cat."

It seemed apparent to Dupont, as he stared at the trio ahead of him, that the two rough riders of the Argentine were indeed afraid of their prisoner, for though she no longer carried a weapon, they rode each at a little distance from her side, and their heads were continually turned toward her as though they expected her to work some calamity upon them at any instant. Yet he knew that the pair were resolute fellows and had for that very reason been picked out by Slinger to accompany him in his rides of inspection. Even these chosen men stood in manifest awe of the daughter of El Tigre.

"Right now," Slinger continued, "that pair are wishin' that they hadn't told me what they knew her to be. They're figgerin' that one of these days El Tigre will sink a knife into 'em while they're sleepin' ... and maybe he will."

"How can he be such a man?" Dupont asked.

"Ain't there enough devil in her to make you see what her father must be?" Slinger asked curiously. He added: "I see how it is. Because she's got a pretty face, you can't see no harm in her. Is it that way, Crisco?"

Dupont shook his head, for he had become very thoughtful. After all, she had been tigerish enough to fill him with dread and awe when he had ridden down upon her from behind. But since that first moment it seemed to Dupont that he had seen glimpses of something more than the fury.

"Blood'll tell," Slinger declared.

Perhaps it would, and yet all her masculine impetuosity seemed merely to accent her femininity to Dupont. And what could be more charming than the careless manner with which she rode between her two guards now, chattering first to the one and then to the other, while they answered never a word?

CHAPTER FIFTEEN

When they reached the estancia, half buried among the trees, the gauchos disappeared at a gallop toward the corral where, no doubt, the whole story would be revealed with many fanciful embroiderings. So Jeff Slinger and Dupont brought the girl into the house and waited there until Señor Don Sebastian Valdivia should come to them.

He came, at last, whistling the air that he had been playing upon his piano, walking in his very erect, sprightly fashion until, coming close to them, he caught sight of the face of the girl. He stopped in midstride and into his eyes flared a light that Dupont had never seen before, saving in the face of a gold digger who had suddenly opened up a richly promising vein. So it was with the estanciero. All the square leagues of his land and the cattle that wandered over it were as nothing compared with the girl he now saw before him. He came up to her with both his hands outstretched. But she drew herself up to her full five feet and four inches and stared at him as at a stranger.

"Francesca Milaro," murmured Valdivia. "This is a moment of which I have dreamed."

"I have no doubt," the girl said acidly. "You have given up war against men, Don Sebastian. It was too hard, perhaps?"

He shrugged his shoulders. "You are determined to be absurd, child," said the estanciero. "How could I make war against you?"

"Your four men have captured, me, señor. And here I am a prisoner."

"Captured?" Valdivia muttered, looking to his men.

"We saw her streaking it … thought she was a boy. We took a run to see who it was … she started shooting at Crisco here. Emptied her gun, and then he rode down and nabbed her. That was it."

"All?" the rancher said, facing Dupont with an odd expression. "The good God of prophecy was truly in me when I first saw you then. For I knew at that time that you would bring me good luck, señor, though I never could have dreamed of such luck as this … such golden good fortune, *amigo*."

He spoke slowly, as a man who selects his words carefully, and even then finds what will only half express his mind.

"However, Señor Valdivia," the girl said, "how will you answer the law when it asks how you dare to detain me here in your house?"

"Are you so friendly with the law, Francesca?" the estanciero asked rather sharply.

She tossed her head. "I have no fear of it, Don Sebastian," she said.

"Nor I," returned Valdivia.

"Against my will … you will keep me?" the girl asked, trembling with anger rather than terror.

"Tush," Don Sebastian said. "Let us not talk of constraint. Let us talk of kindness. But first of all let us talk of food. You will be hungry. As I remember it, you are usually hungry, Francesca?"

"I could not eat in your house, señor. I thank you for your kindness."

"Is there poison in the air of this house, Francesca?"

"To me, Don Sebastian, a great poison."

It seemed to Dupont that the face of Valdivia darkened, not so much with anger as with grief, and, knowing well what was working in the mind of the *estanicero*, Dupont could not help sympathizing with him.

"I must have time to talk with you," declared Valdivia. "In the meantime, my friends, I thank you, for I shall not need you at once again. *Adiós* for the moment."

They turned away and Slinger passed on through the door, but Dupont lingered for an instant. For he felt upon him the wide, despairing eyes of the girl, fixed as though upon a last friend, and yet a friend to whom she could not appeal, the eyes of a captive, longing for escape.

"Tell me only one thing, Señor Valdivia," he asked.

"A hundred, if you wish."

"Have you the right to detain her here?"

"Tush. A right intention makes a right action. Surely you must know that."

"I think so," Dupont said, looking not at him but very fixedly at Francesca Milaro. "Surely I think so, or I should not leave her here with you for a single instant. Of that I assure you."

"Ah?" murmured the proud Argentinean. "You have doubts of me, Señor Dupont?"

As for Charles Dupont, he could not at once answer, for his heart was swelling with emotion until it ached. To bring this girl into the hands of so good and so great a man as he believed Valdivia to be seemed to him to be the finest manner in which he could serve her. And yet the quiet of despair that had fallen upon her was very eloquent. So he swayed in doubt. It occurred to him to wonder suddenly that he should have to come to think entirely of the girl and not at all of the pleasure of Valdivia. But in fact nothing was in his mind saving what should be best done for this daughter of an outlawed man.

Valdivia appeared to read the conflict that raged in the mind of his companion, for he added presently: "We must talk together, I see. I shall give you reasons." He stepped to the wall and there touched with his knuckles a great brazen gong that filled the wide corridor with long and hollow murmurings.

A female servant and a *mozo* came at once.

"The señorita will be taken to her chamber," said Valdivia. "Her rooms will be in the eastern wing. See that she is cared for. Send the girl, Ruth, to attend on her. Do you understand? She is to find comfort in my house."

The two bowed to him, frightened by the solemnity of his instructions.

Francesca Milaro paused for half a breath to give the master of the house a searching glance of scorn and to fix upon Dupont such a look of mingled doubt and hope and appeal that it made his heart leap. Then, without further complaint or resistance, as though realizing that to struggle now would be simply to compromise her dignity, she went on down the broad hallway with the two servants showing the way to her most obsequiously.

Señor Valdivia remained for a time to gaze after her, until she had disappeared through the next door. "She is like a queen, Dupont, is she not?" he said more to himself than to his companion. "She is worthy of being ..." He paused before adding abruptly: "However, what I must say to you is simply this ... you must not distrust me, *amigo*. Do you feel that I would do harm to her?"

"Surely no, señor. But if she wishes to go ... have you the right to keep her here?"

"Tell me, Señor Dupont. If a child wishes to run out into a storm, would you give it free leave to go?"

"I can only say ..."

"Tush, Dupont. You are a fine fellow. You are only worried that you may not have done what is best for her in leaving her here with me. You have already forgotten or forgiven the bullets that the little minx fired at you. And a rare miracle that she did not strike you with one of them, for I have seen her shoot like any man. Even one of your own gunmen, señor. However, you forgive and you forget. She remains to you no more than a beautiful woman, and therefore you wish to serve her. But tell me, Dupont, can you serve her better than to take her from a wild beast of a father and give her into the keeping of a man who will treat her as a father should treat a child ... at least until I have persuaded her to love and to marry me? Can you do more for her than this?"

When a man who may command condescends to persuade, he has won his argument before he well begins it, and that the estanciero was willing to give gentle reasons about such an important matter when he might well have called half a dozen servants to thrust Dupont off the premises was a bit of flattery that the cowpuncher appreciated at its full value. It was of a piece with all that he had seen connected with Valdivia, until at last he began to feel that all that was good and all that was honorable in the character of a man was united to make the excellences of this kindly millionaire. Certainly to make the girl the wife of such a man was to ensure her happiness. And yet what Dupont said aloud was: "She may hate me for this."

"I am vain enough," answered the estanciero, "to feel that eventually she will be very happy. But you must consider another thing. How can I, my friend, compel her to marry me? These are not the Dark Ages when the master of the castle owned the bodies and the souls of those who were within his walls. These are not the Dark Ages," he repeated, and, lifting his head a little, he looked past Dupont as though his vision were piercing to the very heart of the last centuries of armor and chivalry.

"That is very true," the cowpuncher said, a little awed by the solemnity of Valdivia. But, though he surrendered the girl into the hands of so good and gentle a man as Valdivia, he could not help feeling a stinging pang of loss. Perhaps, he thought, he would have felt just the same pang no matter to whom he had given her. There was something more than a mere selfless desire for her well-being. The moment he recognized such an emotion in his heart, he bit his lip in shame, and he withdrew at once, for who was he to rival this powerful and good man?

When he went in to the evening meal that day, he was in the sharpest expectation of meeting Francesca at the table, but she was not there. Instead, Valdivia presided in the highest good spirits. He talked with amazing frankness about the girl.

"She sits at the window of her room," he told them. "She sits there sulking, without a word, without a movement. That is the tiger in her."

Pedro LeBon rarely spoke, but now he said quietly: "The old tiger, Señor Valdivia, when will he be coming to carry her away with him?"

Valdivia shrugged his shoulders. "There is no doubt that he will come tonight. He would consider himself disgraced if he were to allow her to remain in our hands longer than that."

"He will be met, then?" asked LeBon.

"Of course."

LeBon, who was as fearless as he was quiet, smiled in a sinister fashion. "It is an excellent manner to build a foundation of happiness," he said. "To kill the father and marry the daughter."

"Ha?" Valdivia shouted, stung into forgetfulness of his dignity.

"I said," LeBon answered without flinching, "that the daughter will be sure to love her husband after her father has been stifled in the trap. Is it not so, Señor Dupont?"

But The Crisco Kid was unable to answer. He was too deep in thought.

CHAPTER SIXTEEN

When the evening fell, the estancia was under siege although no enemy appeared. But somewhere in the dusk, as everyone knew, El Tigre must be roaming, and perhaps his men with him. So Valdivia made his dispositions for defense like a capable general. To enter through the house itself would be impossible. Twenty armed men garrisoned it under the command of Valdivia himself. The only other direction from which the girl's room could be approached was through the garden and toward her window, and in the garden Valdivia placed his two best fighting men. The one was the majordomo, Jeff Slinger. The other was The Crisco Kid, already growing celebrated in the district around the camp as Señor Dupont, who was "*muy gaucho*." That is to say, he rode like a fiend and he could make a rope do all but talk. He did not use the long *lazo* with its eighteen yards of heavy rawhide that cut the air like a knife, but he carried, like Jeff Slinger, a thirty-five-foot hemp rope and depended upon the speed and the agility of his horse to get near enough to his prey to daub the rope on horse or cow.

These two then, as the sunset flamed red in the west and the first lonely stars began to drop down into visibility, sat at the gate that closed the garden. In the distance, half a dozen gauchos were racing their horses in the open space in front of the line of little houses where the married men lived. The distances were short; they rode either bareback or with only a square of cloth beneath them. And the shrill, harsh voices rose time and again in chattering volleys, over the rapid beating of hoofs. Another swirl of dust with the winner riding back out of it, laughing and waving his hand above his head, while the conquered followed, sawing savagely at the mouths of their mounts. Then the bets would be laid on another match. Money was nothing to these fellows. They worked like slaves from dawn to dark. Then they staked their wages upon the speed of their tired horses. Tonight, a few would go to bed happily and richer. The rest would be lost in the deeps of despair until the next night's racing changed the luck and made all new again. Hard work, a diet of meat, a gambling game in the moment of leisure—this was their life.

Here Pedro LeBon wandered past the garden gate singing softly to himself, walking with fumbling steps.

"Drunk?" Dupont muttered to Jeff Slinger.

"Drunk as a lord."

They breathed deeply of the smoke of their cigarettes.

"Seems to me," Dupont said at last, "that this fellow LeBon does pretty much as he pleases on the estancia. How does that come about? Very clever with the cattle business?"

"He has a head," answered Slinger.

"He has a tongue, too," Dupont added. "He thinks nothing of talking back to Valdivia."

Slinger grinned sidewise at his companion, his eyes squinting, as though he were inviting Crisco to see something that was already apparent to others.

"Maybe you've picked up something, Crisco?" he asked slyly.

"About what?"

"LeBon."

"The gauchos talk pretty freely with me, but they haven't said anything about LeBon. Why?"

"Well, there ain't much use talkin'. I guess he's as much the boss around here as Valdivia is."

"How?"

"I dunno. I'm just guessin' what a lot of others have guessed before me. LeBon has something on Valdivia and Valdivia ain't got the nerve to fire him."

"You're wrong," Dupont answered with great confidence. "Valdivia isn't the man to be run by blackmail. Not him. If there was ever a fine fellow in the world, it's this Valdivia, partner."

Slinger grunted. Having communed with his thoughts for a time, at last he said simply: "Go right on thinkin' that, friend. I hope you don't have no bad luck."

"What are you driving at?" Dupont asked sharply.

"Nothin'. I've said my say. You lay low and wait for Valdivia to show his hand."

Dupont could draw nothing more from his companion, and at this unsatisfactory point he was forced to let the conversation rest. So they watched the sunset deepening and darkening. Finally there was only a delicate rim of light along the horizon—the pale afterglow that comes before the full blackness of the night. From the houses, where the racing had stopped, they could hear the twanging of strings and the lulling sound of singing—deep undercurrents of men's voices and one girl weaving a silver thread of melody over the rest. The hot day had ended. Now a few quiet breathing spaces of coolness and of rest—then sleep.

In twenty minutes the estancia was black with darkness and with silence.

"He'll never come tonight," Dupont said, balancing his revolver delicately in his hand.

"Why not?"

"Why, the estancia is like a fortress now."

"This here is El Tigre ... he ain't no kind of man you've ever met up with before," Jeff Slinger said with a devout meaning.

"One noise of a gun," Dupont said, "will bring a couple of hundred men around the estancia."

"And maybe half of them two hundred are gents that would like to see El Tigre win."

"You mean … even here?"

"That's what I mean, old son."

"It isn't possible, Slinger."

"Ain't it?"

"He hasn't enough money to bribe all these men."

"He don't bribe 'em with money. He's a hero to them. That's what bribes 'em. Besides, he buys 'em up by scarin' 'em to death. You wait and see. I'd put my bet on El Tigre."

It amazed and startled Dupont to hear such a speech. For a foolish instant he almost suspected Slinger himself of being one of the bandit's sympathizers.

"Them two that told who Francesca was," Slinger muttered at last, "they're sleepin' darn' little and darn' cold tonight. And maybe they ain't goin' to wake up no more in the mornin'."

"In heaven's name, Slinger, how could this fellow come at the house?"

"Why not this way?"

"But the first shot we fire …"

"Suppose we got no time to fire?"

"He'll have to hypnotize me, then."

"Maybe he will. Only … don't be too sure when you play ag'in' El Tigre. That devil has brains."

There were two paths winding through the garden toward the house. Dupont sat in one; Slinger, just far enough away in the dark to be a visible shadow, sat in the other. Sometimes they rose to pace up and down and so kept the chill of the night air out of their bodies. Sometimes they walked across to exchange a word.

Until midnight the watch was easy enough, and exciting enough in suspense to keep them easily awake, but after midnight the spirits of even the most determined will suddenly begin to droop. A slumberous ache invades the muscles and the mind grows unnerved. Dupont found himself yawning. The long busy day made his whole body crave rest. Moments of dizziness came upon him, out of which he roused himself with a guilty start, feeling as if he had been asleep on his feet, and all the shrubs in the garden a moment later would again waver and grow blurred.

Like part of one of these moments he suddenly saw Jeff Slinger waver and stagger and then fall backward at full length, though nothing living could have approached him without being seen. Then, among the shrubs just before Dupont, something stirred among the foliage.

That instant he tipped up the muzzle of his revolver, prepared to fire. But no one sprang out to the attack. Only, in the dull night before him, something came with a soft whirring, seeming to sweep toward him like a circling pair of outstretched, thin wings, and nobody between them. He had time to note that and marvel at it with a chill dread. Then he was struck by the flying mystery across the breast. Thin arms whipped around him, tying his hands to his sides. One blow fell upon his chest and another upon his opposite hip, and as he fell backward—just as Slinger had done—he saw two men rushing toward him out of the night. The fall half stunned him. But he knew that the gun was wrenched from his clutching fingers and then a cloth was wrapped about his head, stifling and blinding him.

A voice speaking Spanish of excellent quality—a deep, soft voice—said: "That is well, Pedro. But no knife. There must be no blood tonight. Do you understand?"

A half audible grunt was the answer, and the two men busied themselves tying the hands of Dupont behind his back, and turning him upon his face in the sandy patch.

Then all was silent. Not a whisper, not a stir in the garden until he heard the voice of a girl speaking no louder than a whisper, but audible even to the place where he lay.

"Oh, my brave father."

"Hush, Francesca."

There was a light rustling, as though the open wind of the night stirred the dresses of a woman. Then soft footfalls passed. At the same time a gag was pressed between Dupont's teeth, and the guards who stood over him stealthily withdrew. He decided to count to ten before he made a struggle to give the alarm. But by the time the count had been reached, the thick, half-stifled voice of Jeff Slinger sounded nearby, shouting: "Help! El Tigre!"

A hundred voices, it seemed, made answer. Some from the house—some from beyond the garden. Were those extra watchers or the men of El Tigre shouting to add to the confusion?

Then his bonds were torn away. The rope that held him was cut, and he turned in a fury to join in the pursuit.

All was useless. By the time horses were saddled with those clumsy Argentinean saddles, the wide and silent Pampas had buried the fugitives deeply within its breast. They had the whole starry circle of the horizon before them, but in what direction should they ride? They scattered wildly here and there and everywhere. Some of them did not come back until far after dawn, and Charles Dupont was among these. But not one of the hunters had come upon the traces of El Tigre and his fleetly mounted band.

CHAPTER SEVENTEEN

There are varieties of anger, but the most impressive of all, beyond question, is the silent fury. In such a wordless passion Charles Dupont found the rich estanciero when he returned that morning. Señor Valdivia could not remain seated in one chair. He was forced to rise and pace swiftly, restlessly across the room and back again, and all the while, out of a deathly white face, his gleaming black eyes went to and fro.

When Dupont said that he still could not understand by what mysterious engine he had been struck down in the night and rendered helpless, the estanciero pointed without a word to a *boleadoras* lying upon the floor of the room. There were simply three thongs connecting three balls of lead. One thong was shorter than the other.

As a matter of fact, Dupont had seen them used before. The ball connected with the shortest thong of the three was held in the thrower's hand who, when he had swung the strange little engine and put the longer thongs in violent circular motion, hurled it at the enemy. Its weight carried it forward like a thrown stone; its circular motion served to make it wind tightly around whatever it was thrown at. The primitive Indians had invented that singular novelty among the weapons of the world. They snared game with it. They entangled their human enemies in the same fashion. And now Dupont had received a personal demonstration of what the *boleadoras* could accomplish. Yet, up to the moment he saw the thing of lead and leather lying upon the floor, he could not dream what had happened to him. This was the bodiless pair of wings that had flown at him with a soft, humming sound through the dark of the night.

For the first time the strangeness of the Argentine took hold of his mind. Even the locust pest had been less terrible and less odd.

"He is an agent of the devil," Valdivia said bitterly at the last. "And the devil stands at his right hand. When I brought you with me, Dupont, I could have sworn that I was safe from him. But even you were helpless against him. If it had not been that he came for his daughter only and wished to make sure of her escape first of all, he could have gone on to enter my house and he could have murdered me in it simply enough."

Dupont was silent, as a proud man must be silent when his courage or his skill has been called into question.

Valdivia passed into a sudden ecstasy of grief and rage. "What power but the devil," he said, "could have given her to me for a single glimpse and then taken her away before she had time to more than learn to fear me? But, ah, Dupont, is she not a flower and a fragrance among women?"

"She is, señor."

"It is her mother's beauty and her mother's grace, but her spirit is all her own."

"I have been thinking," Dupont ventured gently, "of something that you once said to me."

The estanciero made a gesture as though to indicate that he heard his companion, though it was plain that he hardly noted him at all.

"It was this ... that a man might come at El Tigre by pretending to lead the life of an outlaw, and doing enough to bring him to the attention of El Tigre himself, until El Tigre might wish to have him in his own band."

"Well?"

"Suppose that I do this thing, señor?"

"It is too late. He knows that you are my man."

"He knows that I have failed you, as you and I know," Dupont said gravely. "And therefore what could be more logical than for you and me to separate after quarreling? Suppose, for instance, that we were to have words at the table today … suppose that I were to leave. Suppose, after tonight, that you were to declare that something had been stolen from your house … is that not enough, señor, to convince others that we are no longer friends?"

Valdivia paused in the midst of his pacing, and, with his head still lowered as though from the weight of his burden of gloom, he glanced up at his companion with glittering, bright eyes. "Dupont," he said at last, "that would be a bold stroke. That would be a very bold stroke. It would bring the danger of the law on your head."

"And it would attract El Tigre, would it not?"

"Perhaps … a little."

"If you were to add a price upon my head …"

"Ha?" the Argentinean cried, and he straightened suddenly.

"Ten thousand pesos on my head, señor. That would make me an attractive target for them to strike at. There would be some hard riding through the Pampas to get at me, would there not?"

"Ten thousand pesos! You would be a dead man, my poor friend."

"Perhaps," Dupont answered grimly. "Perhaps."

"Would you risk so much?"

"With Twilight under me, I might escape from the hunters. Might I not? And, in that case, El Tigre would be sure to hear of me."

"He would. Dupont, I see that you are even a braver man than I have guessed."

"First, if I could hear the exact story of what happened between you and El Tigre …"

The estanciero, his eye still cruelly bright with the rope that had suddenly come to him, stood nodding and thinking. "I shall tell you in a word," he said at last. "I was betrothed to Dolores Servente … to the lovely Dolores. That was these many, many years ago. And my neighbor, who had a small estancia … my neighbor, Carlos Milaro, loved her, also. This, however, he kept hidden from me until my betrothal was announced. Then the man went mad with spite and with fury. One day, he rode over, and, after a little talk, he burst into a rage and denounced me. He said that my money was buying away from him the girl he loved and who loved him. He left my house. On his way to his own home, he encountered two of my men … Pedro LeBon and another.

"He quarreled with them like a savage fool. You understand, Dupont, simply because they were men of mine, he stopped them on the road and began hot talk. They were fellows of high spirit. In a moment, guns were out. This Milaro even then was a devil with weapons. He badly wounded LeBon and killed the other. Then he rode on. After that he was arrested. He told a foolish story … that the two had ambushed him. That story would not hold water. He was condemned to die.

"That same day of his condemnation he broke from the prison and rode to the house of Servente. There he saw Dolores. Perhaps her foolish girl's brain was turned by that romantic position … a condemned man telling her he loved her surrounded by a world of enemies. At any rate, she fled with Milaro. He took her away into the wilds to lead with him an outlaw's life."

"A selfish dog," Dupont murmured, red with anger.

"A selfish dog," Valdivia echoed savagely. "In the wilds Francesca was born, and there poor Dolores died, but the child was taken in the pursuit of Milaro, who had become known even then as El Tigre by his secrecy and his fierceness. She was raised by a relative. And when she was sixteen, I saw her … saw her mother's eyes set in her face. I loved her, and determined to marry her.

"But as though El Tigre had read my mind and waited for that time so that he could break my heart again, he appeared out of the Pampas. He saw Francesca. And he carried her away with him to make her as wild as he. And there, señor, is the simple, the sad, and the true story of my enemy, El Tigre."

He spoke with such a passion and with so broken a voice that Dupont stared at him, and it seemed to him that the wild story came to life, that the figures moved and breathed and spoke before him, and it seemed to him, also, that he could gather out of the darkness the dim beauty of Dolores—like Francesca, but sadder and gentler of face.

He thanked Valdivia for that story. It gave him all the background he required. If need be and chance offered, now, he would kill El Tigre as though the man were in fact as beastly as his nickname. And he would carry Francesca back to the estancia of Valdivia by force if he could. With that determination he made ready to make his start that very day. It was quickly and easily arranged with Valdivia. Then he left the house.

"But," the estanciero said as Dupont left, "what shall I say, señor, to praise your great heart? And if you should will, how shall I reward you for your efforts?"

"With your friendship, señor," Dupont answered. "And consider, also, that I am working for the sake of two people, and not for one. There is yourself, señor, and there is Francesco Milano."

It seemed to him that the startled eyes of the estanciero widened and then grew narrow as though with suspicion, but he did not linger to confirm that surprising idea. He went out to turn over his plans in his mind. But after all, what plans could he form? He was attempting to locate a veteran of the world of crime whose domain might be anywhere within three million square miles of country that was strange to the hunter. He could only offer himself like a ball to the racket of chance to be struck about here and there in the hope that the quality of the name he might make for himself would bring him to El Tigre.

With that in his mind, he went in to the noonday meal. Pedro LeBon was not there and the majordomo, Jeff Slinger, was late, having made a trip to the camp town that morning. So the quartet, including Carreño and Valdivia, sat down together. They had not been at their chairs five minutes before the estanciero started the ball rolling.

"You and Señor Dupont were not lucky last night," he said apparently to Slinger, but looking directly at Dupont.

"A *boleadoras* would cross the luck of any man," Slinger said carelessly.

"Ah?" the estanciero said. His tone was only a trifle raised, but it had a sting of cold suspicion and dislike in it, which made everyone at the table straighten in his chair and caused Carreño to gape like a frightened child as he saw the storm gathering.

"What d'you mean, señor?" Jeff Slinger snapped, ready for trouble at any time.

"I mean, Slinger, that you doubtless did all you could, crippled as you are, and stiffened with many accidents and injuries. But as for Señor Dupont ..." He turned a little in his chair and stared coldly at the cowpuncher.

It was very gross, very broad. Dupont was astonished that a man as neatly witted as the estanciero could not have found a more delicate fashion to open the quarrel upon which they had agreed, but he instantly rose to the bait. He pushed back his chair a trifle and frowned across the table.

"I hope I misunderstand you, Señor Valdivia," he said grimly.

"I hope," Valdivia, "that you had ears to hear me."

Dupont rose from his place. "It is equivalent to calling me a coward, señor, if you infer that I did not do all that could be done?"

"I never make rude inferences when they can be helped."

"Señor Valdivia, I am ready to hear an apology."

The estanciero leaned back in his chair, and, folding his hands together, he smiled so mirthlessly, so cruelly up at the cowpuncher that Dupont felt his blood turn cold. It made the play that he was acting a trifle too realistic. Yet he could have no doubt but that the Argentinean was simply stepping into the role upon which they had agreed beforehand.

"I am waiting."

"You will grow tired, señor."

"You will not retract it, Señor Valdivia?"

"Tush," the Argentinean said, waving his hand. "The man is mad."

"Then," said Dupont, "it is necessary for me to tell you that you are insolent, Señor Valdivia."

Slinger spoke without stirring in his place. "Crisco, you'd better go and sit quiet for a while and think things over."

"I have had ample time for thought," Dupont said. "Señor Valdivia, I will go farther, if it is necessary. I shall wait outside after I have packed my things. If you have any more to say to me or any explanation to make, I shall be there."

With that, he strode from the room with a black face. As he went, he heard Valdivia saying with a laugh: "The fool thinks that I will go out and draw a gun on him."

CHAPTER EIGHTEEN

He did as he had promised. He packed his blanket roll, and outside the house he waited, walking up and down in the white-hot sun, but Valdivia, of course, did not appear. Only, once or twice, he saw the face of a house *mozo* appear at a window, grinning, and disappear again.

So he walked slowly away. His position was already complicated. All that he owned was now carried over his shoulder. Even Twilight was not his, but it might be that he could take the horse before orders reached the corrals.

He went straight to them, therefore, and called Twilight with a sharp whistle. The stallion trotted eagerly across the corral to him, whinnying softly, and then a voice spoke from behind.

"Señor El Crisco."

He turned and saw a gaucho standing lazily against the corner of a shed, with a long rifle leaning against his side carelessly.

"Aye?" called Dupont.

"Have you come to say *adiós* to Twilight?"

The orders had reached the corral, therefore, and the horse would be refused him. It flashed into his mind that he might leap upon the bare back of the stallion and make away, but it would probably mean an interchange of shots with the gaucho, and no matter what he did in his wild career that lay before him, he must not stain his hands with blood.

So he went back into the shed, and, taking down the saddle that, at least, was his, he walked out through the open door past three or four more of the cowhands of the camp, all grinning faintly and maliciously behind their cigarettes. That morning he had been in highest favor with them all, but now the rumor had spread, and he was deserted.

Here, again, was a little too much reality for his comfort, and, as he stepped out onto the thick dust of the road toward the camp town, his mind was blank with dismay. In ten minutes the great estancia was already growing into a solidly compacted and blurred group of buildings behind him. The saddle weighed heavily upon one shoulder and his pack upon the other. There was the burden of the rifle, too, and the heavy Colt tugging down from his cartridge belt. The perspiration began to course down his face in streams.

The Kid turned from the deep dust of the road at last, to find easier going in the fields, and almost at once, as he stepped among the puna grass—that harsh and forbidding provender that only Argentine cattle will relish—he hit something before him with the toe of his boot, something soft and horribly alive.

He looked down and saw a five-inch tarantula, a hairy monster of the insect world, sprawled upon its back with its eight thick legs beating the air. It regained its feet instantly, and, whether blinded with dust and fury or out of tigerish instinct, rushed with unavoidable speed at the foot that had overturned it. He felt distinctly, through the thin leather of his boot, the tug and impress of the horny falces of the creature, and, kicking it far away, Dupont went drearily and shudderingly back to the road, for it seemed to him like an early token of what his adventures were to be. The very dumb things of this country were against him.

There is nothing like perspiration and hard labor, however, to sweep idle moods out of the brain. When he had covered another mile, he came upon a group of willows, or *sauces* as the natives called them. Under these he searched the grass, with the recent horror of the tarantula still in his mind. When he had made sure that all was well, he sat down, but still that creeping dread invaded his mind from time to time.

From this place he could still see the shapeless mound of the estancia in the distance. When the night came, he must go back to it if he could, steal Twilight, or at least try desperately to do so, and by that very act draw down the vengeance of the estanciero upon his head.

But there could be no doubt that they would be on their guard against him. Certainly from the very beginning Valdivia was not making his path easy in the world of crime into which he had adventured. Doubtless there was good reason for his attitude. If Dupont could not conquer such a small problem as the theft of Twilight, how could he be expected to deal with El Tigre, the invincible?

That greater matter made this shrink in importance, and Dupont, as he contemplated it, found his spirits rising. All the while, the heat of the midafternoon grew greater and greater. It seemed to reflect in waves from the ground; the stir of the wind simply served to burn his face and the long hours dragged slowly on until, springing up from a different quarter of the horizon, a touch of a fresh breeze came.

And when the evening arrived at last, what had seemed impossible before grew probable. He waited until the last sunset glow was ending, and then he stepped forward on his return trip. He left pack and saddle behind him. If he could reach the back of Twilight, he would regain this spot where his belongings lay well ahead of the pursuit that would be sweeping after him.

He chose this early moment in the twilight because he felt that they would not expect him until the night had worn toward the middle hour. He might take them half by surprise, and men are surely partly blinded toward that which they do not suspect.

The Kid's course was in a broad loop around the estancia, so that he might approach it from a different direction than that in which he had been seen to disappear. Who could tell what small things might be his saving or his ruin in this adventure? He passed the southern end of the house at a considerable distance; straight before him were the corrals, and he was stealing toward these when, as he turned the corner of a shed, he collided full against a gaucho carrying a saddle. The other, recoiling, tripped and fell into a sitting posture with an exclamation of surprise and of anger. Before he could make out the shape or the face of the stranger, Dupont thrust the cold muzzle of his revolver into the hollow of the man's throat.

"*Diablo*," gasped the fallen man. "What are you?"

"I am El Crisco," answered Dupont, using the name by which he was most commonly called among the gauchos. "Be very quiet. I shall do you no harm ... I hope."

There was a murmur of horror and of anger.

"Stand up," said Dupont, "keeping your hands above your head." He helped the struggling man to his feet. "Now I shall borrow this for a moment." He took the heavy-handled knife that is the constant companion of every gaucho. But there was no gun. The knife he threw a distance to the ground. "The horse," Dupont said. "Where is the stallion, *amigo mío?*"

"You can never take him," said the gaucho, who, like a brave man, was breathing hard and gritting his teeth as he felt the shame of this overthrow.

"I shall decide that for myself," Dupont answered, feeling a little more at ease after the shock of that encounter. "Tell me first where he is?"

"In that paddock just before you, Señor El Crisco."

"How is he guarded?"

"There are four men ... one at every corner of the paddock."

Dupont groaned. Without Twilight, he felt himself stripped of two-thirds of his strength. On the back of that magnificent animal, he could fairly laugh at the horsemen who might follow him. Without Twilight, he was lost almost at once. The superior knowledge of the country that the pursuers were sure to possess would entrap him.

"How high is the fence of that paddock?"

The gaucho indicated above his head as high as his arm could stretch.

"The gate, then, *amigo?*"

"What of that?"

"Is it bars or a gate?"

"A gate, señor."

"Let us go forward together."

"In the name of I heaven, señor …"

"It is too dark for them to make me out clearly. Besides, they will never suspect me if I saunter up at your side. They expect El Crisco to come alone."

The gaucho muttered something beneath his breath. "What is your name?" asked Dupont suddenly.

"Garcia Delav—"

"Garcia," interrupted the cowpuncher, without waiting to hear the rest of his companion's name, "if you are a true man to me … do you see?" He dropped two or three bills into the pocket of the other. "But if you make an outcry or lift a hand to betray me, this gun that I carry here in the pocket of my coat, as I walk a little behind you … do you see? … will send a bullet through your back and through your heart."

"Murder," the gaucho whispered, shuddering.

"What is one more dead man to me?" Dupont said with an affected coldness. "It must be as I say. Do you believe me?"

"I believe you," Garcia answered huskily.

They walked on, therefore, slowly, side-by-side.

"If they ask who I am, what will you tell them? For they must not hear my voice."

"You are ... let me think of that ... why, you are my brother ... Juan Delavero."

"Good."

Presently they could espy the place. It was on ground just a shade elevated above the rest of the plain—a sufficient knoll as they approached to show the posts and the bars of the fence clearly, with a watcher at every corner, and the dim form of Twilight silhouetted against the distant luminous dust of the stars.

They were hailed by two of the watchers at once as they approached.

"Who is that?"

"It is I, Garcia Delavero," the gaucho answered smoothly enough. "And my brother Juan with me."

"Why are you here, *amigos*?"

In spite of the fact that the part he was playing had been thrust upon him, it seemed that Garcia could not help but throw himself into the role that he had been given.

"Perhaps the fun will begin while we are here," he answered. "Perhaps we will see El Crisco come to take the stallion." And he laughed. If he were nervous, his nerves merely served to make the laughter harsh and loud.

"This El Crisco, he is not fool enough for that," answered another of the watchers. "Delavero, keep away from the fence. That horse is a devil and will have his teeth in you."

Twilight, in fact, though accustomed to the four who were now watching him, flattened his ears as he saw the newcomers.

"Well," Garcia said, "he is gentle enough with El Crisco."

"Certainly that fellow has bewitched the horse. He fought like a great cat when we led him up here. Juarez was kicked twice and is in bed. His leg is broken, I think."

Dupont guiding the way, they came to the fence and to the

gate. Against it they leaned. And the mind of Dupont was busy. What he noted most of all was that the wind was blowing steadily and quite strong in their faces—a rising night wind that might be a cold gale before the morning. Then, very gently, lest there should be a scraping sound, he began to push back the bar that slipped into a notch in the post and fastened the gate shut.

"Juan!" cried the fourth watcher at the corral fence. "Juan, you lost money tonight at the racing?"

"A little," Dupont answered in a muffled voice. And he drew the fastening bar clear of the notch, so that the gate swayed gently out against him an inch or so.

"A little ..." inquired the other. "A hundred pesos, was it not?"

"Ten," Dupont answered gruffly.

The other, who had been leaning against the fence, now straightened. "By heavens, Juan, you have grown half a foot since I saw you, or else my eyes are liars."

"The devil is in it," Garcia whispered with a gasp. "I forgot that my brother is a small man, and you, señor, are a giant."

"Come back with me down the hill," Dupont said in the same tone. "Quickly now." He turned away, Garcia at his side.

"Juan!" the sentinel called.

"Your eyes ..." Dupont answered, still walking away with long strides.

"What of my eyes?"

"They are liars, *amigo*."

There was a shout of anger from the watcher. "Juan! By heaven, friends, it is not Juan!"

"Yes?"

"Garcia, it is not your brother?"

"Who could it be, then? Why should I lie?"

"The gate!" came a sudden shout from three voices.

Dupont glanced back. They were at a distance as great as he had wished to reach before he gave the signal, but now he saw the gate was sagging open before the wind and was already a foot ajar, while two of the guards rushed to close it. Then he gave his signal, whistling thin and shrill, and he saw the stallion start so suddenly that there was a wink and shimmer of the starlight along his silken flanks. He came like a thunderbolt. At the gate he swung a bit to one side, so that his shoulder came half against it, and the big gate was knocked wide, tumbling one of the men who had run to close it upon the ground and making the other start back with a shout of alarm. But Twilight was down the slope like a thunderbolt, indeed, neighing joyously as he ran toward the master, the master whose signal he never failed to obey.

He hardly checked his speed as he went by, but Dupont, catching at the mane and gripping it with lucky firmness, leaped onto the back, struggled a moment to grip the slippery hide with his heels, and then shot away into the night with the last words of poor Garcia Delavero ringing at his ear.

"You leave me a ruined man, señor."

Then the guns began to chatter behind him.

CHAPTER NINETEEN

Who can tag the flying tail of a comet? The bullets that were blindly showered after the dim and disappearing figure on the dark stallion did not find their mark. Only luck would have brought them to the target. Neither did the wild hunt through the plains bring them to the fugitive. Not only was Twilight far fleeter and more enduring on the flat, but when a fence rose before him, the strands of barbed wire shimmering like dew-strung threads of spider silk under the moon, he leaped the obstacle that the men behind him would have to pause to cut through.

They came back from that pursuit to a master who covered a secret delight with a mask of fury. He gathered his gauchos, his peons, and his *puesteros* together. He made them a speech in which he laid upon them the whip of scorn. He had been to them a father; they were to him in return ungrateful children. They allowed him to be insulted by a gringo, and then they allowed the gringo to return and steal from his corrals his finest horse, worth all the others. Worth, in fact, the life of a man. After that, they tumbled through the night, pretending that they strove to recapture the thief, but in reality only fearing that they might meet him and come within the range of his guns.

Such was the speech of Señor Valdivia that left all who were in his hearing writhing with shame and with bitterest anger. Carreño was a stricken man, after hearing his master in such a temper, and when he attended Don Sebastian afterward, his fat body was quivering with terror. But even when they were alone, Valdivia on this subject did not open his mind to his servant and secretary. It was a secret too precious and with too much import.

The next day it was learned that the night before, in the nearest camp town, a man riding a black horse had fallen into a brawl with one of the townsmen and shot and killed him. It was at once presumed that the mysterious rider must be none other than El Crisco. So Charles Dupont was outlawed for that crime. It was then that the estanciero put the price upon his head—10,000 pesos. A great fortune to every wild-riding gaucho on the Pampas—enough to support a family forever and in luxury.

One might have said that when he wrote the check for that sum and sent it to a bank where it was to be held in trust until it was claimed by the captor or the destroyer of the outlaw, that Valdivia was closing a noose around the throat of Dupont as truly as any hangman. So felt Valdivia himself, and he enjoyed a thrill of exquisite power as he scrawled his signature.

"Why so much?" asked Carreño. "After all, the horse was not worth so much."

"It's the principle of the thing," the rancher said sententiously. "This Dupont is an extraordinary fellow … an extraordinary criminal. One would never have thought of him as a man of crime … seeing him day by day as we have seen him."

"Certainly not," said Carreño. "And yet there was that first day when we saw him facing that man, Carew …"

The estanciero nodded. "However, being an extraordinary man, extraordinary measures must be taken to apprehend him. Therefore I have offered the big reward. For in a manner it was my fault. I introduced this villain into the country. It is my duty to rid the country of him."

"Señor, you are a great patriot," Carreño said, and he clasped his fat hands together. To him, the rancher was divine in goodness and in selfless justice.

The reward was offered, then, and every day Valdivia waited for the news to come that his check at the bank was claimed in behalf of certain captors. But the reward was not claimed. The money lay unasked for. And the days stretched to a week, to a fortnight, to a month.

"You see," said Valdivia, secretly swelling with delight, but making his brow as dark as possible, "you see that this man was even more dangerous than we thought. Here, in a strange land, he has been able to escape from the hands of the law and, more than that, from the labors of a thousand head-hunters who are eager for the reward that I have offered."

"He is a terrible man!" Carreño exclaimed. "You have heard about the thing that he did yesterday?"

"What thing, Carreño?"

"It makes the blood cold and the heart sick even to name it, or to think it?"

"Very well. Turn my blood cold, Carreño."

"He came to the house of an old man who had two sons. He was hungry and made them cook him a great meal. When the meal was ended, he made them bring him all the money that they had in their home. When he had filled his pockets with their silver and their gold …"

"You told me it was a poor man, Carreño?"

"A very poor man, señor."

"Yet there was a plunder of gold and of silver in his house?"

"I only tell you the story as it was told to me."

"Who told it to you?"

"Word was brought to town. The young Vereal heard the story. He brought it back to the estancia."

"Ah? He heard the story from another man who had heard it, and now you tell it to me?"

"Am I wrong to do so?"

"By no means. Continue to believe all that you hear in this world, Carreño. It will fill your life with variety and with interest, I assure you."

To this exhortation Juan listened, nodding solemnly. He did not quite know what his master meant, but he knew that when he did not understand, the best thing was simply to nod and to pretend agreement.

"Continue the story, Carreño."

"It is too terrible, señor. But it seems that after this devil, this Charles Dupont, had eaten the food of the three poor men and then plundered them of all the money they had, he drew a gun and fired. He murdered all the three."

"Horrible," agreed the estanciero. "Did the neighbors make no effort to attack him before he could escape, after firing three murderous bullets?"

"There were no neighbors. The house stood by itself in the midst of the Pampas. It was not until the next morning that the event was discovered by a chance traveler who went that way and, stopping at the door, found the three dead men and the floor covered with sticky black pools. Is it not a beastly crime, señor?"

"But, Carreño, who were the witnesses of it?"

"Ah?"

"Who saw Dupont do the murder? The house stood alone, and all three who were in it were destroyed. Who remained to give witness against Dupont?"

"You must understand, señor, that only two days before a man on a beautiful horse that looked much like Twilight was seen at the town of Cherasco, which lay only twenty-five miles from the hut where these three were murdered so foully. No, there can be no doubt but that Señor Crisco is the guilty man.

The estanciero placed a hand across the lower part of his face and stared at the floor. "Does everyone agree that it must have been he?"

"Of course."

"Might not some other person have come past?"

"Ah, señor, you are charitable even to those who wrong you and your countrymen ... you are charitable even to terrible bandits and killers of men. Is not that a wrong thing, *patrón?*"

"Perhaps ... perhaps," said the master in a stifled voice. "Then people will have no more regard for Dupont than for a wild beast."

"They will shoot him on sight, there is no doubt."

"Well, he brought it upon his own head," the estanciero said, thinking aloud.

"Ah?" murmured Carreño. "That is very true. His crimes have raised the hands of all men against him. And to think, señor, that you must owe your life to him ..."

At this, Valdivia started a little. "You are a fool, Carreño," he declared hotly.

Carreño was stunned.

"What else have you heard of this ... brigand?" asked the master at the last.

"There is a story that he bears a charmed life."

"Tush! That is foolish talk."

"I only repeat what I hear ... what I hear from honest men. I never repeat what fools might tell me, señor."

"Of course not. A fellow of your penetration knows how to sift the evidence. Is it not so, Carreño?"

Once more a little bewildered, Carreño nodded a slow agreement. "However," he said, "there really cannot be much doubt about the charmed life."

"Tell me, then. What is the proof?"

"In the bar of a *fonda* ... I have forgotten the name of the town, but I think ... let me see, señor ..."

"Never mind the name. Continue."

"There were half a dozen drinking. They were all true gauchos. They all had knives. They all were wearing guns. A masked man stepped into the doorway with a gun in each hand and ordered them to stand up and hold their hands above their heads. They obeyed this robber, but while they stood there, one or two of their friends came to enter the bar and saw the robber standing there. They leaped upon him from behind, and, at this, the six other gauchos rushed at him. But it was like trying to hold an eel. He twisted from their hands as though they were children and he a giant. He leaped upon his horse and rode slowly down the road, as though he scorned them too much really to flee from them. Now listen to me, *patrón*. These eight men took their rifles and their revolvers and fired as straight and as fast as they could ... and all were good marksmen. But they did not strike the horseman. Is not that enough proof that his life is charmed?"

"A very strange thing it sounds."

"A miracle, señor. Not one of the eight men would ever ride to hunt El Crisco again. They swear that he is the devil."

"Tush! This talk of the devil is very silly ... but, well, when was this?"

"Four days ago."

"And where?"

"At a little town near Corrientes."

"What, Carreño? Could this man have galloped all the distance from ... Corrientes to Cherasco ... within two days?"

The eye of Carreño grew vague. "A man with such powers ... who can say what he can and what he cannot do?"

The estanciero smiled very faintly. "True, Carreño." He nodded. "But though this desperate and charmed robber was masked, they recognized him as Dupont?"

"Beyond all doubt."

"By his description?"

"He was a big man. He seemed terrible even behind his mask."

"Ah, yes, and then they had a chance to see the stallion. They recognized Twilight?"

"Beyond a doubt."

"What was the time of the day?"

"It was not quite dark. They could see that it was a large horse, and black. Twilight would look black at that time of the day."

"And these men who had been drinking, shooting in the dusk, were not able to hit the robber?"

"Not with a single bullet."

"Then the case is clear, and we must say that Dupont bears a charmed life."

Carreño, escaping from this interrogation with such flying colors, as he thought, could not help but beam with happiness. "El Crisco has become a famous man in one short month." He added: "He is almost as terrible as El Tigre, men say."

CHAPTER TWENTY

When the imagination of the world is struck, it paints its own pictures and has very little deference for the truth of a matter when it is mixing its colors. It paints strongly, and with a swift brush. It is not always the finest race horse that is the public's favorite; it is not always the best boxer who packs a house; it is not always the ablest politician who collects the greatest number of votes. For, no matter what reason tells a man, it is only when his emotions are appealed to and enlisted that he begins to speak from the heart.

In the world of crime, the same thing is true. Captain Kidd, in some ways, was a very petty fellow. Certainly compared with many and sundry of the old buccaneers, his career was no more violent than that of a bad boy in a schoolroom. The terrible blazing forms of Morgan and Drake make him shrink into insignificance. But something in his career struck the imagination of the world, and from that day to this his name has been synonymous with cruelty, cunning, courage, and all the hard and romantic qualities that go to make up the existence of a pirate.

And so it was with Charles Dupont, now translated into that southern world where he was better known as El Crisco. Just what it was in Kidd that appealed to the imagination would be hard to say.

And what it was in Dupont that stirred the Argentineans was equally
mysterious. Perhaps it was the fact that he had dared to face and insult
a man so great as Sebastian Valdivia. Perhaps it was because of his
mastery of a horse that was as terrible as a loaded gun to all other men.
Perhaps it was the reckless ease with which he had executed his exploit
and stolen Twilight away from Valdivia and Valdivia's guards. Perhaps,
more than all these things, it was because he had brought from the
North all the air and the aroma of a destroyer of men. Carreño had
much to say on that subject; others brought varying reports. And in
short, in a trice Charles Dupont had become a celebrated desperado
at the small expense of a single horse theft.

The truth was that during the first month he remained as
quiet as possible. He had with him—Valdivia's foresight had seen
to that—ample money to care for his needs. He bought what he
wanted, stole nothing because he needed nothing, and drifted
slowly through the country heading, in general, in the direction
toward which he had heard El Tigre had made with his daughter.
How was he to be discovered or suspected? The problem seemed
baffling.

At the rude and solitary hut of some small farmer, some Italian
colonist, or some wild-living gaucho, there appeared in the late
evening a mild-mannered gringo with a gentle voice, speaking
excellent Spanish, desiring perhaps to learn the way to such and such
a place, or to share the evening meal and pay for his share, or to buy
provisions, or provender for his horse. And, in the night, the horse
might be led to a manger in the cattle shed and given its fill of food.

In none of these things could one recognize a desperado whose
hand was against all men and against whom the hands of all men
were raised. Even El Tigre, swift and secret as he was, usually moved
attended by followers, and his form and his grim face were known
from one end of the country to the other—by a scar in the center
of his forehead that gave a lionlike frown to his face, if in no other
way he could be identified. But when Dupont entered a house, his

voice was the gentlest of all voices, and his gun was never in evidence. The ignorant peons, the romantic gauchos, hearing of him, expected to see a man of dash and color, cursing, drinking, raging through a whole town on a horse that lived in the air more than upon the ground.

Therefore, by the very extravagance of the reputation that had been falsely built up around him, Dupont was sheltered. He melted obscurely into the Pampas, and people who were listening for thunder saw him pass without giving him a glance. His utter disappearance, however, helped to make imaginations run riot. He had been seen to plunge into the night mounted upon his magnificent horse, speeding away from the camp of Valdivia. The cannon had been fired and all the Argentine waited for the shell to strike. Because it did not strike, they forced themselves to believe that they saw it descend here and there. That was the original of the innumerable yarns that were built up about him in the short space of two fortnights—stories many of them even more wildly extravagant than the foolish narratives that Juan had told to Valdivia. But few had the critical coldness of Valdivia. The stories were heard, believed, repeated. The great newspapers of Buenos Aires caught up the tales and printed them in headlines. All crimes upon the Pampas were attributed to him, unless the perpetrator was actually seen and recognized. The editors, receiving twenty reports daily, selected the most terrible and printed them. El Crisco had become a tremendous legend within a single month.

But, while his awful fame caromed and cannonaded across the big country, El Crisco himself was working deftly and secretly at the trail. He was hunting for clues that would lead him to the great outlaw, and those clues were hard to come by. By day he slept. But in the evenings he came to solitary houses, or even to little camp towns, and, tethering the stallion in the darkness, he advanced boldly among men in an inn, or *fonda*, and drank with them and talked and listened, ever guiding the conversation toward El Tigre.

In this way he gathered all manner of conflicting reports. He followed them here and there across the land. He was a shuttlecock driven here and there by false news of the bandit. Until, at last, when he was beginning to despair, when he felt like a man adrift on the great ocean in a little boat, he reached his first definite tidings.

He was sitting on the verandah of a little inn in a camp town. The sun was down, and the last of the day was making a dim stain in the west, but overhead, to illumine the sign of the place and lead the thirsty to their drink, was a great gasoline lamp shining like a miniature sun. He had been so burned and scalded by the true sun that day that even the flood of light was a torment. But he was very tired, and the chair in which he sat fitted comfortably into the hollow of his back. Therefore he remained, half troubled, half comforted, listening to the cool clinking of glasses from within the *fonda*, the rumble or the sharp laughter of voices of men. Footfalls sounded heavily on the planked sidewalk. Now and then a horse cantered past with hoofbeats muffled by the ankle-deep dust of the street. He was in one of those moods when the eye wanders and takes only a small part of the attention with it. He saw the signs on the opposite shops, and his eyes read them without conveying into his mind any meaning. He saw the high, false fronts of the buildings and smiled faintly, realizing that behind these imposing masks there were only squat, shapeless hulks of houses. Indeed, looking farther at either side, he could see between the facades the flat, long roofs, and the dull outlines of the main body.

In this mood of idleness, swelling from the heat of the day that still was in the air and that still seemed to be radiating from the corrugated iron roof of the verandah, he began to watch the drift of the people past the *fonda*, of whom a considerable number turned in toward the door. One, at this moment, stopped short, seeming to look down to the planked sidewalk in thought, and then turned and entered the inn.

Something of the dreaminess of Charles Dupont left him, and

he began to realize that, since he had sat there, at least one other had stopped in that same manner as though, passing the inn, a sudden thought much graver than drink had called him into the place. That idea had barely come to him when still another paused, looked down at the sidewalk, and turned into the *fonda*.

Here was something more than mere chance. The dark faces, the bright, suspicious eyes with which the last two had come toward the door of the inn had surely some meaning. And going to the place on the sidewalk where each had found something that arrested him and made him look down, Dupont saw no more than five scratches, such as might be made by the rolling of the sharp rowel of a spur over the wood.

He had not the slightest doubt, however, that this was a sign that had a distinct meaning among a few of the men who passed the place. Therefore, he turned into the *fonda* himself.

His suspicions were rewarded instantly. Four men sat at a corner table, and two of these were the men he had lately marked as they stopped abruptly, and then made toward the hostelry as though summoned by an irresistible power. They had certainly not been drawn together by the call of any convivial society, for, though all were now drinking red wine, it seemed to Dupont that there was surprisingly little conversation, that the faces of all were dark, and that they flashed upon one another, from time to time, glances keen with suspicion. The light from a lamp fell near them upon the floor, and he started a little as he saw, slicing over the dark wood, five spur scratches like those that were on the sidewalk before the *fonda*.

He hesitated only a moment, and then, following an irresistible impulse, he took a glass of wine from the bar and, taking a chair with him, found a place at that corner table. As he sat down, there fell upon him a sharp focusing of eyes that seemed striving to penetrate to his very heart. He paid back those glances deliberately, slowly, turning his glance from one face to another and meeting the gleaming eyes. At this, as though half angered and yet half contented, they looked gloomily down again at their wine.

Certainly no matter how they were called together, they did not know one another, or at least in any friendly fashion. But here a sixth man approached the table and, drawing up a chair, crowded the circle to fullness. He began to take command at once. He was a little man, but very broad of shoulders and very long of arms, and with the smoky skin and yellow-stained eyes of the half-breed.

"*Amigos,*" he said, "I heard that there were only four men in this place. But here are five. Who is the fifth man?"

Instinctively he looked at Dupont, for the fair skin and the clear blue eyes of the latter seemed to accuse him, whereas the complexions of the other four were more like his own. From all around the table the same glittering suspicion looked forth at Dupont. He took a pencil from his pocket and, without a word, drew five short lines upon the table—five such lines as he had seen on the floor and on the sidewalk—the outer ones short, the inner ones longer. Upon this the whole battery of suspicion rested for a moment, and then the latest comer said abruptly: "It is enough, señor. I am happy to have you with us. You have seen the sign in passing through the town. Is it not so?"

"It is," answered Dupont.

"You also have served?"

"I have served, señor," said Dupont.

"One more man is more added strength," the half-breed said gravely. "We meet in one hour a mile from town on the east road."

There was a little interval of silence after this. Finally the oldest of the original quartet said sullenly: "My wife is a sick woman, señor."

"You have time to ride home and say good bye to her," said the half-breed, shrugging his wide shoulders.

"My wife is a sick woman, señor," repeated the other, frowning blackly.

"What is your name?" snapped out the leader.

"Roca."

"Señor Roca, how many times have you served?"

"Three times," Roca answered, staring at the table.

"Then," said the other, "you should know that an order is an order."

"How long is a man to be in this business?" growled out Roca. "Forever?"

"*Bah!*" sneered the leader. "Did you ask that when you tried to join?"

"A young man cannot be expected to think of everything."

"But you are old enough now not to act like a fool and talk like a fool. Señor Roca, mount your horse and within the hour be with us on the east road a mile from the town. Do you hear me?"

Roca rose without a word and stumbled across the floor of the *fonda*, a lumbering, work-deadened hulk of a man. One could tell by the stoop of his shoulders and the helpless swinging of his big hands at his side that he lived by the curse of Cain. Dupont, looking after him, pitied the fellow with all his heart. The more so since this was some illegal business, manifestly, for which men were being gathered from the town.

"Roca!" called the wide-shouldered man.

The other turned and lumbered back to the table, his face more scowling than ever, but a little pale, thought Dupont.

"There is another thing to consider, *amigo*," said the leader, turning in his chair and looking abruptly up into the eyes of the big fellow.

"So?"

"Consider that if your wife is sick, you, too, might become sick … might become even sicker if certain things were not done. That is all, *amigo*."

Roca glowered down at him, balling one heavy fist. Then he turned on his heel and went out from the place.

"Who is this Roca?" asked the leader.

"He works by the day in the town and on the estancias near the town," answered one.

"You," the short man said, and pointed a sudden finger at the youngest of the group, a thin-faced, rat-eyed boy of nineteen.

"*Sí*, señor," muttered he who had been so designated.

"Follow this Roca. There are times when men are apt to talk. You will be so far away that he cannot see you. You will be so close that you hear every word he speaks. And if he talks too much …" He ended by reaching his hand around to the small of his back. It was a significant gesture, for at the back of the belt the gauchos wear their long, heavy-handled knives.

The other rose without a word, but with a grin of pleasure, and went with a light step from the room.

CHAPTER TWENTY-ONE

There was more than one doubt in the mind of Charles Dupont as he jogged Twilight down the road toward the meeting place, but whether the dreadful form of El Tigre were to emerge from this night's affair or not, at least he had entered into the underworld of Argentine crime, and it was in this world that he must expect to meet with the famous bandit.

He found them already assembled. Even Roca must have been there, for, although he could not distinguish faces in the cloudy dark, he could count five men waiting. When he joined them, not a word of greeting was spoken. But they turned the heads of their horses eastward and struck away at a round canter. He could at least recognize the squat form and the wide shoulders of the leader riding in the front. For his own part, he would be content to remain in the rear throughout the adventure. He had no desire to break laws.

For two hours that journey continued, with hardly a word spoken. And the only sound came from the throat of one of the men in whom he recognized, at last, the slender, catlike youngster who had been previously detailed to follow and keep watch upon Roca. He was a happy youth, and as he rode, he could not help breaking out into song so loud and piercing that the leader presently shouted back a harsh order that reduced the boy to humming. A man who sang was a man who would talk. Dupont singled him out for conversation.

He was ready enough to talk and he told a story that was as brief as it was vivid. He had worked cattle until a year or so before; he had ended an argument with the majordomo of a camp by running his knife between the ribs of the man. Luckily the majordomo recovered, and the boy spent only six months in prison for this first offense, but in prison he had learned enough from other criminals to convince him that the way to make money is not to labor for it. So he had looked about him for something to do and had presently found it.

"You could hardly have found a better way of making money easily," ventured Dupont.

"Easily, señor?" said the boy. "Why, we can make money, but no one makes it *easily* when he works under El Tigre. Is it not so?"

The heart of Charles Dupont swelled and sang. Oh, lucky instinct that had led him into this affair. He was on the trail of El Tigre at the last. He might soon even be in the presence of that leader.

Now they came in view of a short line of lights stretched across the horizon, looking much like an oddly even line of stars, but as they drew nearer, the line stretched out on either side, and after a time there could be no doubt that they had come within view of a town. Perhaps they were to be a part of a raid of some importance.

They approached the black and shapeless outline of a house around which there were a number of figures of horses and of men—a small house, part of whose roof had fallen in, as Dupont could tell by the outline against the sky. A voice hailed them while they were still at a little distance, and a form rose out of the ground, as it were, with the starlight glimmering along the barrel of a rifle.

The leader approaching this sentinel apparently satisfied his doubts in a word or two, after which he ordered his men to remain where they were and rode on toward the house.

"It was well done." Dupont said to his talkative companion,

"that manner in which El Tigre took his daughter away from Valdivia."

"*Bah!*" cried the youngster. "It was very simple. Twenty men of El Tigre were among the workers on Valdivia's estancia. He knew the very mind of Don Sebastian, and all the hinges that it turned on."

It was a thing that Dupont had guessed before, and certainly it made the ease with which the bandit and his men had approached the great estancia more understandable. His companion now turned the talk upon the locust invasion, which would keep the cattle of that district eating hay from stacks and silos during the rest of the season. In ten minutes more there was a general stir of men about the ruined house, and their leader returned to them. He gathered his men together in a group about him and told them, briefly, what was planned for that night, and what part they were to take in it.

It was an attack upon a flourishing bank in this little city, a bank that had recently won much hatred and some notoriety by the cruel methods of its controlling directors, for it had shut down with an iron hand upon those whose mortgages were overdue, and had foreclosed on one after another among the small farmers and ranchers who lived on a patch of ground and a handful of cows. Their work was to blockade one part of the main street of the town.

Having issued this statement, he led them on at a round pace toward the town. Other groups were leaving the ruined house and heading in the same general direction. It seemed to Dupont that he could count as many as forty figures. Surely this was robbery on a grand scale. It became almost organized war. How different from the work of a few determined and cool-headed yeggs in his own home country who, unassisted and unprotected, invaded a bank in the night and cracked the safe.

There were half a dozen groups of the marauders. That of which Dupont made a member and each of the others chose a separate street for piercing to the heart of the town. To judge by the section that he saw, it might be a place of twenty-five hundred inhabitants. It had the

hastily thrown up appearance of most Argentine towns, which rise
out of the ground built with adobe and corrugated iron. The unpaved
streets, knee-deep in mud in the rainy season and ankle-deep in dust
in the summer, were rutted and worn by the great ten-foot wheels of
the Argentine carts that carry three tons as a burden. From them, in
the night, as the horses waded through them at a walk, there arose an
invisible cloud of dust, stinging the eyes, choking the nose.

The town slept. There were no street lamps. Only the ugly
houses pushed their facades up against the sky on either hand,
obscure and lumpish forms. Or the windows here and there flashed
back the starlight with astonishing brilliance, like polished steel.
So perfectly did the carpeting of dust muffle the sounds of the
falling hoofs that one could hardly hear the noises from his neighbor's horse as he rode. There was only the squeaking of leather
now and again, or the loud snort of a horse as it cleared the dust
from its flaring nostrils. Neither could they hear a sound from the
other parts of the town through which the various sections of El
Tigre's band were now moving. Silently they were drawing to a
focus where they could work their mischief.

And the successes of El Tigre seemed now more understandable
to Dupont. The leader, having chosen his point of attack, needed
only to send a sudden call into the neighborhood of the place
and summon at once sufficient men for his purposes. Once those
purposes were accomplished, he withdrew suddenly, and all his
forces scattered to the four winds, settling quietly down to their
former lives after they had received the rewards of their labors.

They came into a broad plaza. Two other groups of horsemen
entered at the same time from other directions and all went about
their appointed tasks without friction. The duty of that section in
which Dupont was a member was simply to take up a position across
the mouth of the broadest street that gave upon the plaza from the
east. Here they dismounted, but when the horses were given into
the hands of one of the men, it was found that Dupont would have

to take that duty, for the chestnut stallion could not be managed by any of the others. He stood to one side, his right hand full of reins, and watched his companions take up their places in the shelter of doorways, their rifles cocked and pointing down the street.

All this was done smoothly. Then the little wide-shouldered leader made a low-voiced speech. "We are to be the rear guard," he said. "When the work is finished we are the last to leave the town. Consider, *amigos*, how El Tigre has honored us."

Dupont, his left hand on the muzzle of his horse, watched the bright eyes of Twilight stirring suspiciously as he glanced up and down the street. The other animals stood at ease, on three legs, their heads fallen, resting from their journey. But Twilight was like an arrow trembling on the string, as though he had drunk in the fears and the tremors of the human minds around him.

A window slammed up in the second story of a house at one side of the street. There had been enough noise to disturb at least one person, for a shrill woman's voice exclaimed: "Drunkards! Drunkards! Go home! Who is down there?"

There was no answer from below, but presently, with a frightened gasp, she slammed down the window again and disappeared in the dark of her room. Perhaps she had seen the glint of the stars along a rifle barrel. Perhaps she had seen the group of fine horses, silhouetted against the whitewashed wall.

"Pray this business end quickly," Roca said, his voice husky and nervous.

"Coward," hissed the leader. "If you speak again …"

The street became silent once more. In all the plaza there was not a soul in view—not another of all of the men of El Tigre. Like a cat's brood, how silently they moved, these bandits from the great plains. But in spite of the silence, how was the alarm being spread? Had yonder woman in her room slipped back into her bed, and did she lie there with the blanket drawn over her head, trembling and hoping that the end of the world was not near? Or had she, like a shrewd matron, stolen away to give the alarm in the right quarter?

These thoughts drifted through the mind of Dupont. He handled his revolver, grew reassured, and stared about him again across the plaza. It was deathly quiet. The white marble statue of some patriot glimmered faintly from its pedestal. The false-fronted houses stood gravely about like spectators at a fight.

How long they were about their work—those fellows who had undertaken the task of blowing the safe in the bank? Or did they have the combination? Or was it possible that the muffled noise of the explosion would not carry across the plaza from the interior of the bank?

Then, like a light turned on suddenly in the brain of Dupont, bringing all the sleeping terror of the night to life, he heard the terrible scream of a man who tastes sudden death and dies in midshriek. A thousand voices instantly answered.

CHAPTER TWENTY-TWO

So it seemed to Dupont, at least. All around the plaza men began to shout, and twenty guns exploded with a rattling volley. "Saddles!" shouted El Tigre's lieutenant.

The gauchos shot into their seats as though great invisible hands were hurling them to their places, and then, with rifles held across the crooks of their arms, they waited. They had not long to pause. Across the plaza swept a charge of a dozen horsemen, crowding against one another, the horses weaving with the fury of full speed. Behind them were others, and as these fugitives shot past they yelled: "*¡Todo es perdido! ¡Todo es perdido!*"

Down the street wailed that mournful cry and crashed back from the faces of the buildings. "All is lost! All is lost!"

And again, as another group of El Tigre's men shot past: "Soldiers! Ride, *amigos!*"

Soldiers! That was the secret, then. Against ordinary townsfolk or against even some numbers of police, no doubt these hardy ruffians would not have hesitated to do battle, but against the disciplined courage and no doubt the overwhelming numbers of soldiers, they were helpless. So they rode like madmen back toward the Pampas.

It was no question of courage to stay at such a time. It was every man for himself, and Dupont, turning the head of Twilight in the current of the flight, gave the stallion his head.

After that, it was like riding through rapids in a small boat, safe, but tossed wildly about. For seeing other horses before him, and disdaining to run behind them, Twilight raged like a fiend through the press. Dodging, plunging, twisting, swerving, his ears flattened on his neck, his head stretched out, his legs flying at full speed, he drifted through the mass of the fugitives, whipping past them in groups or man by man, and, before the outskirts of the town were reached, he was running easily in the lead, bringing up his fine head and arching his neck once more in content. To be first or to be nothing was the will of Twilight.

Then they poured out into the broad, dark plain, and funneled out widely. Behind them, solid bodies of mounted men galloped in hot pursuit. Sometimes, here and there, Dupont heard the ringing explosion of a rifle, or the dull, short bark of a revolver. Once or twice he heard yells of pain. The law was laying its whip upon the bodies of the miscreants.

But in ten minutes he was far away from the nearest, and gaining ground at every stride. The first two or three miles of a run merely served, so it seemed, to limber the muscles of this wonderful horse. He stretched away as freely as a ship sailing before the wind. Another few minutes and all sound had died down behind him on the Pampas. They were driving on alone.

Now he drew up the stallion, gave him a breathing spell, and then jogged on again. All his hopes had failed on this occasion. He had been brought within the very shadow of El Tigre, but had failed to see even the claws of that famous man. How many months might it be before he could have another such opportunity?

The dawn and the aching weariness of his body put an end to reflections. He found a little tumble-down ruin of an adobe. There was good grass nearby for the grazing of Twilight, and, having hobbled that king of horses, he threw further caution to the winds, rolled down his blankets, and was asleep instantly.

He dreamed, at last, of fire beating against his face, and then of a kindly hand striking the flames away and covering his eyes with blessed shadow. At this, he wakened and found that the slant afternoon sun was shining boldly into the place, only broken by a figure in the doorway. Dupont came to his feet with catlike speed.

The stranger, at this sudden movement, drew hastily back into the outer sunshine and there stood shading his startled eyes and staring into the interior of the broken-down hut. He was a tall old man with bent shoulders and legs bowed by many and many a day spent in the saddle. His long, thick, drooping mustaches were a dirty gray with age and with dust. In the distance an ancient horse stood with hanging head, too spiritless to crop the grass.

"Señor," explained the old fellow humbly, "I saw a horse ..." He pointed to the magnificent form of Twilight. The gallant stallion, as though the work of the last twenty-four hours had been a mere pleasure jaunt, stood as lightly as a cat with his head high and his inquiring ears pricked at the stranger. Yet, had the hobbles been removed from his legs, Dupont knew the chestnut would have flown at the man with a devil in his eyes.

"You surprised me," Dupont answered amiably. "Come in, *amigo*, and escape from the sun."

The other hesitated for an instant, and then came with caution into the doorway, scanned the interior with careful eyes, and finally thought it safe to squat, bowlegged, in a corner and roll a cigarette.

"You are making a long journey," he asked Dupont.

Questions were by no means what Dupont wanted. He decided that he would avoid any more of them by a partial avowal of the truth.

"I have had only one long ride," he said. "I rode from Nabor last night."

"Nabor!" cried the old man, and it was plain that he had heard something of the troubles in that city.

"I was riding on the trail of El Tigre's crew," Dupont said smoothly enough.

"Ha?" cried the other, more astonished than ever. "You rode *alone* behind those demons?"

"No, no. For every one of them there were four of us."

"Even those odds are dangerous against such wolves," said the veteran. "I once had a son ... ah, *amigo*, I once had a son ..." He broke off, his voice falling gradually away, and his eyes, misted with age and the thought of this old sorrow, looking far off toward a happier time. He added: "But you were riding with the men of Nabor?"

"Yes. We followed them. But they scattered like the leaves before a wind."

"I have heard how they use that old trick."

"First there would be a dozen men before us. Then they would fan out ... one here, another to this side, another to that, and still a group of four or five left flying in one direction, and most of the pursuit centered on them ... do you see?"

"It is a very old story. El Tigre teaches his men the tricks of foxes."

"The fastest horses were kept straight ahead, drawing the others after them, while the men on the slower horses ducked off on each side."

"Of course."

"So we began to find that where we had started to chase some four dozen ..."

"Four dozen? Señor, señor! I have heard honest men swear that there were between two and three hundred of the rascals."

"I tell you how many I saw when we were riding behind them. There may have been others who made off in other directions. Of that I know nothing."

"That is true, of course. And yet I understood that they all rode out of the town together."

"But as I was saying, I saw them thinning out before us. So at last I decided to take after a rascal on a small horse that turned off to the right. But apparently he did not turn off because his mount was slow. I sent my horse hard after him. You may see that my horse had good looks, and he is as fine as he is handsome. However, he was tired by a long day of work. I worked him hard, but this villain managed to keep well ahead of me. At last, when the dawn began to come, both my horse and I were tired out. I came to this place, and here I went to sleep." This concluded his tale.

"Then you can tell me all that happened in Nabor?" asked the old fellow, his eyes beginning to shine like diamonds in the greed for news.

"I can tell you what I heard and saw and did," said Dupont. "I had just come to the *fonda*, and was dismounting from the saddle ... because I had had a late start yesterday ... when I heard a blast of guns, and then a scream, and then there was shouting. 'El Tigre.' You can imagine that I was in the saddle again at once, and that I rode out to find out what was the matter. Everywhere men were saddling and mounting. Everywhere they were yelling and waving weapons. I followed in one current of hard riders. It took me out into the fields beyond the town. There I could see a crowd of riders. And we followed them as hard as we could, every man hoping that he might have the luck to help capture El Tigre. That is the story ..." He stopped.

The old man was rubbing his hands together impatiently. "That is all you know?" he asked.

"No, one thing more. As we were riding, I heard that El Tigre had tried to rob the bank."

The old fellow waved such slight news into the thinnest air with a gesture of disdain. "Then you have not heard what really happened?" he shouted. "I shall make your heart warm. If you have ridden after El Tigre, this will make your blood as warm as wine." He nodded to himself for an instant, still rubbing his hands, and smiling, while the delight in his narrative began to rise in his eyes like water brimming in a pitcher under the faucet. "This is what I heard from my cousin," he said. "My cousin came out from Nabor early this morning. Fifty of us sat about and listened while he told the story. All of it must have been true. Who would dare, do you think, to lie to fifty men? No, that would be too dangerous, *amigo*."

"Very dangerous," Dupont assented, and began to manufacture a cigarette.

"First keep in mind," rambled on the storyteller, "that there was a man named Roca. You will not forget that?"

"I shall not forget that, my friend." But he started a little in spite of himself, for what had Roca to do with the success or the failure of this expedition?

"This Roca," went on the old man, "had worked under El Tigre before, and he was called on to help when they rode for Nabor. But he did not like the thing. He had a wife who was sick, you see?"

"Ah?" murmured Dupont, remembering the sullen face of Roca in the *fonda*.

"When he wished to get out of the task, he was threatened, so that he saw he must go or else have a knife stuck between his ribs as a traitor."

"One can understand how that would be."

"He went home to his sick wife. But he dared not speak a word to her. One never can tell. Even the air has ears when one speaks of El Tigre. Is it not so?"

"Undoubtedly."

"But this Roca was not a fool. He wrote on the wall ... 'El Tigre hunts tonight down the east road ... I think toward Nabor.' That was all, and that was enough. His wife could not read, poor woman, but, after her husband was gone, she called in a neighbor who was a wise man, and he saw the writing. This wise neighbor went to the police, and they telegraphed to Nabor. There were soldiers camped five miles from Nabor, and, when the telegram came, they were sent for and hidden away in houses near the bank, for it was guessed that at the bank El Tigre would strike. When he leaps, it is at a bull. Is it true?"

"That is very true, of course."

"In the middle of the night, horsemen began to steal into the town. Some guarded the plaza. Others went into the bank. They had keys for the door. Someone in the bank had been bought, it is said. But when all was ready, the word was given. The colonel of the soldiers himself gave the word ... by stabbing with his sword one of the bandits. His scream was the signal for the others. The soldiers ran out into the street, shooting as they went, and rushed for the bank. And what do you think they found there?"

"Some of El Tigre's bloodhounds, I suppose."

"Yes, yes. Some they killed, others they wounded, and a dozen of them threw themselves at one big man ... and they took him alive. Who was it, señor?" The old gaucho was rolling himself from side to side in the height of his excitement.

"I cannot guess, of course."

"Señor, it was El Tigre!"

CHAPTER TWENTY-THREE

It was news that at first seemed to Dupont so great that the blood rushed into his face. Here was the major half of his work already done for him. El Tigre was taken. But a moment of reflection altered his views a good deal. With El Tigre gone, his daughter would disappear. Perhaps she would flee into the mountains with one of the lieutenants of the outlaw chieftain, and, having married the man, her life would be ruined and ended as perfectly as though a bullet had struck her down.

It had been hard enough to come on the traces of even so notorious a figure as El Tigre. It would be a thousandfold more difficult to reach Francesca. Indeed, if he hoped to find the girl, he could not reasonably retain that hope if her father were removed behind the walls of a prison awaiting his death, which would surely follow soon.

"Is it not a great deliverance, señor?" the old gaucho asked.

"People will not forget last night," agreed Dupont gloomily.

"We are coming to better days, señor. The great El Tigre is taken. Soon we may hope that the other pest … the other murderer will be taken."

"Who is he?"

"Can you ask? Can you ask, señor? I mean that man who is

more wicked than El Tigre. For El Tigre, if he stole money, gave much to those who were poor. He was a man who might have been a good, peaceful fellow if he had had better luck. But this other is a devil who murders sleeping men ... El Crisco!"

"So?" Dupont declared, stung by the horror and the anger in the voice of his ancient companion. "Well, this El Crisco has done many bad things, I hear. What manner of man is he?"

"A young man and a big man," said the other. "With ... why, señor, much such a man as you are. But he is to be chiefly known by his horse ... Twilight."

"I have heard of his horse, too."

"A very great and wonderful stallion, señor. There are some who say that there is magic in that horse and his rider. I, however, believe no such tales. Some will tell you that bullets cannot strike either the horse or the man."

"Well," Dupont murmured, anxious to turn the subject as soon as possible, "that is an odd name for a horse."

"It is because he is of an odd coloring. A black chestnut, señor, like ... like ..." He looked about him while his mind fumbled for a striking comparison, and, so doing, his glance passed out through the door and fell upon the splendid figure of the stallion, with the sunshine glimmering along his silken flanks. "Why, señor, his horse is of a color exactly like your own horse."

Here the truth, it seemed, burst suddenly upon him. His hand remained frozen in its position in midair as though fixed in a solid substance, and, while the blood ran out of his cheeks and left them a sickly sallow color, he stared with bulging eyes at his companion. It was as though he were beholding a bodiless ghost in the terror of the midnight.

There was small chance to outface such conviction as that which he heard in the voice of the gaucho, but Dupont made his best effort to succeed. "What is wrong, *amigo?*" he asked.

"El Crisco!" gasped out the old gaucho, and at the same time his shaking right hand reached behind the small of his back, while he set his teeth with the white lips strained back from them. He was like an old dog that meets a mighty timber wolf in the forest and, seeing no hope for escape, prepares with a growl to sell his life as dearly as he may.

The heart of Dupont was touched. Suddenly he said: "Take your hand from your knife, my old friend. Do you think that is any use against this?" And he touched the butt of his revolver hanging loosely in the holster.

The glance of the gaucho wavered down to the gun, and he shuddered. "Señor El Crisco," he said huskily, "I am an old man, and there are many sins upon my shoulders. Give me only enough time to pray that God may receive my miserable soul into his mercy and ..."

Dupont shrugged his thick, strong young shoulders. "What is your name, old man?" he asked.

The other called back his dim eyes from the contemplation of the wickedness of his long life. "Perez," he said faintly. "My name is Perez."

"My good Perez, listen to me. There are many lies floating in the air about El Crisco. Among others, they have called me a murderer. I swear to you, señor, that I have never taken the life of any man in the whole of the Argentine. Shall I begin murder with you?"

"I pray God that you will not, señor."

"But if I let you go, Perez, you will fly to the nearest town and give the alarm."

"I?" The thin arms of the gaucho were thrown wide in a protestation of innocence. "God strike me with his lightning if I could do such a thing to my benefactor ..."

"Hush," Dupont said sternly. "Do not lie. However, you are free to go your way."

"Señor El Crisco ..." He choked and could say no more.

"*Adiós*, Perez."

Perez rose to his feet, trembling so that he could hardly stand,

and, walking from the shack, he crossed the space toward his horse slowly, shaken now and again with strong convulsions of terror and glancing back over his shoulder as though he expected to see a leveled rifle behind him. So he gained the saddle and turned the head of his weary horse down the road. For a hundred yards he jogged slowly. Then, looking back and seeing that El Crisco had made no motion toward saddling the black chestnut, he clapped the spurs to the sides of his ancient horse and brought that steed into a rickety gallop.

Dupont, gazing after him, could not help breaking into laughter, but his mirth was short-lived. Before long Perez would have spread the tale of what he had seen and heard, doubtless embroidered with many miraculous details. And some scores of swift, keen-eyed riders would swarm out onto the Pampas to hunt for the outlawed man.

So, gloomily enough, he saddled Twilight and rode on his way. That way was straight back toward the town of Nabor, for, at the very moment when he was drawing the cinches tight, he had formed a reckless resolution. It was sufficiently wild to have made even the fabulous El Crisco, who haunted the dreams of honest men, tremble and grow pale.

CHAPTER TWENTY-FOUR

There was no work in Nabor on this day. It was a holiday that had to be observed with as much religious zeal as the day of the birth of the republic. For on this day had occurred an event that would lift Nabor forever out of oblivion. Never again would a citizen of that prosperous little municipality, visiting Buenos Aires, have to explain to those he met where the town of Nabor was situated and what was its population and what were its industries. No, it would be known henceforth as the place where El Tigre was, at length, taken a prisoner, and removed from his wild and dangerous life.

Wherever they went, the men of Nabor would be welcome guests, for it would everywhere be hoped that they could give new tidings about that famous event. Accordingly the shops were closed and the bars were opened and the town of Nabor—male and female, girl and boy—busied itself with the important affair of learning all that was to be known of the history of that great night, and all that was not known about it.

No one hunted for truth. Everyone was interested in the picturesque only. All was put under a microscope and the result was then painted in the wildest colors. And the wine circulated. What is more inspiring to the inquisitive brain than a touch of alcohol? The good men of Nabor used it plentifully, and they found that it indeed made their wits fertile. There were times when the numbers of El Tigre's handful of followers reached the magnificent proportions of five and six hundred men—a stout army that had only been vanquished by the brilliant genius and the stout sword and the gallant discipline of Colonel Alfonso Ramírez.

Nothing could have been better to the purpose of Charles Dupont than the festival spirit that now lived and breathed in the air of the town of Nabor. The eyes of men and women were dimmed to all but one topic. Looking in the air for stars, one cannot see the danger at one's feet. And rejoicing for the glory of a recent victory, how many armies have been suddenly routed by the surprise attack of a new and unexpected foeman?

So it was with the town of Nabor, which, while it swung its united hat and cheered for Alfonso Ramírez—long might his name be glorious throughout the land—was so blinded with the tears of joy that it did not see stalking through the streets a monster hardly less known to fame—El Crisco himself.

El Crisco, and walking through the streets of the town in the light of the sun. Certainly it was madness. But El Crisco was a calm-brained Anglo-Saxon, willing to take desperate chances like others of the cold Northern races, but first counting up those chances deliberately and finding some hope for a success. The very madness was what he hoped might blind others around him.

In addition, he had done what he could to hide his distinctive features. Some days before, he had secured some dye and stain, yet he had hesitated before this to use it. And the thought of staining his blond hair black, for some reason, angered him. However, he could not neglect a precaution so important on this day of days.

In the first place, he did not enter the town with Twilight. That was, of course, a madness a little too great even for an Anglo-Saxon gone berserk. But in a shed on the outskirts of the town, a shed that stood behind an abandoned house, he had placed the great black

chestnut and smoothed his dappled hide like the sleek skin of a
jaguar. Who could tell how dearly he would need the stallion on
that night—or whether he would ever so much as see him again?

And so, running his hand lovingly down the arched neck of
Twilight, he whispered in the quivering ear: "Old-timer, it's you
who dragged me south to this country. It's you that dragged me into
all this trouble. How the devil will you ever pay me back, you rascal,
when I'm salted away with cold lead?"

With this farewell he went into another part of the shed and
continued his work. It was a laborious process, but he performed it
with some neatness and at the expense of a good hour of his time.
At the end of that period there issued from the shed, instead of the
blond, fair-skinned fellow who had entered it, one with shining,
coal-black hair, and with a skin as dark as walnut juice would turn
it. Even the eyelids were darkened, and the very eyelashes had been
carefully blackened. And the arms and neck of this transformed
adventurer were as dusky as the skin of a Malay.

About his neck there flamed a crimson bandanna of immense
proportions, spotted with splashes of blue and of yellow. It caught
the eye blocks away, like fire in the dark of the night. But it was
the theory of Charles Dupont, on this occasion, that the bolder his
attire the greater his chances of success. They would not be apt to
think of another outlaw now that El Tigre was in the prison. And
after the downfall of that great leader, surely they would expect to
have their town shunned by every other bandit as long as Nabor
stood under the sun or the eternal stars.

Such was the opinion of Charles Dupont, but as he swaggered
down the street, his heart was cold and small in him, and every eye
that fell upon him seemed to be prying at his soul, and as every
person passed, it seemed to Dupont that they were turning and
glancing back over their shoulders at him.

However, having entered upon his task, he would not draw
back. He went straight to the center of town and entered the

plaza. There he found the reason for the fairly deserted streets through which he had just been passing. For the entire population of Nabor, very nearly, had gathered here where all might see and be seen, talk and listen, and taste the new delightful rumors and reports as swiftly as they were born.

He sauntered through the blinding sunshine toward the nearest saloon. There was no room inside. Little tables had been brought out upon the verandah and under the trees nearby. Assistant bartenders, hired for the nonce at ridiculous salaries, were busy here and there, making mistakes in change, cursing themselves and their tasks, and then taking comfort out of a stolen bottle. Here, in a corner against a wall of the house, he found a place where an upturned box served him as a seat. He could watch the swirl of life along the plaza, he could hear the snatches of talk from passersby, and just opposite he could see the municipal building with its stately, broad flight of steps.

It was in that building that the distinguished prisoner was now being guarded, and guarded by no other than the indomitable Colonel Alfonso Ramírez himself. But for that matter, one could have guessed that El Tigre was in that place by the frequency with which the gossipers turned their eyes in that direction and by the steady stream of people who flocked up the steps.

Dupont began to give ear to those who were buzzing so busily around him. Most of it was the rankest nonsense. In this fashion was rumor born.

"A thousand pesos to ten," said one fat-faced peon as he tippled his wine, "that those soldiers who wrestled with El Tigre wished that they had tried a wildcat sooner."

And as he left the table, another sat down in his place.

"What news?" he asked.

"We have been hearing how El Tigre threw the soldiers around when they jumped at him," he was told.

"Ah, yes, he must have broken some heads. He is as strong as

any three men. He must have thrown them around." He departed
in his turn.

In five minutes the same theme was taken up again. Only one
of the original group around that table remained.

"We have had news of El Tigre at the moment when he was
captured," he told the newcomers.

They were instantly reduced to a reverent silence.

"They jumped on him from every side. His hands were clogged
with their bodies, you might say. He had no room to turn himself
about. He had to leave his weapons with them as he tore himself
away. But he could not get clear. They swarmed after him again
like ants over an ant hill. What a man he is. He took one … a fat
soldier … and threw him the length of the room. They say that
man's skull was broken. He took another by the heels and used him
for a club. He has the strength of at least four men, you know. But
finally some twenty of them spilled over him like water over a roof.
He was washed to the floor by men falling on him as thick as drops
of rain."

And as that story was received with shouts of surprise and delight,
Dupont grinned behind his broad hand that held his cigarette. He
tasted his red wine, and suddenly he saw that the table at which
the gossip had been circulating so busily was empty. Everyone who
had heard that last amazing tale had scattered here and there and
everywhere to repeat what he had heard. Behold, a new sensation
had been added to this day of days in the honest town of Nabor.

Here all talk ceased suddenly. At the head of the wide steps of
the municipal building there appeared a tall and resplendent figure.
It was a tall man in military uniform—his hat, his coat, his trousers
fairly encrusted with gold lace and his narrow breast decked with
medals. One hand rested upon the hilt of his narrow sword, the
other doffed his hat that glistened with yellow metal as he bowed to
the plaudits of the crowd.

And what plaudits these were. Everyone was instantly up from boxes and chairs and shouting, yelling, raving, waving hands and hats and silken handkerchiefs of bright colors.

"Colonel Ramírez! Colonel Ramírez!"

This was the great man, the savior of society, the queller of that dragon, El Tigre. Good reason to shout. They opened their throats and strained their lungs with their acclaim.

"Colonel Ramírez!"

The colonel walked slowly down the steps. A throng engulfed him before he reached the bottom. He struggled with amiable violence through it. A file of soldiers thrust into the jam and pushed back the struggling crowd with their rifles—in vain. They opened a channel that was instantly closed again. Women came running and held up their children to see the famous hero. Those in back pressed upon those in front.

"Colonel Ramírez!"

They pushed the soldiers, shouting, laughing, before them. They were around the colonel again, shaking his hand, blessing his courage and his wisdom.

At length he reached his horse, a dancing bay mare, beautiful in the sun, tossing her bridle and all its polished silver ornament. Behold. He is raised to the saddle by twenty hands. He is seated with his hat cocked over one eye. The mare starts away. She dances sidewise, as though delighted by her burden. And the brave colonel is gone down the street, with a crowd rushing out before him, and closing in behind regardless of the heels of the bay, which dart out now and again as she prances along.

But the brave colonel, the good colonel—how could even his horse do harm to the people of Nabor?

CHAPTER TWENTY-FIVE

Like birds roused from their sleep by a sudden squall of wind that shakes them on their chilly perches among the trees, the good folk settled back to their boxes and to their chairs once more. Two jovial gauchos, come in from an estancia to take part in the celebration, settled down at the table where Charles Dupont sat.

"There is a man," said one.

"He could be a king," the other said.

"Perhaps he will be? Or a president?"

"He will be a general for this."

"Yes. If he is not promoted for this, there is no justice in the Argentine."

"A kind man, too."

"And modest."

"Did you see him pat the head of the old man?"

"And he kissed that little boy whose mother held him up."

"Yes, one can see that the colonel is as good as he is brave."

"If he looks fierce, it is because he is terrible only to his enemies."

"If there were a war, there is only one general for our country."

This sample Dupont heard close at hand, but the same talk was going on everywhere. Waves of quieting noise swept through the plaza back and forth and back again. Then the gauchos turned to Dupont. They would buy him wine. But he had luckily forestalled them and ordered a vintage three times as expensive as their pockets could afford. An excellent Médoc, old enough to have something of that musty taste that is dear to the heart of the wine lover.

They drank it slowly, smacking their lips after the first swallow.

"You know wine, señor!"

"Oh, a little. Only a little, *amigos.*"

They grinned more broadly. That word had placed them definitely in their own class, out of which the quality of the wine had seemed to lift him for a moment. He was only a gaucho like themselves, they decided—a gaucho with something in the purse and a free hand to spend it.

"You are working near Nabor?"

"I have been traveling west. Now that El Tigre is gone, one may travel safely, eh?"

"If there were only El Tigre. Well, he is not the last. But the other will soon go. People will not endure him. He is a mad dog … a wild wolf …"

"Who, *amigos?*"

"Why, who but El Crisco?"

"Yes, yes. To be sure, there is El Crisco. But his hand is not as strong or his arm as long as El Tigre's."

"Perhaps not. But he is poison. He is a tarantula. Poor El Tigre. After all, he was a kind man. But this El Crisco … however, you have heard of what he did only this morning?"

"Not I."

"Well, the news has just reached Nabor. He is a devil. May he die by inches, the dog!"

"What has he done, this El Crisco?" Dupont asked curiously.

"What has he done? There is nothing more devilish. He caught an old man, a harmless old fellow named Perez. I myself know this Perez. He is very old. *Muy criollo,* too. Very good. This El Crisco catches him in a little hut. He is afraid that if Perez gets away, he will raise the people of the next town. So this El Crisco decides to murder Perez. That is bad, but the rest ... *bah!* It is the way he determines on the murder. He will enjoy the killing, this El Crisco. He ties the poor old man to the wall of the house, very tight. There is nothing but iron and adobe in the house. He piles what wood there is around the feet of the old man. Then he goes away a little distance to collect more wood. While he is gone, Perez gets strength from God ... or from the fear of being roasted alive. For that was Crisco's plan ... to burn that old gaucho alive. *Faugh!* Is that not a fiend? But Perez gets strength, pulls an arm loose from the ropes, and so cuts his way clear, and runs out to his horse and rides away, with El Crisco shooting after him until he rode out of range. Poor Perez ... he showed them a hole through his hat when he reached the town."

This recital was greeted with grunts of savage fury by the companion of the narrator. As for Charles Dupont, he felt like smiling, but he forced a scowl upon his face. "Such fiends should be given such a death as they prepared for others," he declared, and he was heartily agreed with.

"They hunted for this El Crisco, then?" he asked.

"Half a hundred men hunted. But, of course, his stallion has wings. It flies over the ground. The devil who befriends El Crisco puts his strength into that wild beast ... that horse that kills men even as its master does."

"Which way did the trail run?"

"Toward us ... toward Nabor."

The perspiration rolled out on the forehead of Charles Dupont. For suppose the trailers were to come upon Twilight in the shed? However, he forced that unhappy thought from his mind. There were more immediate dangers.

Here a fresh clamor rolled up the street. The colonel was returning, and in spite of all the enthusiasm that had been expended upon him before, there seemed an equal store remaining. Again he passed through a small triumph. Again the crowd flocked with him up the steps of the municipal building and, after he had disappeared, cheered until their throats were hoarse. After which, unable to speak in more than husky whispers, they rushed back for more wine to recruit their enthusiasm.

When it was quiet again, Dupont started from his place and, sauntering across the street, joined the mob that filed steadily into the municipal building and out again. All was noise and confusion in the great hall into which he stepped through the front doors. People milled up and down like cattle in a corral, or collected in small groups and exchanged opinions and gossip busily until tall gendarmes hustled them on their way because the traffic was blocked. The line of those going in was kept thin and steady by police supervision, and, falling into his place in it, Dupont progressed slowly toward a door on one side of the hall.

On the way, the whole line was talking at the top of their voices, but when the door was reached, men and women seemed to shrink in size. Hats were automatically removed. All voices hushed to utter silence and so, in his turn and time, Dupont stepped into a big, high-ceilinged chamber where the quiet was like the quiet of a museum—the Egyptian rooms of a great museum where the past breathes upon the present a musty and stupefying perfume, and all that is great in history seems dead and never to live again.

There were the same whispers, the same focusing of eyes, the same cautious footfalls. And yonder sat the object of all this attention. Behind his chair, four soldiers leaned upon their rifles. On either side of him, four more soldiers stood at ease, their eyes gloomily fixed upon their prisoner, their shining bayonets extending above the muzzles of their guns. Twelve men to watch one, and that one bound with steel chains.

His wrists lay in his lap, handcuffed, and from the handcuffs to his ankles ran another chain, strong enough to have held a ship at its moorings, and around the ankles were fitted other bands of steel, and to his anklets was anchored a great ball of lead of forty pounds weight. So secured, the authorities of law and order exhibited their prisoner to the eyes of the curious world, and the townsfolk and all who had ridden in from the surrounding farms and estancias went slowly, softly by, staring in awe at that face that had frightened their children to sleep on many and many a night.

After all, he was not extraordinary when analyzed. He was not much above six feet in actual inches, perhaps. He was less than Charles Dupont in poundage. And upon his face and his shoulders were stamped the writing of some fifty years. Neither was there anything brutal in his expression. It was rather a thoughtful face, a noble forehead, lips compressed as though by pain and worry, and sunken eyes of thought. Yet there was about him that which made him a giant. Seated as he was, he overshadowed the stalwart guards, the chosen men of the regiment who stood post around him.

He was neither sullen nor defiant, or threatening. Instead, he regarded the slow movement of faces past his station with a considerate look of one who has read in human nature as in a book all the days of his life and continues to read until his last breathing moment. He seemed almost on the point of speaking, now and then, as someone who passed excited a keen emotion or brought some thought to him.

But after the first sharp glance Charles Dupont saw only one thing. It was a fleeting shadowy thing—no more than the flick of a bird's wings across a windowpane, and the bird gone on singing. But into the mind of Dupont there flashed a glimpse of recognition, and a feeling that he must have seen this face before. And then the knowledge came strongly back upon him in a cold wave that rolled across his heart and his brain. The shadow of recognition sprang from a ghost of similarity between this man and his daughter Francesca. No, it was not in the features, handsome though they were. It was in his spirit. And the spirit is that which cannot be exposed or explained through the facts of the flesh.

He went on out from the room, his mind whirling, his feet moving in a fumbling manner until he was again in the outer hall. There, the instant they issued from the room, the rest of the line broke into exclamations, subdued to whispers at first, under the influence of the awe that had so lately and so heavily weighed upon them, but presently rising to shrillness as they realized they were released from the curious, searching eyes of the great outlaw.

What comment they made then, as they came out.

"Did you see his eyes? Like a lion's in a cage, studying us so that he could remember and tear us to bits if he ever met us again."

"I wouldn't go back in that room for a thousand pesos!" This from a woman, of course. Her husband laughed at her, but in a sickly fashion.

"And his hands, José. Did you see his hands?"

"Like a woman's hands ... so slender and so small."

"That's why they can move so fast."

"Well, he's' still the quickest man in the world with a gun."

"*Bah!* That's because he frightens people to death when they meet him. They can't endure to be in front of him. He made me, for, instance, feel like a little boy."

"Someday somebody might have beaten him in fair fight, but I don't think so."

"No, I think not. There was never anyone like El Tigre."

"I was almost sorry ..."

"At least the colonel was not afraid of him."

"Oh, no, the colonel would laugh at the devil."

"Yes, honor is everything to a man like ..."

"Thank God, that there are such men in the Argentine."

"Yes, he should be ..."

Charles Dupont stepped away from this group. He passed others. It was the same everywhere up and down the hall. The talk was all of the terrible El Tigre in his chains. And of the brave colonel.

And something grew cold in the great heart of Charles Dupont. How strange it was, he thought, that in this crowd there was not one who appreciated the horror of showing such a man to a crowd and making a show out of his downfall. For, great though the sins of such a man might be, at least he was brave, and courage is a virtue that wipes out the worst of vices, to some extent. Brave? Yes, it seemed to Dupont that he had never before seen such courage as this iron man showed, looking at his tormentors with calm eyes, banishing from his face every trace and taint of the shame and the horror and the fury that must be raging in his soul.

So, having seen his man and having blushed for looking at him, Dupont prepared himself for the last steps in the great venture.

CHAPTER TWENTY-SIX

One could easily tell the room in which the colonel sat by the quality of the people who passed through a certain door in front of which stood two sergeants, fellows in their dress uniforms with their medals on their breasts, proud soldiers and brave soldiers who carried their guns as if they knew what shooting and being shot at meant. For those who passed through that door were all of the quality of the land. There were rich estancieros, the officials of the town, the bankers, the great men of the community, dressed in their best, proud of themselves, a little frightened at going into the presence of such a person as the colonel had so recently proved himself to be. They went in stiff and awed. They came out smiling, glancing at one another, exchanging pleased comments. Evidently the colonel was a man who knew how to receive others with a certain social grace. He was not all the stern warrior.

How many votes was he preparing on his behalf should he ever decide on a political life? At least, in Nabor, he could have been elected king the next day.

Dupont walked up to the door. Two rifles were crossed before his breast instantly, the bright bayonets glittering, close to his eyes.

"Your pass, señor?"

"I have very important business."

"The lieutenant is in the next room. You may go there. But the colonel is …"

They spoke as men speak when they use the name of the deity, and do not use it profanely. Apparently this colonel was not a god to the outer world only; he was respected even by his own troops.

Dupont retired. He had paper and an envelope with him. What wanderer goes without them? He wrote:

Brave Colonel Ramírez,

Today you have done a great service to your country. There is another service equally great, which may be performed. I wish to see you and to speak to you, and to you alone.

When I say that I take my life in my hands by telling you the secret that I carry in my breast, you will understand why there may be no other person in the room when I address you.

Of that secret, reluctantly, I commit one word to paper. It is about El Crisco.

Señor Colonel, you have captured El Tigre. I dare say that is a bright day in your life. How much brighter if, on the same day, you were to strike down that other fiend and murderer, El Crisco. At one stroke to liberate your country from two terrible calamities, two devils in the form of men. Colonel, that would be glory, indeed.

Brave Colonel, I dare swear to you so much. If you will admit me to your presence, I shall give you the opportunity of seeing the terrible El Crisco face to face. Señor, if you value glory, see me and hear me. I shall show you the way to El Crisco. Need I say that I have taken my life in my hands to do so much?

But to whom should I carry my information except to

the man who has already proved his valor and his wisdom by capturing El Tigre?

Señor, I commend my prayer to your own wisdom. Banish everyone from your room and bid the soldiers at your door admit the writer of this note.

Guess, therefore, at the dread with which I commit myself even to your hands, señor, when I inform you that I dare not sign to this note any other signature than that of One Who Has Seen and Admired Colonel Ramírez.

This singular epistle, written to the best of his ability in a purely Latin and romantic strain of extravagance, he sealed duly, addressed to the colonel, and placed in the hands of one of the soldiers at the door.

"Señor," he said to that man of war, "I commend this letter to your hands. It is for the colonel only. Should another open it, it will be a calamity to me, to the colonel, and to your country."

This he said with the greatest dignity and complacency, so that the sergeant, blinking a little, laid aside his gun and, clutching the envelope tightly, made his way through the door at the same time that a fat estanciero came out, grinning his pleasure at the world on account of the pleasant reception that he had found within the room.

There followed an anxious interval. There was a possibility, a very great possibility, indeed, that the colonel would not be too interested in this strange epistle to commend it to his secretary, order the writer of the missive to be arrested and examined to discover what the tidings that he bore might be. But there had been something in the carriage and in the dress of the colonel that assured Dupont that the worthy officer had had his head turned by the taste of much glory easily acquired and that he would be greedy for more gains of the same kind.

Eventually there was a pouring forth from the inner chamber. In a single group a dozen issued from that sanctum and came rather blankly into the great outer hall.

After this, the soldier to whom he had given the note approached him again, and with much respect offered him a military salute that he returned to the best of his ability.

"Señor," the sergeant said, "it is the pleasure of the colonel to see you. Follow me, señor."

So, drawing a great breath, and telling himself that he was now stepping into the very jaws of death, Charles Dupont followed the brave sergeant into the inner sanctum, heard the door close behind him, and found himself alone with the colonel in person.

The colonel sat behind a desk. Why he should have needed a desk seemed odd, but it was an oddity that would not occur to the average person entering that room. But it is an old truth that when men wish to appear dignified, they wish to get their legs out of view.

The colonel was now leaning back in his chair, his hands resting upon its broad arms, frowning gravely at his visitor. At close view, and being seated, he was even more lean of body and face than appeared from the distance. He had one of those birdlike faces, the nose long and thin and curved sharply down at the end, his mouth very small, with no red of the lips showing, his forehead slanting sharply back and covered with deep wrinkles, his black glossy hair sleeked down with oil. Much exposure had given him a healthy tan. Otherwise his emaciation would have suggested consumption.

"You are," said the colonel, "the man who wrote this note?"

The letter was spread upon the surface of the desk before him, and he tapped it with a clawlike hand, the back of which was covered with a knotting of blue veins. The hands were very white—gloves had scrupulously kept them from the sun. The hands seemed to belong to another person.

"I am he," Charles Dupont said, holding his hat in both hands. And he bowed his erect, strong shoulders a little, after a fashion that he had noted before in very respectful, rather frightened men. He felt the eyes of the colonel taking note of this attitude, and relishing it.

"In this paper," continued the man of war, "you hint, my friend, at an important revelation."

There was a tall screen in the corner of the room, used, perhaps, to shut out the sun when the window was left open in the late afternoon, for the windows looked upon the west. Toward this screen Dupont cautiously rolled his eyes.

The colonel took the hint at once, and with a smile he rose from his chair and moved the screen. "You see," he observed, returning to his chair, "that I am above artifice and …" He probably was about to add "fear," but changed his mind and said: "You need have no scruples in opening your mind to me."

"Señor *el coronel*," Dupont said, "I am a man who has taken his life in his hands."

"My good fellow," said the colonel, smiling again in a rather smudgy, disagreeable fashion, "I have hoped to demonstrate that I am capable of giving protection to those who have a wish to serve their county … or," he added with a strong emphasis, "to see it served by others."

"It is true," Dupont said. "The world knows what Señor *el coronel* has done. It is for that reason that I have found the courage to offer this information to him, and this opportunity. None but so brave a man would dare to use it."

The colonel bristled with satisfaction. "You speak good English, young man," he said. "You have been schooled?"

"Somewhat, señor."

In what place?"

"In the United States, señor."

The colonel lifted his dense black eyebrows. "Ah," he said. "I did not think … however, you are of the Argentine?"

"No."

"However, I see by your tone that you will be. For a brave young man, there is a career in the army. And for you … you will trust me now with your name?"

"Señor *el coronel*, ten thousand pardons. The time has not yet come for that, I beg you to believe."

"No?" grumbled the colonel, prying at the face of Dupont with his sharp little birdlike eyes. "And why not?"

"Because, señor, it would come to you as a shock."

"Nonsense, my man. I am one raised to endure shocks."

"First, Señor *el coronel*, there is the promise which I made to you."

"Exactly. If I admitted you to my presence, you were to bring me face to face with this devilish murderer ... this same El Crisco. Well, my friend, I ask for no more. Let me be brought to this man and he shall cease to trouble the republic. So much I promise you. Now, then, continue with your story. We are alone. The walls are more than a foot in thickness, and there is no possible means of communication with those outside the door than through the touching of this bell. Very well, you may speak with entire frankness. In what way are you to lead me to El Crisco?"

"Señor," Dupont said, drawing out the expected moment with a singular enjoyment, "I assure you that you have underrated this man. He is truly dangerous, because he is truly desperate."

"Tush," replied the colonel. "I have had experience with these braggart desperadoes before. And though I have encountered many of them, I have yet to meet one from whom I would shrink ... do you hear me? From whom I would shrink even single-handed. I trust, my friend, in the speed of my hand and in the surety of my eye as much as any outlaw who ever rode across the Pampas."

So saying, the colonel leaned back in his chair and modestly lowered his eyes toward his cigar, as one who would permit another to stare in uninterrupted and unembarrassed admiration upon his heroic features.

"Ah, señor," said Dupont, "it is such a man that is needed to face El Crisco."

"You need say no more," the colonel said with some irritation. "I have heard much about this villain. I have heard of his courage, his insolence, his deadly surety with weapons, his devilish malice. But all is nothing to me. Where I find the good of my country is to be served, there shall the hand of Ramírez ever be found."

He could not help losing his voice a little in the expression of so noble a sentiment. When the echoes had died away from the tall and somber walls, Dupont moved a little closer and leaned as to whisper the great secret.

"Señor *el coronel*, with so brave a man I no longer have the slightest hesitation. I at once admit you to the privilege of seeing this villain, this murderer. Señor, the man you see before you is El Crisco himself."

And with this, the hat fell from his hand and the brave colonel found himself looking down the throat of a black-muzzled Colt of .45 caliber, gripped by a large and strong hand in which the weapon trembled no more than if he who held it had been a creature of stone.

CHAPTER TWENTY-SEVEN

A pause came upon the room and upon the conversation in it—such a pause as comes upon armies when the foes are in sight and the lines are marshaled, but the first hurricane of death has not been loosed from the guns. Into that interval there came from the hallway, beyond the stout door, a faint, faint roaring, which represented all of the confused chattering that was able to penetrate from the hallway where the hundreds swarmed and clattered. And from the square, loud single voices of revelry and acclaim burst in from the windows.

The colonel laid down his cigar and allowed it to smolder unheeded, weltering in the thick varnish that covered the surface of the room and sending forth a pungent odor through the air. Then he moistened his pale lips. "You," he said rather faintly, "are El Crisco? I see that you are something of a practical jester, my friend."

"And you, señor," Dupont said in a changed voice, "I am glad to see are just the man to appreciate my jest."

"El Crisco, for instance, has the pale face of a *gringo*."

"Exactly," Dupont said, and, drawing out a handkerchief with his left hand, he rubbed it over his hot face. It came away covered with a dark-brown stain. And he saw the eyes of the brave colonel widen.

"It is enough," said Ramírez.

"Your bravery, *Coronel*, is only surpassed by your wisdom, I assure you."

"In what manner, señor, can you be served by braving me in …"

"The lion's den?"

"You see for yourself. It may be called a lion's den. There are soldiers at the door. There are soldiers everywhere around the building. There are soldiers in the plaza."

"That rear door," Dupont said suddenly. "Where does it lead?"

"To the side of the building. The entrance is also guarded. Even that side entrance is guarded."

"Does it open upon the plaza?"

"It does not."

"Señor *el coronel*, I begin to believe that there may be a way out of the lion's den."

The colonel shrugged his shoulders in spite of the leveled gun. In spite of that gun he smiled, and there was an acid edge of malice in his smile and an evil glint in his eye. "You are confident, Señor Crisco," he said.

"All desperate men are confident."

"But now, having bearded me in the den, so to speak …"—the colonel's face grew devilish with shame and with fury—"what have you gained?"

"You are a man who has always served, *Coronel*."

"It is my pride."

"And I trust, therefore, that I may find a way in which you will serve me."

"Ah?"

"You are a man of honor, Ramírez."

"It has never been doubted."

"But you are also a man who loves life. No, you are not one of those who will throw away a great deal of life for a very little bit of honor." Dupont spoke slowly and judicially.

"You are wrong," said the colonel with some heat. "I …"

"Slowly," cautioned Dupont. "The point is about to be tested." With the toe of his boot he fumbled for his fallen hat, found it, and raised it to his hand. "I am about to retire behind that screen," he said. "From that position I shall have a full view of you and you of me, but I shall not be seen by a man entering the door. Is that plain?"

"Perfectly plain, Señor Crisco."

"How great is that distance?"

"Five paces, I presume." The colonel, if pale, was astonishingly steady of voice.

"At ten paces, señor, I blow the heart out of an American dime. At five paces, *Coronel*, do you think that I would miss, say, one of those medals that hangs over your left breast … over your heart?"

The worthy colonel started a little. "I presume not," he said.

"Having retired behind that screen," Dupont explained, "I shall issue certain directions, and you will obey them … to the letter … to the exact letter. At the least deviation, señor, from my instructions, I kill you certainly and instantly."

The colonel, for the first time, lifted his eyes from the fascinating muzzle of the revolver and looked into the face of the tall young man who stood before him. "I believe you … implicitly," he muttered.

"For to me," Dupont said, working up a mood of savagery that he knew would be reflected instantly in his countenance, "my own life is now not worth a copper coin. At what valuation, señor, will I place the life of another man … even of a brave colonel in the army of the republic?"

"You are extremely clear," said Ramírez. "Now … to your point."

Dupont stepped backward slowly, until he had gained the place he desired behind the screen.

"Señor *el coronel*, it is my painful necessity to request you to summon an orderly. When he appears, command him to have your red bay mare and another horse … the best in your string … led around to the side entrance upon which this door at the rear of the room opens. Do you understand?"

The colonel closed his eyes and swallowed hard. Then, nodding, he stretched out his hand. "Have I your permission to ring?"

"You have. Consider, also, that when the orderly enters, with one word you can condemn me to certain death and win for yourself immortal fame ... and equally immortal death. For, at the instant you speak, I press this trigger and ... well, *Coronel*, you have seen war." He added in the same iron voice of mockery: "My trust is that you will leave such immortal fame to ... the dead, señor. Now call the orderly."

The button was pressed by the trembling hand of the colonel. The door opened; the heels of the orderly clicked as he gave the salute.

"Let María and the black gelding be led to the side entrance on which the rear door of this office opens. Let them be tethered there. Then the men who bring them may return to their other duties."

The click of the heels with the answering salute, and the door closed softly.

The eyes of the colonel turned again to his tyrant behind the screen.

"Again I see," murmured Dupont, "that you are a very wise man, *Coronel*. On account of this wisdom I prophesy for you a great career ... in politics."

The colonel saw fit to overlook the last portion of this biting speech. "You see," he said, "that I have added to your instructions. I presumed that you would not wish to have men waiting at the heads of the horses?"

"Your insight," Dupont confirmed, "is admirable. And yet, when you were giving the added instructions, your soul was one one hundredth of an inch from eternity."

The colonel grew paler still and hastily reached for the cigar, but, finding that it was securely stuck to the varnish by this time and that his hand shook extremely as he reached out, he changed his mind and locked his fingers tightly together, resting them upon the edge of the desk.

"Now," Dupont said, "we proceed to the next step. You will send for El Tigre …"

At this the colonel's coolness of nerve was completely shattered.

"You will send for El Tigre," Dupont repeated with his face set in a terrible frown.

The colonel sank back in his chair, his eyes closed, his hand against his heart.

"You will send for El Tigre," Dupont continued, his voice more iron than ever. "You will order that the keys to his irons be brought with him. You will declare that you wish to examine him in private. Do you hear me?"

The colonel opened his eyes. He was a sick man. "I have heard every word," he said thickly.

"You will have the ball removed from his feet. The other fetters may remain. He can walk in them. But the keys must be brought with them."

"It is very clear, señor." He stretched out his hand toward the bell.

"Wait!"

The hand dropped as though struck down by a club. "In the name of heaven, Señor Crisco, what now?"

"Have you anything to drink near you? Have you a flask of brandy?"

"I have that thing."

"In which drawer?"

"The upper on the right."

"You may open that drawer. If you take out anything other than a brandy flask …"

The colonel opened the drawer; he was breathing hard.

"Uncork it and take a good swallow."

The colonel obeyed with a military precision, and coughed as the hot liquor stung his throat.

"Restore the flask to the drawer."

It was done.

"Your color is already better. Now send for the next orderly."

So the bell was touched again. Again the door opened, and the voice of the colonel repeated the dictated order.

There was a gasp from the orderly. "Sir," he asked, "was it El Tigre you named?"

The colonel leaped to his feet and beat on the surface of the desk. "Fool and dog," he screamed, "have you ears to hear? I said El Tigre ... and at once! At once!"

The door closed with a bang. The colonel fell back with a groan in his chair.

CHAPTER TWENTY-EIGHT

To the ear of Charles Dupont there was never a sweeter or more solemn music than the chiming of chains as the door opened and let in from the hall the rattling of astonished voices, and that sound of steel on steel.

"Halt!" the colonel said suddenly.

There was the click of heels that announced an abrupt halt.

"Put the keys on that table."

A faint jingle made due answer.

"That will do."

"Sir …"

"Ha!"

"Alone in this room … with this man … even if his hands are secured …"

"Out of the room!" thundered the colonel. "Ten thousand devils, have I to teach you discipline … or what danger is? Will you begin to teach me?"

The orderly fairly fled, and the guard that had brought in the prisoner with him. When the door was closed the heavy silence began again, but now the colonel was looking straight before him at the man in irons and not at the muzzle of the leveled revolver.

"Señor El Tigre ... Señor Milaro," said the colonel, correcting himself hastily, "a friend of yours is waiting for you." And he waved toward the screen.

Dupont stepped out with his gun.

"It is to be murder, then," said the deeply musical voice of the prisoner, a voice that thrilled the very heart of Dupont.

"It is a fool's attempt at freedom for you ... and for him," snarled the colonel, whose cheeks were now flushed by the brandy he had drunk.

"Your hand, however," Dupont said, "must complete the work of much grace that you have begun, Señor *el coronel*. There are the keys. You will free Señor Milaro."

And then he heard the deep breath of Milaro drawn. But there was no word from the prisoner. And again the heart of Dupont swelled.

As for the colonel, he fell into a black passion. "I had rather lose my life here and now!" he cried. "Pull the trigger, and the devil take you. I shall not liberate this man with my own hands."

"Tush," Dupont declared coldly. "I still believe in your discretion. Now that there is so much noise and so much confusion in the hall, I swear that I believe that a revolver shot would not be heard. However, I have another thought. Let the keys remain where they are for the moment. Call the orderly again. Tell him to have the trumpet sounded and the drums beat in the plaza so that the soldiers will fall in at once. At once, señor."

And the colonel pressed the bell. Once more the door opened, once more the order was given, word for word.

"Now," said Dupont, "you may begin." And he waved toward the prisoner.

As for the colonel, he made a long pause. And that pause was a great tribute to his courage. But discretion proved again the better part of valor. He advanced at length, took up the keys, and set about the work of unlocking the fetters.

Dupont, standing behind the colonel, could look at the prisoner, also, for the first time. And he studied the bewilderment, carefully subdued, in the features of the outlaw. Bright hope was beginning, too, in his eyes, and his jaws were set.

"And you, señor ..." he said at last to Dupont.

"It is El Crisco!" snarled out the colonel.

At that, such a flood of light poured across the features of El Tigre that he became for the instant young again. "Ah, Señor Dupont," he said, "my daughter has told me ..." He stopped short. The last fetters were freed from his wrists and he stretched forth his long and powerful arms. That gesture and a single great indrawn breath—so it was that he welcomed the hope of liberty again.

At the next moment the bugle began to blare in the plaza and there came the sound of rapid scuffling of feet in the hallway. Through the windows they could see the surprised soldiery falling in, the ranks forming as if by magic, while the astonished people of Nabor thronged thickly about the men of war, as though wondering what new enemy this preparation could be against.

"There is one final courtesy," said Dupont, "that we can offer to the colonel. Señor Milaro ... there are the fetters."

El Tigre favored his young companion with a flashing glance like the look of an eagle, and, catching up the chains, he advanced upon poor Ramírez. As for the latter, his spirit was already broken, and, falling into a chair as he saw this last indignity about to be offered to him, he covered his face with his hands and submitted without a word or an effort. For his fame was torn from him, and great as he had been today, tomorrow he would be fully as crushed and small as the meanest man in his regiment.

He submitted to the chains. He submitted, also, to the gag that was presently forced between his teeth, and, lying back in his chair, he saw El Tigre take the two gold-mounted revolvers that the colonel's own regiment had presented as a token of faith and affection to their commanding officer.

"I take them as a memento, señor," said El Tigre. "I take them as a happy memento of the hours that I spent in the room in this building where I was exposed, señor, to the eyes of the good people of Nabor and the gentry from the estancias around about. They will also serve to remind me of the happy moment when men shall break down the door of this office and, coming in, find the famous Colonel Ramírez lying in his chair bound with the chains of ... El Tigre."

So saying, he smiled down upon his victim, and showed two rows of perfectly even, perfectly white teeth. It was a smile that made even Dupont start, and once again he could recall the tale that he had heard from the estanciero, Valdivia. That there was good in this man he could not have doubted, after having once looked upon that magnificent forehead or into those deep-sunk, big eyes. That there was an infinite capacity for evil, also, he could not doubt from this instant.

That reflection hardened his heart and enabled him to look forward to the other work that must lie before him if he were to complete all that he had set out to accomplish. It seemed morally easy, no matter how physically difficult it might prove. And with all scruples removed, his strength was doubled. Besides, he told himself, it was impossible to doubt the goodness of Valdivia as an essential thing, and, granting that goodness, it was impossible to doubt with equal strength the essential evil in Milaro, who the world called El Tigre.

The last of the stoic in the staunch colonel had been quite exhausted by the taunts of El Tigre, and now he writhed in his chair and struggled against his gag to yell for help until he choked and his face swelled with purple blood. Disregarding this useless violence, El Tigre and his deliverer stepped to the window and looked forth upon the square. The last of the soldiers were falling in, the drums were still beating, and the inhabitants of the town were gathered thickly around the place, admiring and cheering.

"There are two horses at the door to which that entrance leads," explained Dupont. "One of them belongs to the colonel. I am sure he would not object if you rode it."

The bandit laid his hand upon the shoulder of the younger man. "My son," he said, "to be free is a wonderful thing, but to be freed in this fashion is the best of all. To ride from Nabor on the horse of the colonel …" He made a gesture that indicated that his satisfaction was complete.

"Let us go now, then," urged Dupont.

"Not yet. They are still gathering. The plaza is now a theater. They flock to it. When the drum has beaten another minute, every man and child in Nabor will he gathered, and we will have no interruption on our way out."

There was no good argument against this statement, yet it was nervous work to remain there in the office of the colonel, knowing that before long he would be asked for. Or would they dare to ask for him, knowing that he was closeted with the great outlaw?

At length, when the plaza was black with people, El Tigre gave his assent. They waved farewell to poor Ramírez, and, passing through the rear door of the room, they came upon a flight of steps that went steeply down to the ground outside the building. There at the entrance they found the bay mare, María, and beside her a tall black gelding, a magnificent animal. And up and down the alley, which ran past the municipal building and passed into the plaza, there was not a human being in sight. All the population of Nabor, it seemed, was gathered in the public square, waiting to see what this military festival might mean.

So they mounted and rode up the narrow street. All was empty before them. There was no apparent need for a wild gallop that might attract attention as they rushed along. In the whole course of their ride through the town, they encountered only two children playing in a by-street, and one old woman walking with a bundle at her back, her steps propped up with a crooked stick. So they reached the shed where Twilight had been left. There was no one near it. The big horse whinnied gaily at the sight of his master, and, leaving the black gelding behind them, the two were soon cantering across the open Pampas.

Still there was neither sign nor sound of a pursuit from behind. That critical departure from Nabor that Dupont had looked forward to as the most difficult and daring part of his adventure had been accomplished with ridiculous ease.

One thing nettled him a little, and this was the small attention that Carlos Milaro paid to his savior as they journeyed together deeper and deeper into the bosom of safety. For neither by look nor by word did the famous outlaw pay the slightest heed to his companion. He seemed to be lost in the exploration of the broad plains that stretched before them. Or again, he talked to the beautiful mare that he was riding—talked like a child, commenting to her upon her paces, building a future for them both.

"So," he would say to her, when the noble creature strained at the bit and looked anxiously forward to the horizon as though, beyond it, she sensed a destination that they could not conceive with their mere human minds. "So, my dear. There is time. There is time for everything. You cannot race into the sky, my beauty. Run as fast as you will, you may round the world, but you will still be running upon dirt. Gently. Gently. They have trained you like a racer. But I shall feed you till you have a belly that means endurance. Ha, girl, we shall have our times together. We shall have our times together. There shall come a day when those good people of Nabor shall see that the whole price of their town is not worth the mischief I can do with such a witch under my saddle. Softly, my girl. We are coming to know one another ... but slowly, slowly. Men and horses are not books ... we cannot read one another or learn by heart."

So he would talk softly to the mare, until she began to cant back an ear toward him as if she were listening and striving with all her might to understand that gentle human voice. For perhaps the only language of men that she had been called upon to understand, before this, consisted of the pricking of spurs and the stinging of whips. She was all fire, ready to fly away and race until her heart broke. But under the care of El Tigre, she would learn other things.

When they camped, they made their meal off the provisions that Dupont carried in his pack, and afterward the bandit, wrapped in his blanket, sat with his back to the stump of a dead willow tree and looked beyond his companion and into his own thoughts. Black thoughts, perhaps, for they kept his forehead creased with dark care.

Perhaps he was meditating on the method of his revenge for the late indignities that he had undergone. And Dupont, watching his face covertly, decided that he had found, at last, a man who he felt worthy of fear. And, for all the wild things that he had seen and done in his days, for all the strong men with whom he had matched his own strength, he felt that in this somber and silent man he had encountered one stronger than himself. It was a disagreeable thought, a thought that translated itself into a weight felt at the bottom of the stomach.

He rolled himself in his blanket to sleep, but, before he closed his eyes, he heard the deep, quiet voice of the bandit say: "Señor Dupont, I have always thought of death as the most horrible thing in the world. But I was taught today in Nabor that there are worse things. When I think of you, Señor Dupont, it shall always be as of one who rescued me from something far worse than death."

In that speech he summed up his gratitude. After that instant, he never again referred to this day. One might have thought, from this moment forward, that he had never seen Nabor and brave Colonel Ramírez.

CHAPTER TWENTY-NINE

In the weeks that followed the disappearance of El Crisco, Juan Carreño found that history and his master's moods were revealed to him by flashes of lightning.

In the first place, he received strict orders to collect all reports extant concerning the doings of Charles Dupont. He set about busily performing this service. It was much to his liking. In his fat body there was hidden a fat, sleek soul that sometimes dreamed of itself performing great things. He never received in humility one of the whiplash corrections of his master without dreaming the matter over when he was alone and seeing himself as the master, Valdivia as the secretary. Those moments of dreaming were his consolation. When he was alone with his thoughts he was always brave as a lion and often as terrible as that beast of prey. If he shrank from danger in the day, the day also gave him a dream in which he was a hero. Such is the compensation of cowards.

Following the meteoric career of El Crisco, he found himself compiling a strange and wonderful narrative. It was drawn from many sources. There were the newspaper reports from Buenos Aires and from other large towns through the country. But best of all were the word-of-mouth reports. Men were constantly telling tales of

El Crisco to the employees of the great estancia, and the smooth-tongued gauchos never lost an opportunity to repeat these stories, with some added embellishments from their own inventive wits, for they could always get a silver coin from the secretary of the estanciero, and the wilder the story the larger the piece of money. Having learned this, the result was inevitable. But Carreño never thought of doubting the honesty of the narratives that he gleaned out of the newspapers or from the gauchos on the ranch. He wrote out every report in his own style—crisp, concise, naming every detail without emotion. But though his language was dull and dry, how greatly his heart often swelled as he penned these relations. For now, when he daydreamed, he was always in the boots of El Crisco, riding the matchless chestnut over the Pampas, wherever his wild will led him.

Besides the pleasure that he got out of this in itself, he had the constant knowledge that his master was even more interested than himself. When he read one of his reports to Valdivia, Don Sebastian was sure to favor him with the most absolute and childlike attention. He would nod over the high points of horrors.

"And think, Carreño" he would say. "It is I who brought this horror into my country and launched it like a pestilence upon my poor fellow citizens."

After which Carreño would assure him that it was the will of God in the execution of which he was only a humble agent and no more. But sometimes the remarks of the master were a trifle disconcerting, as for instance when he said at the end of the third week: "How many men have been killed, they say, by this wild marauder, this El Crisco?"

Carreño had that very day added up the total. "Seventy-one," he could answer glibly, very proud of his promptness,

"Seventy-one," Valdivia echoed quietly. "Well, well. That is a holocaust indeed. But, Carreño, one can hardly believe that for three weeks on end a man can average three slaughters a day? Do you not think so?"

"Ah, señor," Carreño answered, "this fellow is a strange and terrible man."

"To be sure he is, and nothing that he has done, to my thinking, is more terrible than, on the very same day, within five hours, to kill two men in Corrientes and three more eight hundred and fifty miles to the south and the west of that city."

Carreño considered this problem. It did not for an instant occur to him that it could not be solved.

"One cannot understand everything in this world," Carreño said at the last.

That was a maxim with which he shifted many a weary load of perplexity from his shoulders and left it for the wisdom of other sages to lift up. But he continued to collect the reports concerning the deeds of the outlaw. Within a single fortnight his first scrapbook that had been set aside methodically for that purpose was jammed full from cover to cover. After that, he established a little filing system. It was cross-indexed by the industrious Carreño. He could, in an instant, discover what El Crisco had done at any time either by date or by name of those plundered and destroyed or the locality in which he had worked.

"You will become the historian of El Crisco," Valdivia said to his secretary one day. "Perhaps you will be remembered for this work when everything else about you is forgotten."

After that, the fat man had something else to dream of. Only part of the time, he now saw himself as a wild and destroying brigand. The rest, he imagined large headlines in newspapers announcing the goings and comings of Juan Carreño, the celebrated author. He even read a grammar and two books on style, preparing himself for his future labors when all the evidence concerning El Crisco had been collated.

"You should draw up a map of the wanderings of the brigand," suggested the mischievous Valdivia on a day.

It was a tragic suggestion to Carreño. He labored until many a weary midnight trying to fit the facts to the map or the map to the facts. But how can a man be in three places in one day? And according to the reports, El Crisco had done this very thing and committed horrible crimes in each of the three places.

Carreño carried his problem to Valdivia.

"What can I say," said the estanciero very gravely, "except that, to use your own words, some people are capable of very strange performances. Is it not so?"

Carreño was so delighted to hear his master quote one of his observances that he forgot his despair. But after that he gave up the making of the map. It remained where he had begun it, full of criss-cross lines and big question marks.

When the greatest news of all arrived, he had the good fortune to be the first to carry it to the ears of the master. For Valdivia had risen late on this morning and Carreño had a chance to read the papers first. He could hardly wait until Valdivia issued from his room. He met the estanciero at the door of the breakfast room,

"Señor, señor!" he cried. "This exceeds all the rest. You remember that El Tigre was captured?"

"How could I forget, blockhead, when I received that news only yesterday? If you have come to tell me that the villain has escaped … wait until I have finished breakfast."

But Carreño, though he trembled for fear of the wrath of the master, was urged forward by the exquisite malice of the gossip. "It is the very word. He has been rescued!"

"A thousand devils," groaned Valdivia. "You rogue, you say it as if you were delighted."

"I, delighted?" gasped out Carreño, trembling with pleasure and impatience. "No, no. I am covered with grief for your sake, señor. But guess by whom this miraculous thing was done? Guess who, when El Tigre was a prisoner, surrounded by guards, entered the room of the Colonel Ramírez, the hero, held a gun at his head, forced him to order El Tigre into his presence, forced him to order horses prepared at the side door of the municipal building, forced him to have the troops assembled in the square, forced him with his own hands to free El Tigre, and then with the irons of El Tigre bound Ramírez ... guess who has done this?"

"Guess who has done this?" exclaimed the estanciero, staring. "Why, only the devil could have done it."

"You are right as ever, señor. It was a devil in human form ... the worst and most brilliant of devils ... it was El Crisco himself who rescued El Tigre and rode away with him over the Pampas."

This information turned Valdivia to stone. Then he struck himself heavily across the forehead and uttered words that were quite incomprehensible to the secretary.

"They have joined hands," groaned Valdivia. "They have joined hands. And now, I shall be ruined. Oh, what a fool I have been to trust in a ... Carreño, get out of my sight. And if you ever again mention the name of El Crisco, I discharge you that instant from my service."

It was a thunderbolt for Carreño. Here was his dearest delight reft from him at a stroke, and his career as a chronicler cut short. However, even if the master refused to listen to his tales as he gathered them, he determined to continue his work in private. Fame would eventually reward him. And what was even the praise of Valdivia compared with the applause of the millions of his countrymen who would read his great book with fascinated attention?

But, very naturally, he never again mentioned El Crisco willingly. He could not understand how the master should show such keen interest in all the exploits of the new outlaw except his very most daring and brilliant one. He could not understand why Valdivia refused to read or hear the details of an exploit that, as the gauchos said freely on the ranch, proved El Crisco to be as great a man as ever El Tigre had been in that bandit's most flowering prime. But he continued to work on his book, and as for the eccentricities of Valdivia, he laid them down to the curse of money. How could one expect the rich to be like the poor—logical? They could afford to be different.

The days immediately following were rich in the annals of El Crisco, as Carreño wrote them down. As fast as his pen could work he had to reproduce from the newspapers half a dozen reports every day. There was the result of the exploit of Nabor. The worthy Colonel Ramírez, for instance, had been at first heartily laughed at. But there was a sudden change of feeling. Who, it was said, could be expected to handle at the same time such fiends as El Crisco and El Tigre? It was more than could be hoped from any human. It was only a miracle that Ramírez had escaped with his life. He had been given a vote of thanks by Nabor. And the town had subscribed from its own pockets enough money to replace a certain pair of costly revolvers that had been stolen by the wicked and lucky Carlos Milaro in his escape.

Who could have expected fortune to swing back to the colonel after his fall? More than this, the military department had commissioned the brave Ramírez to continue the hunt and take charge of the chase after the two desperadoes who were now considered to be a national danger.

Yet all of these precious tidbits the good secretary was unable to convey to the ears of the estanciero. There were other things as well. For instance, the cunning Ramírez had, first of all, in working for his revenge and to reinstate himself in the confidence of his countrymen, succeeded in locating Francesca Milaro. He had put a secret watch upon her, confident that her father would attempt to return to her as soon as he was free again. Nor had he been wrong. El Tigre came, and El Crisco with him. There, at one grasp, both the villains had nestled within the closing fingers of the hard hand of the law. But that strong hand had closed upon a bunch of nettles. Stung and outraged, the fingers had opened again, and the two daring outlaws had cut their way through to safety—and more than that, they had carried away with them Francesca the beautiful.

But even this marvelous tale could not be carried to the estanciero. He refused to read even the papers. He closed his ears to the facts. And yet something weighed so upon his spirits that he daily grew pale and paler. His brow was contracted until there was a continual furrow between his eyes. He developed a furtive look. One would have thought that calamity hung over his head.

Pondering upon these matters, one night, the good Carreño walked in the garden breathing deeply of the fragrance of the hidden flowers, and listening to the distant singing of the laborers from the *puestos*, their harsh voices softened in the night wind. And in the midst of his half sad, half pleasant thoughts, he heard a light step behind him, light as the footfall of a woman. He turned with a smirk, and found himself confronted by Charles Dupont— El Crisco himself.

Terror supplied the place of a gag. Poor Carreño could neither speak nor stir.

CHAPTER THIRTY

It is one thing to dream. It is another to see one's dream turn into a fact by day or even by starlight. It seemed to the trembling secretary that blood dripped from the fingers of the bandit. Those hands presented neither knife nor gun at his breast, and that absence of threat only emphasized the cruel complacency, the omniscience of the miscreant.

"Juan," the American said with his usual gentleness, "you are so happy to see me that you have lost your voice. Well, well, there is nothing to fear. I shall not harm you. Do you hear? I shall not harm you, Carreño."

Carreño could only gasp.

"Wake up, man," the bandit said, a little irritated. "I am not entirely a wild beast ... in spite of reports. Tell me where your master is?"

For once Carreño became almost a man. "Señor *El ... Dupont*," he said sadly, "God forbid that I should betray my good master."

"Betray ... in the name of heaven, Carreño, do you think that I have come here to murder him? Nonsense, you talk like a fool. Don't you understand that all of this was undertaken by his express ... However, let it go. If there is a way to come at him without exposing ourselves to anyone's view, take me to him instantly."

"I? Never!"

El Crisco uttered a faint exclamation of anger and admiration commingled. "Brave Carreño," he said, "would you have so much courage for yourself? I think not. However, this is what I shall do. Lead me secretly to his door. Then you may enter by yourself. If, after you have told him that I have come, he is not willing to see me freely, and alone, I shall turn and leave the place. In fact I wish for nothing, but what do you say to that, Carreño?"

The secretary pondered it feebly. He saw danger. And yet he thought that there might be something almost generous in this proposal. Before he could finish his thinking, the heavy hand of the outlaw dropped upon his shoulder.

"Come! Start at once. I have small time to waste, *amigo*."

So Carreño led the way into the house by a side door and up a narrow and dark corridor to the library where he knew his master was at that moment. There he tapped timidly, and the voice of Valdivia answered him and bade him enter.

He turned to El Crisco. "Your promise, señor?"

"I keep it to the letter. Go in and tell him that I wait to see him."

Carreño could not help but obey, having advanced so far. He opened the door by slow jerks and at length stood in the presence of his master. The door he closed behind him.

Valdivia considered him with a faint smile, above the edge of a book. He seemed to be still following the print with half his mind while he prepared to talk with his secretary. "You look, Carreño," he said, "as though you had come to ask for an increase in pay. Is it that?"

"Señor ..."

"Well, I see that I have hit the nail on the head at the first attempt. You don't have to blunder and delay about it, Carreño. Always speak out your mind freely with me. Because ... it is a mind that I delight to follow."

"Señor, you are a thousand times kind to me."

"You have the increase. Leave the sum of it to me ... it will greater than you would dare to ask for yourself."

"God bless you, señor."

"You talk like a widow's son. No, you talk like the widow herself. Now get off with you and don't trouble me with thanks."

"Only one thing, Señor Valdivia."

"The devil. I hate habits, Carreño, and particularly the habit of begging. What else is wrong with you?"

"El Crisco ..."

The Argentinean hurled the book across the room. "You rascal!" he thundered. "I swore that if you dared to mention that name to me, I would discharge you that instant, and, by the heavens, you will find ..."

Carreño clasped imploring hands.

"Well," Valdivia said in tones far other than a gentleman should use, "what have you to say for yourself? I grant you ten seconds to explain what you mean."

"He himself ..." In his terror Carreño choked. But it was enough to make Valdivia start to his feet.

"What is it, Carreño?" he asked in a lowered voice, changing color a little.

"He himself ... El Crisco ... he has come."

Valdivia changed color. "Are you mad, Carreño? Where is he, then?"

"There," whispered the panic-stricken secretary. "There ... outside the door."

There was a drawer of the big library table standing open near to the estanciero, and without a word he caught out from it a revolver. "Are you armed, Carreño?" he asked, whispering as the secretary had done. "And will you help me face him?"

"Until I die, señor."

"And yet ... how did he come to let you pass if he is there?"

"He told me to tell you that he has come, and he swears that, if you do not wish to speak with him, he will go just as he has come and do no harm."

The estanciero started. Once or twice he started forward and then drew back again, and the color flooded into his face and ebbed swiftly out of it, until at length he came to a determination, and, throwing the revolver into the drawer, he dropped into his chair. "Tell Dupont that I'll see him," he directed.

"But not alone ..."

"Alone, Carreño. Leave me."

"I shall gather men below ..."

"Fool," sneered Valdivia. "If the wretch has come to murder, what do I care for vengeance after I am dead? Leave the room and tell him to enter. If this is mere effrontery and devilishness, this fellow is a great man."

So Carreño left the room, and, as he stepped out, Dupont came in and closed the door behind him. He removed from his head the wide sombrero that he had worn until that moment.

"Señor Valdivia," he said, "I have brought you good news. Milaro and his daughter are within your power."

In great crises, the mind flies off at wild tangents. When death stares men in the face, some think of all the swift procession of their lives, or of nothing, but rarely of death itself. And when this great tiding came to Valdivia, he could see nothing but that first picture of the tall young cowpuncher as he had stood in the corral at the side of Twilight.

Then he rallied and rose from his seat. "Dupont," he said, breathing hard, "I have always thought you an honest fellow. Let me be equally honest with you. The whole world knows that you have allied yourself with El Tigre ... rescued him from prison and certain death ... helped him to regain his daughter, and now you come to say that you have placed them both in my power? Can you expect me to believe that this is not a trap?"

It was so frankly spoken that Dupont, though he reddened with anger, was instantly calm again. "Valdivia," he answered with equal directness, "do you think that I could play the hypocrite and the traitor to two men?"

The estanciero hesitated, as a general hesitates before he gives the order to charge. Then he pointed to a chair, and, when his visitor was seated, he said: "If this is true, it is the great day of my life. You know, Dupont, that my wishes are ... but let that go. I have trusted you, *amigo*, as I have never trusted another man."

Again the dark blood swept into the face of Dupont. "For you, Valdivia," he said coldly, "I have lured a brave man into a trap. He is brave, I know. He is generous, I know. He is kind in everything that I have seen of him. But ... if he is a good man, you are a scoundrel."

"Ah?" murmured Don Sebastian with an indrawn breath.

"And that," said Dupont, "I know you are not."

The estanciero relaxed again in his chair.

"When I gave you my word that I would do my best to bring Francesca to you, señor, I made that promise because I was convinced from what you had told me that her father is a beast ... a wild beast, Valdivia. So I have drawn him into the trap. If he is taken and if I should find out afterward that you have lied to me ... then, Valdivia, I swear to you that I would never rest, day or night, until I had put a bullet through your head. Because from what I have seen with my own eyes, this Milaro is a king among men. But I have your word against him. And I have trusted your word."

There was a slender-throated decanter on the table beside Valdivia, and now he tipped a swallow of golden brandy into a glass and drank it off, quite forgetful of offering the same to his guest. But he needed that stimulus before he spoke again and was able to smile at the American.

"Why, Dupont." he said, "when I first saw you, I knew you were worth your weight in gold as a fighting man ... and if I needed proof before tonight, at least now I am sure that you are worth your weight in diamonds as an honest man. If I am unworthy of your trust ... God forgive me."

He raised his hand as he spoke, but though he strove at the same time to look upward, he found that he could not lift his eyes from the grim face of the cowpuncher. For a long moment he felt the boring scrutiny of Dupont, then the big man drew his handkerchief across his wet forehead.

"I believe you," Dupont said faintly. "And yet ... when I came here, I half hoped that I would not be able to believe. Tell me, Valdivia," he added suddenly in an outbreak of the anguish in his mind, "is treachery ever pardonable? No matter what the end may be, is treachery ever excused ... do you think?"

"It is a matter of the case," Valdivia said, biting his thin lip. "If you needed treachery to get the girl to me, and if you felt that I could make her happy, and if you felt that she was worth the betrayal of her father ..."

"Worth it? She is worth all the rest of the world," Dupont said in a trembling voice.

The answer of the estanciero was sharp as a cutting knife. "You have a keen appreciation of her virtues, Dupont."

"I love her," the American answered simply.

The eyes of Valdivia grew dull and dazed. "You love her ... and bring her to me?" he muttered.

"I am not a fool," said the cowpuncher sadly. "She is a jewel. What sort of a setting could I give her? And besides," he continued, arguing aloud with himself, "though she might begin by hating you, she could not help but love you in the end. My trust is in your own fine nature, Don Sebastian."

The Argentinean coughed. "You shame me with your modesty, *amigo*," he said gently. "But remember that what you have done is not wasted time. If I am rich, it is not ..." He saw the big hand of Dupont raised sternly.

"This," said the cowpuncher, "is not to be paid for ... except in her happiness," he added, sighing, "except in her happiness, I pray to God."

"It shall be the work of my life to make that happiness, my generous friend."

"You will succeed. I have gone over the thing every night until I was half mad ... it is not your wealth alone, but above all your fine soul, and your honor, Valdivia."

Don Sebastian hastily waved that praise aside. Besides, it was rather a heartfelt judgment than mere words of praise. "As for Milaro ..."

"As for Milaro," the American broke in hotly, "if it were not that liberty for him means death for you, Valdivia, why I ... I would risk my own life a hundred times over rather than give him up." He groaned aloud and bowed his head. "Rather than betray him, Don Sebastian. What a thing it is to live with a man, eat with him, hear him open his mind, feel his trust like a hand on one's shoulder ... and then betray him at the end. And yet, if he is not secured, you will never live to make Francesca happy. And she? She should have the life of a queen, and who can give it to her but you?" He made a gesture of despairing surrender. "If I am wrong," he said, "God strike me. I have done my best to be honest. But this thing more. You are rich, Valdivia."

"Whatever you ask ..."

"Hush. It is not for me, but for Milaro. You are rich, as I said before. Valdivia, justice can be turned aside with money. There are great brains in the law that may be hired. There are newspapers that may be influenced. Could you secure ... say a long term of imprisonment ... for Milaro?"

"I could," said the estanciero. "And I would, my friend. Put your faith in that." And hastily he poured himself another dram and tossed it off, then shrugged his shoulders and was able to face his companion once more and to proceed with the conference. Now," he said more briskly, "let me hear the plan?"

"It is simple ... and devilish," Dupont said heavily. "When I ride off tonight, follow behind me with half a dozen of your best men. Do you understand? I shall lead you to a small shack not five miles from the estancia. On your own ground. Keep your men back until you hear a pistol shot. It will mean that I have secured El Tigre and it is safe for you to ride in. Or else it will mean that I have failed to secure him and that he has put a bullet through me. God knows which would be for the better."

CHAPTER THIRTY-ONE

A half dozen would not suit with the mind of the estanciero. From the *puestos* there were called forth a full dozen and a half of well-tried and trusted gauchos, and they were mounted and carefully equipped with revolvers and with rifles. For who could tell what the night would bring forth? And, when this was done, with the trembling Carreño beside him, Don Sebastian himself set forth at the head of the troop and followed the dim figure of El Crisco, who rode before them through the chill starlight.

They saw a hut, its squat outlines half lost against a gentle swell of rising ground. To that hut rode El Crisco. They saw a door or barrier in place of a door, opened enough to let forth one red ray of firelight. Then El Crisco disappeared into the interior and the long wait began, with the ears of Don Sebastian straining to catch the expected report of a revolver—straining foolishly, for he knew that, if a shot were fired at that distance, he could hear it as clearly as the booming of a cannon.

As for Dupont, he entered the hut and found El Tigre sitting like an Indian, cross-legged, before the small fire, while in the corner at some distance lay Francesca, wrapped in a blanket. At this sight, the cowpuncher began to step on tiptoe, but El Tigre smiled at him and shook his head, as much as to say: "It is no use. She will waken."

Indeed, at that instant she sat bolt erect among the blankets and laughed at Dupont in the very midst of a clumsily cautious step.

"I have lost the knack of a light step," said El Crisco, finding himself unable to smile.

"You will find, Charles," said the outlaw, "that a woman can always hear the step of some one man ..."

"Father!" cried Francesca.

"Ah," said the father, "I have struck out a spark and started a fire."

"What did you say?" Dupont asked, frowning.

"Nothing for the ears of a deaf man," said Milaro. "Ah, Charles, someday ..."

"Father!" cried the girl again, and shook off the blanket and half rose.

"Well," muttered the older man, chuckling softly, "I have said more than enough for some. But for the deaf and the blind ..." He broke off, still chuckling.

Dupont, looking at the girl, saw that she was a rosy red, frowning and smiling at once, and looking at her father rather than at him.

"What is it all about?" he asked.

At this, she flashed a glance at him and began to smile suddenly. "Nothing," she said. "Nothing, of course. It is just one of father's old-fashioned jokes."

"As old," El Tigre said, "as the story of man and woman."

Dupont stared at him, bewildered. To his heavy conscience there seemed to be a grave meaning hidden behind this playfulness. What could they have guessed? But if they had guessed at the truth, though the grim Milaro might smile, surely the girl would not be able to. At length, he shook his head and gave up the problem. He sat down by the fire and stretched out his hands toward it.

"You are cold, Charles," said the older man. And he tossed some fresh wood upon the fire, while Dupont writhed inwardly. From the very first, upon the smallest occasions, these touches of gentleness in the celebrated man-killer had moved him to the heart, but tonight it was a touch of the most exquisite misery.

"I am well enough," he said tersely.

Francesca, rising from her bed, swept a blanket about her graceful body. She stood above them, the firelight playing softly over her face. "It is hard to warm a cold heart, Father," she said. "You are wasting the wood on Charles."

The cowpuncher glanced up to her and he saw what portrait painters have seen before, that a woman is always loveliest when her face is viewed from beneath. Oh, cunning flatterers who paint the lady descending the staircase, her slender hand upon the balustrade, her head proudly lifted. So stood Francesca, one hand held above the fluttering warmth of the fire. He hastily abased his eyes. But looking down, he could not shut her beauty away from his heart of hearts.

"Why, my girl," the outlaw was saying, still chuckling as he spoke, "these Americans take fire slowly. But when they begin to burn, the fire never dies."

"Hush," Francesca said, and stamped.

But when the cowpuncher glanced up at her again, surprised at this small passion, he saw that she was smiling through her anger. Her glance touched his with a pleasant shock, and he wondered as he saw her hastily avert her eyes.

Here the outlaw jerked up his head. "Was that the neigh of a horse?" he asked sharply.

"Yes. It is a horse pasture that we are in," answered Dupont calmly enough, though his heart was thundering.

The first alarm still kept a frown upon the face of the older man for a moment, but presently he nodded. He had formed the habit of accepting the judgments of his younger ally without question since that miracle in Nabor.

"You are very gloomy, Charles," he said at last in that gentle tone with which he usually addressed his rescuer.

"I?" protested Dupont. "Not at all."

"Yes," said Francesca. "He has come to Argentina. But he has left his heart behind him. In the hands of one of those cold-faced American girls. I know."

"What do you know, Francesca?" asked the father.

"That she is not worthy of Charles." She leaned a little. "Tell me," she commanded. "Is it true?"

"You mean," murmured Dupont, taking his mind from his sad thoughts and letting it brood with a mournful pleasure over the beauty of the girl, "you mean that I have left behind me ... a woman I love?"

"Yes, yes."

He shook his head. "No. I have not." He raised his head and looked fairly at her, playing with a double truth. "I have never met a girl, indeed, that I cared for a tithe as much, Francesca, as I care for you."

"Aha!" chuckled El Tigre. "He is catching."

But the girl only sighed. "I believe it. Ah, Señor Dupont, how strange that so brave a man should have so cold a heart." And she turned abruptly and covered herself in her rudely improvised bunk.

Dupont stared after her in alarm. "How have I angered her?" he whispered to El Tigre.

The outlaw answered: "Any woman would know. But I shall not tell you. And now," he added, "tell me what luck you have had in your exploring tonight. I suppose it was to skirt around the house of Valdivia that you rode out?"

"It was for that, of course."

"Come, my son. Is it not time to tell me what plan has been in your mind, to draw you here into the mouth of danger?"

"The time has not yet come."

"And yet, Charles, you are sure that the spoils will be worth this trip?"

"I think so."

"Can you tell me nothing?"

"Only this. That I shall be able to use this before I am through." He drew from his pack a pair of shining handcuffs.

The eyes of El Tigre enlarged. "I think I understand," he said. "You, too, have come to have Valdivia. You intend to take him a prisoner, *amigo?*"

Dupont shrugged his shoulders. "I am afraid that I have been a fool and got handcuffs that are too large for his skinny wrists and hands. These, señor, would fit you."

"No, I think not." He looked down to his brawny wrists and shook his head.

"Let me try them, however," insisted Dupont.

The eyes of El Tigre lifted from the manacles and fastened upon his companion with a penetrating brilliance.

"What is wrong, Señor Milaro?" asked Dupont.

"Nothing ... I had a thought ... but of course I was wrong. Try them on my hands if you will." And he extended those powerful hands almost eagerly toward his companion, as though anxious to show that his distrust had been the thing of an instant only, an instinctive recoiling.

"It is a small thing," Dupont said. "However ..." And reaching forward, with two sharp metallic clicks, the handcuffs settled into place, fitted snugly over the skin, and pressed into it. At the same instant, he reached to the holster of the outlaw and snatched the revolver from the holster, then he fired his own gun into the ceiling.

The glance of Milaro flashed upon either side, as though he sought desperately for a means of escape or an offensive weapon. Then, seeing nothing and hearing in the distance the rapid roaring of approaching hoof beats, he settled back in his place, regarding his captor with a sort of sad curiosity.

Francesca was on her feet, crying out in alarm: "What has happened?" Then, seeing the thin steel bands that bound the hands of her father, she said: "Is it a jest, Father?"

The older man looked up to her with a strange smile. "Listen."

A breath of silence passed over the hut; the noise of the approaching horsemen was distinct.

"Our dear friend, the brave Charles, has saved me and has saved you so that he might offer us up as a ransom to the law."

The girl leaned against the wall, white with grief and horror. Why did she not catch up a weapon, like the little wildcat that she was? wondered Dupont. But she made no stir to resist. This blow that had fallen upon her seemed greater than she could even attempt to ward off.

"We are the price he pays," the outlaw said bitterly, "to make his peace with society. Ah, to think that in twenty years I have trusted only one man … and he should prove a traitor to me."

Dupont, sick at heart, but knowing not that he had irrevocably committed himself, stood before them with the two guns hanging loosely in his hands.

"Señor Milaro," he said feebly, "God be my judge. I have tried to do what is best for Francesca."

The girl started, and stared at Dupont with what seemed to him an inexplicable commingling of dread and hope.

"For Francesca?" the father said. "Listen, child, we shall find that there is still honor in this man. It is to save her from this wild life that you have done this thing, Dupont?"

"It is, señor. And to give her into the keeping of a good man."

"Meaning yourself?" El Tigre inquired sneeringly.

"Meaning the same man who has sworn to me that he will spend money, like water, to get you a sentence of imprisonment, but not death."

"He must have more than money in his power to do that. He must be able to work a miracle. Continue, Charles. Who is this man?"

"One who will devote his life and his power to the happiness of Francesca. Alas, Señor Milaro, a man so full of generosity and goodness of heart, that I gave him my word to serve him, even to the betrayal of you, Milaro."

"I begin to have a thought," groaned Milaro. "Francesca, it is the dog, Valdivia!"

"No, no!" screamed the girl. "I will die ..."

Out of her hand the knife was torn by Dupont, who stood panting and stammering above her, holding her close and helpless with his arm. "Do you hear?" he pleaded. "In the world there is no finer man and no truer gentleman. He is ..."

But Francesca, clinging to him suddenly, wept upon his breast like a child.

Closer swept the noise of the horses, the shouting of the wild riders.

"Listen to me, Charles," El Tigre said in that same dull and hopeless voice with which he had been speaking before, "you have been tricked by a cur."

"Señor Milaro, I would not have spoken of it ... but confess that when you robbed him of the woman he loved ..."

"Robbed him? I?"

"Did you not? And try to murder his men?"

The voice of El Tigre rose to a hollow thunder. "In the name of God, Charles, what are you saying?"

"Did you not? Confess, Milaro. One of them is still living. LeBon is still living."

"He is one of the two rats who laid an ambush for me. Did I steal Dolores? Ah, Charles, he would have bought away from me the woman who loved me, and when she fled with me, he hounded us both with his men. It was his pursuit that drove us out and away just before Francesca was born. It was exposure to the night that killed my sweet Dolores. All of that was the work of Valdivia. Charles! Charles! I have told you that he was a cur. You will feel his teeth yet."

As he spoke, the barrier at the doorway was torn down. Into the hut crowded half a dozen men, coming with staring eyes of terror, with rifles and revolvers extended stiffly in their hands, so great was their fear of the two men who they saw.

"Señor Val-Valdivia," stammered one of the leaders. "Here is a great miracle. Here are both El Tigre and El Crisco. Not one … but both."

And the answer of Valdivia rang high with exultation in the rear of the party: "Seize them both and make them safe. This is a great day for the law of the land. My lads, the reward … every penny of it is to be divided among you."

CHAPTER THIRTY-TWO

It was done in a trice. That last command had stunned Dupont and left him momentarily helpless. Before he could recover, the girl was plucked rudely away from him and he was bound hand and foot. He did not recover from his daze until Valdivia himself made his way into the hut, his face white, his eyes burning with an ecstasy of pleasure. That roving glance flashed across the hut and settled instantly on the girl. He could not speak. He could only point, and, in answer, a gaucho leaped at her as though she had been a wild young tigress. He caught her by the arms. At the same moment the loaded butt of Valdivia's riding crop crashed on the fellow's head and dropped him on the ground.

"Gently," Valdivia ordered. "It is the lady of the estancia who you see before you. Gently, my lads."

"Señor Valdivia," Dupont said, the blackness of helpless rage beginning to sweep across his eyes, "is this a jest? Am I to be bound like a criminal?"

"*Faugh!*" snarled out Valdivia. "The murdering gringo wishes for different treatment. He shall have it." And he struck him a cutting blow across his face with the lash of the quirt. It required the strength of four men to hold back Dupont as he lurched at the Argentinean.

"You see, Charles," said El Tigre, who had submitted to fate without a murmur, "you see it is as I have said. He is a cur, and now you feel his teeth. Is it not so?"

"Be silent," Valdivia snapped. "Carlos," he added, with a voice whose incredible malignity made the blood of the younger man turn cold, "I have waited … and waited … but now God gives you into my hand. It is enough. Yes, it is almost enough to have made the waiting worthwhile. My men, take them out. Señorita Francesca, will you come with me?"

He reached to take her arm, and, with a glance of unutterable loathing, she submitted. They passed out from the hut into the night leaving behind them one loiterer with a stunned face and dull eyes—Juan Carreño.

The sound of horses began and grew faint in the distance. Still, with the dying firelight upon his face, Carreño pondered and struggled to understand, and could not. That destroying wraith, that soul keen and terrible as a sword, that same El Crisco who had been the hero of all his daydreams of late, had been taken, unresisting, before his eyes. It was not possible, and yet he had seen it. The foundations of the universe, for poor Carreño, were shaken to their base. The world was now chaos indeed.

He was like some reader of Homer who, having come to love the noble Hector, reads with disdain and with disbelief, how that hero shrunk from the spear of fierce Diomedes. It could not have been.

So it was with Carreño. How could that bold, wild spirit of El Crisco that had made a trail of destruction across Argentina be reduced without so much as a single blow?

Then a cold and dismal explanation crept into the slow mind of the secretary. It was treason. It was the basest treachery that had disarmed the great warrior. And whose treason? That of Señor Don Sebastian Valdivia himself. It was not possible for Carreño to digest this thought in a moment.

He rode wildly back toward the estancia, but, as his horse galloped and the wind of its running struck into the face of the poor secretary, he saw the truth more and more clearly. The thing from which he fled stood up in his mind's eye, clearly.

He had listened at the door of the library. He had heard enough snatches of the talk of his master with El Crisco to understand what was planned. All for Valdivia, El Crisco had planned this coup. And now, by Valdivia, he was undone, and taken a prisoner to be swung at the end of a rope at the due pleasure of the cruel law.

The words of another great man dinted upon the brain of Carreño, El Tigre saying: *I told you he was a cur, and now you feel his teeth.*

He recalled still more—the conversation of Valdivia in that New Orleans hotel—how long ago it seemed. But that had been merely many words strung together, and words did not have much meaning to Carreño. Here were actions that even a child could comprehend.

He reached the estancia, where he was called at once into the room of Don Sebastian. There he found the estanciero walking back and forth, singing to himself in an ecstasy of happiness.

"It is ended, Carreño," said the rich man. "The work of twenty years is ended. The triumph of El Tigre has failed at last. Now I have the second self of Dolores in my hands, and El Tigre himself is a dead man."

"Dead!" gasped out Carreño.

"To all intents and purposes. Sit down, Carreño, and write this letter."

It was not a long letter. It had the modest brevity of a conqueror, informing the authorities that, by the grace of fortune and owing to certain stratagems and finesses, Don Sebastian had been able to put his hands, at one stroke, upon both of those terrible miscreants—El Crisco and El Tigre. They were now resting at his home. They would be safely guarded there until a strong escort arrived to remove them to prison.

"Señor," breathed Carreño. "You are not sending even Charles Dupont to prison?"

"Not? Of course I am, Carreño."

"But this service ..."

"Why, my lad, for the services of Dupont I am very grateful ... to my own adroitness that knew how to use the gringo. But now he ceases to be a tool. His existence begins to be a danger to me. Therefore, I make all haste to remove that danger from my path. Very good. By the day after tomorrow, at the latest, the escort will arrive. And ... you, Carreño, will receive a part of the reward. And the reward upon the heads of both these men will be a fortune for every one of you, even when it has been divided into eighteen parts. Remember that."

Carreño went stumbling from the room to make a clean copy of that letter, but, as he worked, he found that his pen was stammering and halting. Three times he blotted the page shamefully and finally he sat back and rested his poor head between his hands. He was going mad, he felt. He looked over the three attempts he had made. The words had come out upon the paper in spite of himself.

"Gentlemen," ran the first version, "it is my happiness to inform you that by treason ..."

He had, of course, started a new letter at that point.

Gentlemen,

El Crisco and Carlos Milaro, the celebrated outlaws and murderers and thieves, have today been fortunately captured on my premises through treason ...

Why could he not write it just as the voice of the estanciero had dictated it to him?

But the third attempt ran:

Gentlemen,

It is my pleasure to inform you of an event of some importance to the republic. Charles Dupont, known as El Crisco, and Carlos Milaro, the two famous outlaws, have been captured on my premises. It was accomplished by the assistance of a dozen of my men acting under my supervision. They were betrayed by foul treason …

"I am going mad," Carreño gasped out, and started up from his chair. "The pen is bewitched. It writes of its own volition and out of its own mind. What has come upon me?"

He went to the window and leaned into the cool of the night, but still there was a fever in his thoughts. The bewildered face of handsome Charles Dupont rose before him, as that hero had stood in the hut, surrounded by his captors. And, following an irresistible impulse, he went to confront that captain of the Pampas face to face.

The cellar of the estancia had been converted into a prison. There were certain deep storerooms built of strong blocks of stone, damp, cold, and unhealthy. In two of these the two prisoners had been confined. The masonry was strong enough to hold them, and, if they dug through the masonry, they would have solid masses of earth beyond. And if they strove to break through the narrow gratings that brought air into that subterranean chamber, or if they strove to come out through the doorway, they were hemmed in by armed guards, standing watch not more than two hours together, and then changed for another set of watchers, so that the sentinels might be always fresh. To make surety doubly sure, they were kept in strong ropes.

In the long, low corridor that ran past the rooms that now served as prison cells, Carreño found none other than Pedro LeBon in command. Night and day until these important captives were taken from his charge, LeBon was to stay by them. He was stretched now upon a cot that had been placed in the corridor for his repose, since he could not be expected to keep his eyes open both day and night, but at the first alarm he was to be wakened. A man was stationed constantly at his side for that purpose, and to transmit any orders that he might give.

There was no opposition to Carreño when he entered the corridor. The hardy gauchos twitched up their thick eyebrows, surprised at seeing the delicate secretary among such dank and moldy surroundings. But he was so known to carry the will of the estanciero that they would as soon have questioned Valdivia himself as to have stopped his secretary.

He went straight to LeBon and touched his shoulder. The manager of the great estanciero opened one eye, then coughed and sat up straight, frowning at the secretary.

"Well, Carreño?" he asked.

"I am to be admitted to El Crisco."

"You? Alone?"

Carreño frowned in turn. He knew how to take upon himself dignity, not for himself but for the sake of his master.

"At once!" he said sharply. "And let me have a lantern, LeBon."

The manager hesitated no longer. However strange this might be, it was folly to question the authority of the secretary in any matter whatsoever. Who in the household did not know that Valdivia chose to unburden his mind to this stupid, fat fellow and to him alone? With his own hand he unlocked the door, gave the lantern, and closed the door again behind the secretary.

CHAPTER THIRTY-THREE

If Carreño had not been trembling before, the chill and the dank smell of that chamber would have set him shuddering. He raised the lantern. Its dimly circling light, with a core of shadow in the center, fell upon the form of the big cowpuncher, lying bound, hand and foot, in a corner of the room, just as he had been thrown down by those who carried him to this place. His head was jammed against the wall, so that his face was turned up to the secretary, and his big, unwinking eyes stared back at the trembling Carreño.

The effect upon poor Carreño was almost as if he were encountering a bodiless spirit. He shook so that the lantern light fell in quivering waves across the face of the fallen man.

"Ah, Carreño," the cowpuncher said with perfect good nature, "they have made you a guard to inspect me? You see that I am kept safely, and without a pillow."

He lay, in fact, in a thin pool of seepage water that covered that corner of the floor. The water had soaked up through his clothes. If he could survive such conditions for twenty-four hours, it would be proof of an iron constitution indeed.

"I have not come to mock at you, señor," Carreño said, when he could speak.

"I believe you," said the prisoner calmly. "You are a good fellow serving a bad ... well, let that go."

"You would have said ... serving a bad master, señor?"

"I won't try to convince you of that. In fact, Juan, I admire fidelity."

The secretary lowered the lantern. "Señor El Crisco, God has sent me a plague of doubt."

"Ah? Doubt of what?"

"God forgive me for it. Doubt of my master."

Dupont said not a word. He could not, in fact, believe his ears.

"And I have come to you to talk to you about certain things. I do not think that you would lie to me, señor."

"Why, Carreño, would you trust the word of El Crisco?" asked the cowpuncher, somewhat moved by this sudden turn of the conversation.

"I know," Carreño said, trembling again as he spoke so that the lantern ring jingled lightly in the lantern top, "that you are a strong and terrible man, señor, and yet I have seen you make a horse love you like a dog, and I have seen you risk your life for the very same man who ..."

He paused, unable to fill in his sentence, and Dupont said: "For the same man who now throws me to the dogs, Carreño."

"It is a strange thing," Carreño said sadly. "I have struggled to understand it."

"And I, too, Juan."

"What can be his purpose?"

"To give me up to the law. There is no reasonable doubt of that."

"But why should he fear you?"

"Because, Juan, I believe that he has lied to me about El Tigre. Between you and me, I believe that the great lie was spoken there. If the truth were out, it might be seen that El Tigre was really in the right. And if I were free, and found out that Valdivia had lied to me and used me as a tool to capture a man who really needed more sympathy than persecution … why, Carreño, your master knew that I would do my humble best to run him down and kill him like the rat that I begin to suspect that he may be."

To this terrible talk, Carreño listened with starting eyes and recoiled a little from the speaker. "That cannot be," he breathed.

"Why else has he treated me … like this, Carreño?"

The secretary sighed. Then he shook his head.

"You see," said the cowpuncher, "that before morning there will not be much left of me for the law to hang. The ropes are so tight that they have stopped the circulation in my arms and legs. You may look for yourself."

The secretary, fascinated with horror, stepped closer and then groaned with sympathy, for he saw that the hands of the big man were swollen with purple blood. "It is terrible," he whispered. "May God help me to understand."

"Isn't it simple? At one stroke, he gets rid of El Tigre and of me, and the girl is left in his hands." The calm of El Crisco left him, and he ground his teeth. "The cowardly devil will force her to marry him …"

"Señor," breathed Carreño.

"Ask yourself. Do you think that he will not?"

It was a question that the secretary had hardly dared to put to himself, but when he asked it now, the answer from his heart of hearts was exceedingly simple and straightforward. "Yes." There was no doubt about it in his mind. All that could be done to put a pressure upon the poor girl would be accomplished by Valdivia. "But h-how," stammered Carreño, "can he force her against her will?"

"You are too kind and true a fellow to understand. But suppose, Juan, that he offers to have her father's sentence commuted from death to life imprisonment?"

Carreño struck a hand against his fat forehead. "I could never have thought of that."

Dupont said nothing, but he watched the acid work, eating deep and deeper into the soul of the poor secretary of Valdivia.

"How can I be sure?" he said.

"'Of what?'"

"That my master truly had wronged El Tigre as he has … as he has, I fear, wronged you, señor?"

"What would you do if you knew?"

"The dear God would teach me what to do."

"Let me have Pedro LeBon alone for five minutes with my hands free. I would force him, I think, to say whether or not he attacked Carlos Milaro that day twenty years ago, or whether Carlos Milaro attacked him. The whole crux of the matter is there. Did Valdivia lay an ambush to destroy Milaro? Or did Milaro like a mad fool attack the men of Valdivia for no cause except that he was furious with jealousy. Think of that, Juan."

The secretary lifted his head, and his fat face was quivering with emotion. Never did a small soul struggle so manfully to comprehend a great and wicked truth. But by degrees he began to understand.

"Whether he is evil or good, it depends on that," he said at the last. If he had paused, he could not have found the courage to do the thing. But he did not pause. He took out a knife, opened it, and in a trice he had slashed the bonds of El Crisco. The latter, gasping with astonishment, struggled to his feet. "God forgive me," panted Carreño, shrinking away as the big man rose before him. "What have I done?"

The strong form of Dupont melted to the floor again. His limbs had no strength, so long had the circulation in them been stopped. He lay on the wet stones, propped upon one shaking elbow.

"You can undo what you have done, Juan," he said heavily. "I have no strength now. I am completely in your hands."

The courage of Carreño returned again, and with the courage there came a warm flood of pity. For here was his wild hero so stripped of strength that he was for the nonce no more than a woman. He dropped upon his knees and began to chafe the swollen hands of the outlaw. It was not long. The purple blood began to disappear.

Strength came back to him in waves. And at last he rose to his feet. He tried himself with a few steps. Then he stretched his long arms.

"I am ready, Juan," he said, "for whatever you may have in mind."

"I will bring LeBon," Carreño said. "It is for you to make him speak the whole truth for us."

He passed out into the corridor. He was still trembling, but it was no longer shuddering from fear. A strong anger was taking hold upon him, and there was born in him a stern desire to find out the truth together with a fear of the truth itself. He was like a man awakened, and the strength of the newly born creature called Juan Carreño amazed him.

Never had there been such surety and command in his voice as when he said to LeBon: "Pedro, I need you in the room with El Crisco."

"Why?" LeBon asked, dark of brow, for he had ever hated the smug-faced secretary so often vested with the authority of the master of the estancia.

"I can tell you that when you are there. There is something that must be found out …"

A flash of understanding crossed the face of LeBon. His grin had the purest essence of evil pleasure. "Ah?" he said. "If that is the case, with no more than these little cords twisted around the fingers of this El Crisco, we will make him speak about whatever you choose."

Carreño, sickened and angered, turned his back hastily to keep the manager from reading his expression, and so he led the way back into the room, past the gauchos who stood like a fierce and irregular soldiery along the corridor.

He passed through the doorway. He shut the door hastily behind him, and at the same moment he heard a horrible choking noise. When he turned, he saw Pedro LeBon stretched upon his back along the floor. Over him crouched the terrible El Crisco with the throat of his victim caught in the crook of his arm. Carreño looked on with wonder and with terror. So it was, in his dreams, that he had seen El Crisco work. But to see the fact was far more marvelous than a dream. Here was a strong man reduced to silent surrender in the space of half a second.

El Crisco stripped the weapons from his prisoner. Then, jamming the muzzle of the revolver against the throat of the manager, he said in swift Spanish: "Señor LeBon ..."

"You will die for this, El ..."

"No man can die twice, no matter what he has done. Now, LeBon, we'll have the truth about a certain day twenty years ago. On that day, LeBon, you were shot down by Carlos Milaro. Your companion was shot, also. Tell me this ... did Valdivia send you to murder the man, or did Milaro attack you?"

"I have told you a hundred times ... Milaro attacked me ..."

"You lie, LeBon! I know enough of the truth to tell when you are speaking it. Tell me again. What happened on that day?"

The face of LeBon was working with fury and fear. "Carreño," he said, "step back. I'll not speak out before both of you."

"But you will," Carreño insisted. Suddenly his voice grew thick and passionate. "Dog of a LeBon," he snarled in his throat, "I begin to guess ..."

The fury of the little fat man seemed to terrify LeBon even more than the strength of El Crisco or the reputation of that outlaw. The story broke at once from his lips.

"If I speak, am I safe, El Crisco?"

"You are."

"It was Valdivia. He called me in and opened his heart to me. He said ... 'LeBon, you are a young man ... there are many between you and the managership of the estancia. But do what I tell you to do, and you become manager in a month. What would not a young man do for such a prize? I told him only to command me. He looked at me a moment as though he wondered how far he could trust me. Then he told me the whole story quickly … how he had been betrothed to Dolores Servente … how he had come to learn that Dolores did not love him because she herself had begged him to withdraw in spite of the engagement that her family had made of her hand to him. She had begged because she loved Carlos Milaro. And Valdivia wanted to brush Milaro out of his way. He told me to take another man who I could trust and wait for Milaro. And I did it. But the devil was in Milaro. His horse dodged at the moment we fired together out of the brush. Before we could take aim and fire again, he had killed my friend and shot me down, and left me there. He left me for dead.

"Afterward, Valdivia found a way to make that fight the ruin of Milaro. That is the truth. You, Carreño, let the master know that you understand a word of this truth and you are ruined in his service just as much as I am ruined. I know too much. He cannot shake me off!"

CHAPTER THIRTY-FOUR

Joy is a sweet intoxicant, and Valdivia was so filled with it that he could not remain quiet. When he sat down and strove to read, the words blurred into a smudge or danced before his eyes. He was filled with music, but when he tried to sing, his trained voice made a poor interpreter of the spirit that was musical within him. He walked up and down through his room, but walking was not enough.

With all his soul he wanted to talk with Francesca. Even if she raged at him, her passion would be beautiful, and there was in his mind the perfect confidence that he knew with what silent, delicate weapon to subdue her spirit when the time came. Yet he had resolved that he would not see her on this first night. He would wait until tomorrow.

But in the meantime, he was raging with excitement. All the old Castilian blood in his veins thrilled with the exquisite joy of tyrannical cruelty. What is so keen as hate? And what hatred is so perfect as that which men have for those whom they have injured? What robbed man hates the thief so much as the thief hates his victim?

So it was with Valdivia. When he thought of the one man whose life he had ruined twenty years before and who now lay helpless in his hands, his heart swelled. That was the source of his music. And when he thought of him who had been his blind tool to bring El Tigre into his power, he could hardly keep from song. It was terrible, it was beautiful, and it was perfect.

But he must break the silence that lay too heavily around. He pressed the button that rang the bell in Carreño's room. There was no response. He opened the door and shouted: "Carreño!"

There was no answer.

"The fat fool has gone to the wine cellar," Valdivia muttered, and strode into the secretary's room to make sure of his absence. He would make the rascal sweat for this. He would cancel that promised increase in salary.

He opened the door—the secretary was not there and on his desk were several sheets of paper, with a few lines scribbled upon each one. He leaned above them and read:

Gentlemen,

It is my pleasure to inform you of an event of some importance to the republic …

This Carreño, the master thought to himself, *is the master of more power of style than I had thought.*

He continued to read:

Charles Dupont, known as El Crisco, and Carlos Milaro, the two fatuous outlaws, have been captured on my premises. It was accomplished by the assistance of a dozen of my men acting under my supervision. They were betrayed by foul treason …

The estanciero started back and gripped instinctively the handle of his knife, for he was enough a citizen of his country to know and love the uses of that grim weapon. He felt, at first, that he had lost his reason. But when he leaned again, there lay the written words of the incompleted last sentence before him.

What he first felt was a touch of cowardly fear. What he next felt was a wave of blind, tyrannical fury. He would crush Carreño until the fat little coward squirmed and shrank in his terror.

He went out from the room and the first thing he encountered in the great hall of the house was a group of his gauchos, armed to the teeth and lolling in the old Spanish chairs, upholstered in fine old leather.

"Well?" asked the estanciero, furious at this sight. "Who has sent you here?"

"Señor Carreño has sent us."

"Is the fool drunk?" the great man snarled out. "Is the blockhead gone mad, or simply drunk? *He* sent you up here?"

"He did, señor."

"For what purpose? To wait for your turn to stand guard?"

"We have been standing guard, señor. It was his will …"

"To bring in a new change?"

"No, señor …"

"What?" yelled Valdivia. "Is not the corridor in the cellar guarded now?"

"For only five minutes, señor, since he told us …"

"Death and hell, I am served by fools or devils! I will have your skins for this! I'll have your skins! Not guard the corridor?"

"We were sent to wait here … there was something about interviewing Señor El Crisco …"

A shout came from the lips of Valdivia. "Interview! Who would interview him? Who would dare to speak to him or enter the room where he is kept without my authority?"

"Señor, God knows we have always thought that he came carrying to us your own mind."

"You are fools to think so … my mind … in that fat idiot … that … but the heavens above me, what has happened? Some of you down to the cellar … five minutes did you say? I have lost my wits and the whole world has lost its senses at the same time.

Down to the cellar. Some of you follow me."

With this, he whirled upon his heel and darted off toward the farthest wing of the house, followed by half a dozen of his gauchos, who ran, pale with fear on account of the fury of the master, and half guessing at calamity before they came to it.

He reached the door of the room of the girl.

Two armed men stood guard before it.

"Have you heard a sound in there?" asked the estanciero.

"Nothing."

"Now, heaven be praised. However ... to be doubly sure ..." He rapped at the door.

There was no answer.

"Francesca?"

Not a word of reply.

Snatching a revolver from the hand of a gaucho, Valdivia shattered the lock with a bullet and cast open the door—in time to see Francesca Milaro in the act of whirling a cloak around her shoulders and leaping into the deep casement of her window that overlooked the garden of the house, and just beyond her, illumined by the pale moonlight, the astonished estanciero saw none other than the face of El Tigre, plainly distinguishable.

He had time no more than to cry out, and then he received a stunning blow in the face that felled him like a log in the very pathway of his men, who stumbled over him as they struggled through the doorway. Half a dozen shots were fired, but the fugitive was already hurtling through the window in the rear of the girl and her father. It was the second captive—it was El Crisco—and with a yell of dismay the gauchos recognized him as he fled. Their guns were useless in their hands from that moment. If he and El Tigre could wish bonds of stout well-tied ropes off their limbs and melt away through thick walls of stone, it was as foolish and dangerous to oppose them as to oppose the devil.

They recoiled. They ran in a scattered group to the window,

with the estanciero shouting and cursing as he staggered to his feet and followed.

What they saw was a group of four horses, swiftly mounted at the garden gate, and bearing four forms away through the night beneath the stars and across the long mystery of the Pampas.

* * * * *

They stood at the prow of the old tramp freighter as it nosed its way between the rolling hills north of the Golden Gate and the stern, rocky bluffs to the south of that famous entrance to the harbor of San Francisco Bay. They stood in a close group, as old companions do when they enter upon a strange land. There was Carlos Milaro standing in the very angle of the bows, in front as he must always be, no matter what was on hand. At his right hand was the fat form of Juan Carreño. He was not quite so fat. His face was a little browner. And there was a new expression of manliness perceptible in his features, as though he had grown years older in the last few weeks. But in his eyes there was the same light of quiet and contented worship. He had found a new god to replace the lost deity from his domestic heaven. It was Carlos Milaro, upon whose rugged features his gaze dwelt in quiet contemplation. And what joy to poor Carreño that this great man, this unspeakable hero, should lay his knotted hand upon the soft shoulder of Juan as they came thus into the new land.

As for Mrs. Charles Dupont and her husband, though they stood very close to the other two, it was easy to see that there was a wall, a great boundary dividing them from the companions. It was, perhaps, the happiness that they were breathing even out of the air—a mysterious ether, for their benefit created. It was, perhaps, the difference with which they looked upon the land before them.

"Francesca, you come into a rich land with a poor husband."

"Ah," she said, "I hate money."

"But we will make it together."

"Of course we will, my dear."

"And, Francesca …"

"Yes."

"I hardly know what I wanted to say … except … what a beautiful world it is."

And as the ship drove on, they passed through the Golden Gate and came into view on the wide, blue waters of the bay, dancing in the bright sun of California—and far off, like a flare of gold on the Berkeley Hills, the fields of poppies in the east.

THE END

ABOUT THE AUTHOR

Max Brand is the best-known pen name of Frederick Faust, creator of Dr. KildSare, Destry, and many other fictional characters popular with readers and viewers worldwide. Faust wrote for a variety of audiences in many genres. His enormous output, totaling approximately thirty million words or the equivalent of five hundred thirty ordinary books, covered nearly every field: crime, fantasy, historical romance, espionage, Westerns, science fiction, adventure, animal stories, love, war, and fashionable society, big business and big medicine. Eighty motion pictures have been based on his work along with many radio and television programs. For good measure he also published four volumes of poetry. Perhaps no other author has reached more people in more different ways.

Born in Seattle in 1892, orphaned early, Faust grew up in the rural San Joaquin Valley of California. At Berkeley he became a student rebel and one-man literary movement, contributing prodigiously to all campus publications. Denied a degree because of unconventional conduct, he embarked on a series of adventures culminating in New York City where, after a period of near starvation, he received simultaneous recognition as a serious poet and successful author of fiction. Later, he traveled widely, making his home in New York, then in Florence, and finally in Los Angeles.

Once the United States entered the Second World War, Faust abandoned his lucrative writing career and his work as a screenwriter to serve as a war correspondent with the infantry in Italy, despite his fifty-one years and a bad heart. He was killed during a night attack on a hilltop village held by the German army. New books based on magazine serials or unpublished manuscripts or restored versions continue to appear so that, alive or dead, he has averaged a new book every four months for seventy-five years. Beyond this, some work by him is newly reprinted every week of every year in one or another format somewhere in the world. A great deal more about this author and his work can be found in *The Max Brand Companion* (Greenwood Press, 1997) edited by Jon Tuska and Vicki Piekarski. His website is www.MaxBrandOnline.com.